Make Me Blush

OIL BARRONS BOOK 3

MARIE JOHNSTON

LE PUBLISHING

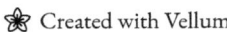

Emery

Dating is my last priority when I move my kids to a small town after a sudden divorce. It'll be easier to be a single, working mom of four, and I won't have to watch my ex with my former coworker. So when I get away for a night to throw myself a nice little pity party in a neighboring small town, I don't expect to get hit on by the tastiest guy I've ever seen.

We talk about everything but the important stuff. I live a little and steam up his backseat windows. I'll never see him again, so why not? But I forgot what a small world Coal Haven can be.

Holden

I don't like my reputation of being a commitment-phobe, but I earned it. So why can't I forget the woman who slipped out of the back seat of my pickup—and my life—in the most effortless way possible? I barely got her first name.

When my cousin coerces me into coaching an elementary school football team, I give in. But I come face to face with my hookup...and she's my worst nightmare wrapped in all my wildest fantasies. A single mom with no time for me or my BS. Maybe it's time to get more than her first name.

One

Emery

I worked on catching my breath as I tugged up my pants in the back seat of a pickup that wasn't mine. My orgasm-numbed brain logged back into my good sense.

What had I done?

My elbow poked a hard rib. Jeez, was there anything on this guy that wasn't chiseled from granite? "Sorry."

"No problem." Holden leaned back in his seat to button his pants.

At least I knew his name.

I mimicked Holden's movements, trying to suck my gut in so I could get my leggings up all the way. The struggle of getting dressed in the back seat of a pickup dimmed the postcoital glow I'd probably be too panicked to enjoy anyway.

Could I even call this a one-night stand? I was in my thirties. I thought I was long past my back-seat-sex days.

I straightened my bra and rolled my shirt down. Some of

my hair had fallen out of my topknot. I puffed it out of the way and caught Holden's eye.

He'd righted his clothing and was reclining against the door, his arm slung across the headrest. His satisfied expression resonated down to my toes as if he hadn't just had my entire body throbbing.

The darkness of the cab covered the flush warming its way up my neck to my face. What *the hell* had I done?

Other than have some amazing sex with a guy I'd just met. In the back seat of his really nice pickup, no less.

I didn't know what he'd done with the condom. I didn't —God, I didn't know anything about this. I didn't go to bars. I didn't do one-night stands or hookups. Even worse, I had no clue how to extract myself from this moment.

And I had no idea if it was bad that I didn't want to.

He didn't appear to be in a rush to leave. The way he was sitting was like an invitation. I could curl up next to him. We could stick to safe topics like we had in the bar. Where we'd gone to college. What we'd majored in. College sports teams.

Maybe we could have sex again.

Whatever impulsive streak possessed me to leave the little bar with him and hook up in the darkness of his pickup cab had vanished. I was the responsible one in my life. I had to be.

Stricken with self-consciousness and unsure what to do next, I said, "So..."

His laugh was good natured. "You were serious when you said you don't do this."

I didn't have sex, period. Not since long before my divorce when I learned my cheating husband was banging the young nurse I'd been training. I wasn't spared from the stereotype. My husband hadn't been an arrogant surgeon when I met him. He'd saved that for after I had worked to support him while he was going through medical school and his residency. He'd waited until I carried his ass to a stellar paycheck—then he'd fucked someone younger, perkier, and more clueless.

My temper flared and there it was, that impulsive streak. I had the urge to strip Holden down and lick the muscles that had flexed behind me when he'd been thrusting us to a simultaneous climax.

Like...I didn't know that was possible.

My ex hadn't been horrible in the bedroom. He'd gotten me off. I'd gotten him off. But we'd reached a place where the spontaneity and excitement were rare and other obligations were numerous.

Still, I'd been happy. Mostly. In the overstressed way that a couple can be happy when doing demanding shift work and trying to keep the magic in our relationship.

"No, I really don't do this," I admitted. "What comes next?"

I didn't have to go. Tonight was my night. The one night I gave myself to go out and have a little pity party. My plan had been to have a couple drinks and get pissed at life.

But before I had finished my first beer, Holden had entered the bar. I didn't think a guy like him would acknowledge me. It wasn't like I'd dressed up. Technically, I lived in a neighboring town. I had just moved to Coal Haven and hadn't wanted my pity party to be witnessed by people I might see the next week in the clinic. So I'd come to Crocus Valley in my leggings, a T-shirt, and a jacket, and found a quiet bar.

"We could stay here." His lopsided grin sent tingles through my body. Did he take a bath in sex appeal every morning? Or was I in that much of a dry spell? "If we go back in the bar, the other two customers would guess what we've been up to."

"Are you saying I can't be chill?" I gave him a playful scowl. Was I flirting? When had I last flirted? Maybe that was why I was divorced. The thought sobered me.

Holden's easy laugh swooped in for the rescue. "Nah, Em, not saying that. But we should wait for the flush to leave your cheeks."

I touched my hot face. I did get red when I orgasmed. My neck was probably all blotchy too. No, I'd never play it chill.

He brushed my cheek with the backs of his fingers. "I like it." He dropped his voice to a rumble. "Cuz I put it there."

"Yeah, you did." We both snickered like middle schoolers.

"You're fun, Em."

"You're the only one who thinks that on the face of this earth." Because he didn't know me or the obligations Henry bitched about when I asked him why he'd checked out of our marriage.

"If you're talking about your ex, I can tell you he's wrong."

Holden had noticed the tan line on my ring finger when we'd first started talking. My divorce was as far in my private life as I'd gone with him, and he hadn't pried. For the last couple of hours, I'd been freed from ruminating on my divorce and how I was going to make it work without a second income and with a mass of student loans I had to share with Henry.

"Well, thank you." I twisted my hands together. Would it be weird to curl up with him? To enjoy being held for a while. To pretend that I wasn't alone for a little longer.

Crocus Valley was quiet. Any traffic went by a block in front of the pickup. Behind the vehicle was an open lot and the railroad tracks. Holden said he liked to swing his pickup around and drive straight out when he was done at the bar. There were no buildings and no security or doorbell cameras. The privacy might've been more of a draw than the parking.

Had he done this before? Wait. I didn't care. I wasn't interested in a relationship or dating. I had too much going on in addition to moving to a new town and starting a new job.

Yeah, I could cuddle. He wasn't pushing me out and looking for his next conquest. There was nothing wrong with enjoying tonight like the single woman I now was.

I opened my mouth to ask if he minded if we just hung out in the privacy of his pickup for a while when buzzing caught my attention.

My fleece jacket had gotten tossed on the floor when the groping began. I yanked it up and dug in the pocket. "Sorry, I gotta check this." I smashed my lips together in case I said more and burst the little fantasy bubble we'd created.

I missed the call, but a message popped up. **What do you want me to do for vomiting?**

"Shit." I closed my eyes for a brief second and stuffed my phone back in the jacket pocket.

"Everything okay?"

If I could record his voice and play it back when I was in bed after an especially stressful day, I wouldn't worry so much about how I was going to survive the next twenty years.

"I don't know. I'm really sorry. I've gotta go." I wrestled my jacket on. My shirt bunched around the shoulders and not in the sexy way it'd done earlier tonight. I grabbed the door handle and gave Holden an apologetic smile.

He quirked a brow, but I didn't miss the doubt in his golden eyes. "Need a ride anywhere?"

"No, I'm just around the corner." I selfishly let my gaze

devour his long, lean body. Might as well carve this moment into my memory. I wasn't getting another opportunity. The text showed me that this was a fluke. I was given a break just to get laid, and now it was back to reality. "Uh...thanks."

"You're welcome," he said dryly, his head cocked.

I slipped out, ignoring the doubt etched into his expression. Was he starting to think that was my MO? Play it innocent and then ditch him?

Before I shut the door, I tried again. "I mean it. Thanks for tonight."

An eyebrow arched. Yeah, he didn't believe it anymore, that this wasn't my usual routine. I didn't want to make things more awkward, so I shut the door and scurried to my car. By the time I reached my Traverse, the fantasy had faded. I was back in the real world.

I sent a reply. **How bad is it?**

I didn't want to drive past where he was parked, so I made a turn in the middle of the road and headed toward my normal life. Tonight might not have meant much to Holden. He might get lost in the women he was with until he found the person he wanted for forever and never thought about me again. And long after he forgot about me, I'd remember the hot guy who'd made me feel wanted again.

* * *

After the twenty-minute drive to Coal Haven, I pulled in front of the little two-story rental house that smelled like wet basement and old smoke. I didn't park in the garage. It was full of crap from the $1.2 million home that had just sold. Henry had wanted the house, but I wasn't letting him move his young nurse into the home we'd shared.

We hadn't been in the house long, and most of the sale went right back to the bank. But I took what little profit I got as my part of the settlement and rented this old house. Last I heard, Henry was in St. Martin with his new girlfriend, spending his share.

I rushed up the steps, and the door opened before I reached it. My mom's eyes were wide.

She hugged her robe around herself. "Oh, Emery. You didn't have to come home. Riley and I would've figured it out." Guilt flashed through Mom's eyes. "I think she had too much sugar."

Big surprise. Mom was used to being the grandma that flung treats around like she was in a parade, but now that we were around more, she'd have to leave her candy stashed. Part of my reason for moving was to live in a town with a slower pace and to have her help. She'd moved to Coal Haven for work and a more affordable cost of living a few years after my dad died.

I stepped around Mom and took my coat off. "How's she feeling?"

"Better, but I thought maybe you'd have some Pedialyte or something."

By kid three I had given up trying to stock special drinks, but Mom had always sworn by the stuff. Just another log to toss on the crackling fire under my guilt.

No, I wasn't going to work myself up over this. The kids had had their grandma to themselves for a few hours, something that hadn't happened much when we were a busy family an hour away.

"How much did she throw up?" I toed out of my shoes and padded down the hallway and up the stairs to Riley's room.

"Just the once. And then again right after. I guess I'd count them as once, but in the moment—" Mom made an exasperated sound. "Well, it seemed like more. So much for a tiny little body."

I entered the room. My one-and-a-half-year-old was sitting up in her crib. "Hey, nugget," I said softly.

She reached for me. I felt her forehead. No fever. Relieved it was likely nothing but a gut ache from Nana's goodies, I picked her up and went to the glider rocker in the corner. Riley rested her head on my shoulder, her dark curls tickling my nose.

Mom hung in the doorway. The hallway light was on. "Do you need me to get anything?"

"No, I think the worst has passed. I'll get her settled back down. Why don't you get some rest?" I had planned to be up late, not her. But tonight had taken all different turns. "Is the couch okay, or did you want to take my bed?"

"Oh, no. This old lady can still sleep on a couch." She adjusted the edges of her purple robe. "You didn't have to rush home."

"I know," I said on an exhale. Maybe I had latched on to the excuse. The longer I stayed with Holden, the more I would've kidded myself about what was really going on. I couldn't risk thinking there was anything real about what happened. Mutual pleasure. Nothing more. "I wasn't really doing anything. Don't worry."

"Oh, I'll always worry." She closed the door so only a crack of light shone through.

I rocked Riley until her breathing evened out. She'd expect to be rocked asleep tomorrow night too. Henry had been gone a lot with his long hours, but the upheaval had upset her. She was clingier and prone to tantrums.

I'd like to be clingier and prone to tantrums, but that was never my relationship with Henry. Looking back, it was clear he'd wanted four kids, to be the successful surgeon who could support a big family, just not the actual work and logistics of raising them. And it had been the same for me as his wife. He didn't have time to comfort, and there was always his job.

So rocking Riley to sleep would comfort me as much as her. I laid her down in her crib, softly shut the door, and turned.

A bleary-eyed eleven-year-old stared at me. I jumped and pressed my hand over my mouth before I shouted and woke Riley. "Avery. You scared the crap out of me."

Avery blinked and screwed her face up. "I thought you were getting lit tonight, Mom."

Oh, I'd gotten something, but my preteen daughter was the last I'd talk to about that. "Do you know what getting lit means?"

She shrugged.

I wanted to keep it that way for a while. I ruffled her hair. "I had one drink and came home."

"Mm." She pressed into me for a bear hug, then stepped back just as quickly. She shuffled to her room across the hall.

I brushed a strand of hair out of my eyes. It fell back in. I gave up and took the band out as I followed her.

"It's not fair that I have to share a room," she mumbled as she crawled into the twin bed with her powder-blue bedspread.

I went to the other twin bed on the opposite end of the room. There were three feet between the beds and enough leftover room for a dresser. The closet was so full, I'd probably lose a child when the door was opened.

"How was Afton tonight?" I ran my fingers lightly over my six-year-old daughter's dark hair. All the kids had hair darker than my light-brown tresses.

"She threw a fit when Nana didn't cut her grilled cheese the right way."

Yeah, that sounded about right. Riley learned to throw tantrums from the best. At least Afton had mellowed since the move. I was around more and she wasn't being shuttled to day care by nannies who changed as often as the toilet paper roll. She'd get used to her grandma's presence.

"You guys get some rest. We'll do some unpacking in the morning." I slipped out of the room as Avery grunted her disapproval of tomorrow's activities.

By the time I got downstairs, Mom had curled up on the couch and turned the living room light off. I kept the hallway light on until I reached one of the two bedroom doors at the end. I opened it. The light cut through to the twin bed tucked into the corner. Landon flipped over and sat up. His wiry nine-year-old body was clad in Nintendo pajamas. "Mom? I thought you were staying out late?"

"Eh, wasn't that exciting." Liar.

Landon nodded. "Guess what?"

The corner of my mouth ticked up. "What?"

"Football starts in two days."

Another reason we'd moved. I'd never be able to get my kids to anything after school if I wasn't lucky enough to find a nursing position that was Monday through Friday, no weekends, and no holidays. Which I'd found at the small clinic in Coal Haven. The kids were a few blocks from everywhere else in town, and I wasn't working far away from home, school, or after-school activities.

"We'll go over the route tomorrow so you can walk to practice," I said. And I'd choke back stifling mom emotions about how he was old enough to be in football *and* get himself home after. They were growing up, but I hoped they could be kids longer in Coal Haven.

"You'll be at my first game, right?"

"Of course." It was nice to say that and know for certain I'd be there. I'd missed so much, working shifts the last year and hiring a seventeen-year-old nanny to help with school and sports.

"Good. Will Dad be there?"

Too bad Henry wasn't around to answer for himself. Not that I wanted him to be here. I was over my ex-husband. But I would've liked him to be more present in his kids' lives. It hadn't been promising so far.

"I'll let him know the schedule." I wouldn't shit-talk their dad, but I wasn't covering for his absentee ass either. He'd settled for every-other-weekend custody without a fight, and his lawyer had been better than mine regarding child support.

It was over. I'd moved on, and we were doing fine.

I went in to kiss Landon good night and then went to my room. I tossed my hair band onto my dresser and sank into my bed. My bedroom didn't have any more room than the other bedrooms had. I'd had to downsize to a queen bed. The king-size bed was in the garage, and since I thought Henry had had sex in it with Jenni, I would have to burn it later.

I flopped backward and eked out a sigh as I stared at the white ceiling fan. Glow-in-the-dark stars were stuck to it. I had a little show every time I shut the lights off.

What a fucking night.

I wasn't jaded enough to think I couldn't date again. I hoped society had come far enough that a thirty-two-year-old single mom wouldn't repel men. But I was realistic enough to know that a thirtysomething divorced mom of four would be like pepper spray after tasing to single men. It was best I didn't start my life in a new town with my kids with the false hope that I'd find someone willing to join the chaos.

Two

Holden

"No. No fucking way." I didn't let up glaring at my cousin Stetson. We were sitting at our normal table in the back of Rattler's Brewhaus. The supper crowd was clearing out.

The big oaf grinned and leaned back in his chair, crossing his arms in a way that usually drew a girl's attention and distracted her from whatever reason she'd been pissed at Stetson. But I wasn't a girl and I sure as shit didn't get sucked in by Stetson's muscles.

The noise of Rattler's Brewhaus drowned out our argument.

"Yes," he insisted. "You're the only one who can help."

I shook my head. "Nope."

"Do it for the kids."

I ground my teeth together. I wanted to stay far away from the kids.

Stetson shrugged and took a long pull of beer from his mug. "They're not babies."

"I know, but I don't want to be responsible for them." Never again. I could invite my other cousin Liam's twin boys over. Squeeze his new baby's chubby cheeks when it was born. But I wasn't holding it, rocking it, or singing any damn lullabies. I wasn't going to wonder *what-if.*

It didn't help that Stetson was asking me to help him coach a fourth-grade football team. I didn't need to be surrounded by a bunch of nine and ten-year-olds.

"You won't be. I'm the head coach. I just need you there offering pointers and making sure kids get the instructions down."

Leave it to Stetson to find the technicalities. "Why don't you ask Remington?"

Our buddy Remington pulled out a chair and plopped down next to me. His black chef's coat and black pants didn't hide his size, but he wasn't as built as Stetson. His muscles were lean, just shy of wiry. His sleek black chef's hat, not puffy like a stereotypical white one, the small gold hoops in his ears, and his dark scruff capped off his look. When the place first opened, a kid asked if he was a pirate. "Ask me what?"

"He's got this place to worry about," Stetson answered, ignoring Remington. "I already asked him."

Remington glanced between us, his blue eyes judging how tense the atmosphere was at the table. "I do."

"Football," Stetson said without taking his gaze off me.

"Ah, yeah. You have practice right when things get exciting here." Remington was a homegrown boy who'd moved around the country and come back to open Rattler's with a buddy he'd met in Chicago. He pushed out of the chair. "I told Stetson to give me a call if you ever have practice at nine in the morning."

A girl called his name from across the bar and he swaggered away. If I ever wanted to get laid more than I did, I'd have to open a bar and grill. It worked for him.

Or I could do what I did last night. Try to find Em.

Then get fucking ditched.

I switched my scowl from my cousin to my mug of beer. I could dish it out, but apparently I couldn't take it.

Stetson broke into my thoughts. "You're not thinking about the kids anymore."

I rubbed the back of my neck. "No." I wasn't one to kiss and tell, but last night had gotten under my skin and rubbed me raw. "I met someone last night."

"You meet someone most nights."

Not most nights, but enough to keep from feeling neglected. And infrequent enough to make me wonder what it would be like to not go home alone. But I didn't need someone around just for sex. When a relationship was founded on that, it broke apart quicker than a graham cracker dipped in milk.

I rotated my mug on the Rattler's coaster. A picture of a rattlesnake wrapped around a mug played peekaboo as I moved the glass. "Not like this."

Stetson snorted. "So she said no."

Oh, Em had shouted yes several times. I turned my thoughts around before I got myself stuck at this table with an erection to hide. "She pretended she had to leave right away after."

There was a beat of silence before he sputtered, then dissolved into wheezing laughter.

"Thanks a lot, fucker." I kept rotating my mug.

"Seriously?" He coughed to catch his breath and pounded the table. Heads turned toward us, but most people knew Stetson and weren't fazed by his jovial nature.

"She got a message, said she had to go, and bailed. Like, she'd barely pulled her pants up before she raced away."

"Your skills are getting dull."

Nope. She'd come so fast and hard that I'd ended up coming just as fast and hard. We barely had time to steam up the cab. We'd gone from light kissing to devouring each other. She had unbuttoned my jeans and things went lightning fast after that. I'd spun her around and yanked down her soft leggings, and damn. She'd been hot and soft in all the best places. In fifty years, I may never forget the peaches-and-cream smell of her hair.

"I barely got more than her name. I swear, she was a pro at bailing. She'd put you to shame."

He didn't take the bait and get offended. "She would not, because I actually date the girls I sleep with. You, sir, do not date. Sounds like this girl doesn't either."

"Whatever. I got played."

"Don't feel good?"

I glowered into the amber liquid. "I don't know why I care. It wasn't like I learned anything about her, other than she went to college in Grand Forks and is divorced."

His eyes narrowed. "How divorced?"

My mood darkened. "Newly divorced."

"There ya go. Don't take it personally. Some other guy fucked her over." Stetson inspected me. "So, why aren't you glad she nailed and bailed?"

"Not used to it, I guess." I'd told myself that whoever I was with knew the deal. I wasn't looking for a relationship, I wouldn't be looking for a relationship, and I wasn't open to being changed. There wasn't a magic pussy out there that would convert me.

But there was a moment of disappointment when I propositioned Em and she'd accepted. I'd almost wanted to sit and get to know her better. She hadn't given out identifying information, but she'd been open and easy to talk to. We'd skipped past the awkward small talk where we scrabbled to find common ground and went straight to easy laughter.

She liked watching college football better than the NFL, and despite where she went to college, her favorite was the NDSU Bison. When I said she must be local since she pronounced bison with a Z and not an S like the rest of the world, she said she'd grown up a few hours away from Crocus Valley. Which could be anywhere in the state.

I hadn't thought having sex would be the end of the night. I had been wrong.

And I'd wanted to cuddle, dammit. I didn't cuddle. I didn't spend enough time in bed to hold someone. Too many reminders.

There it was. The reason I was so salty. A tiny crack had opened in my willingness to get to know someone again, and I'd been shut down hard.

"So, about the team." Stetson wasn't giving up. He was the biggest nag when his mind was set on something.

Stetson knew my hang-ups. He wouldn't put me in charge. All I had to do was be the fun guy and make sure kids got into the right positions. I could do that. "You fucking owe me if I do this."

His cocky grin made me want to shove him off his chair. "Knew you'd do it. Practice starts tomorrow."

* * *

Stetson shoved a clipboard at me. "Want to make sure we have all their emergency information while I run through and see who wasn't here last year?"

I could handle that. We were surrounded by scrawny little kids. They'd get introduced to us, learn about the positions, and then get their gear. In an hour, I'd have one practice down, too many fucking more to go.

I read the list of names. Most I recognized from around town. I'd gone to school with their parents or now did business at their folks' places of work. If they didn't have parent names filled in, I could do it. I'd have to grab a few phone numbers. I hit one name that was missing an address.

Huh. I didn't recognize the last name. With the oil refinery, the gasification plant, and the coal mine nearby, Coal Haven had several families coming and going.

I walked down the line. "Landon Halliwell?"

A small boy raised his hand, his eyes wide like he thought I was going to flog him in front of the team. He had a mop of dark hair that made his eyes look a lighter brown than they were.

"C'mere." I walked to the end of the line of kids without checking to see if he followed.

When I turned, he was right behind me, staring up at me with those big eyes. My heart twisted. Fucking Stetson. He should've known better than to ask me to do this.

"You're a lot taller than my dad," he said, his voice filled with awe.

I felt like a dick. While I was thinking about how much I didn't want to be here, the kid was impressed by me just because I was tall and wore a gray T-shirt that said Coach.

I squatted down to keep from intimidating him. "I get that a lot." I didn't, but it seemed like an okay thing to say. "Speaking of your dad, what's his name?"

"Henry."

"Henry Halliwell?" Emery Halliwell was listed. As long as one parent's name was filled in, I didn't need the other's. The parent column was already filled out; I was just being a nosy fucker. Landon was new to the team, and, I suspected, new to town. Wouldn't hurt to get to know him since I'd probably run into his parents, maybe even do business with them. The town was too small not to.

The kid bobbed his head, and a dark lock of hair hung over his eyes.

"Okay, Landon. Do you know your address?"

He shook his head.

I gave him an exaggerated surprised look. "How don't you know your address, man?"

He sniffed and looked at the ground. "We just moved."

That would explain why the column was empty. It wasn't critical, but it'd help if other points of contact failed. "Wanna let your mom know we need your address?"

He nodded, pumped that he wasn't in trouble. "Do we have a game this Saturday?"

I smiled and remembered being excited for my first game. "Not until next Saturday. Gotta have time to teach you how to play first."

"Okay, good. My dad's going to try to be there." He grinned, then ran back to the group of kids surrounding a kneeling Stetson.

A familiar tug in my chest happened with his words. I got the feeling Landon had experienced what I had. Looking around for a dad at a big game and he wasn't there.

But I didn't know why Landon's dad couldn't make it. Maybe he did shift work or mandatory overtime at one of the plants or the mine. The dad could be a deadbeat like mine had been, thinking his precious job was more critical than his kid, or he could be a hardworking Joe who missed out on a lot to put food on the table.

Landon had seemed so excited his dad could come to the first game. For the kid's sake, I hoped that no matter what category his dad fit in, he'd be there.

Three

Emery

"What do you mean you can't make it?" If I could reach through the phone and strangle Henry, it'd have happened a year ago. I was in the parking lot beside the track. Parents and kids were exiting vehicles around me. The little boys were already in their gear like Landon had been. I'd watched him run to the track, promising I'd be in the stands before the game started. Then I called Henry.

Because the first thing Landon had noticed when we pulled up for his first game was that his dad's Suburban wasn't in the parking lot.

"I'm on call, Emery. You know how that is."

"You mean like I know that in order to take vacation to St. Martin you had to trade the only days on which your son asked you to give a damn?" I'd emailed the schedule when I signed Landon up two months ago. The trip to St. Martin was sudden. Henry wouldn't admit it, though. "It's his first game."

"You're not being fair."

"If you cared about fairness—" I bit my lip. Arguing with Henry and throwing his behavior back at him wouldn't make him more engaged in his kids' lives. "Can you at least call and apologize to him after the game?"

"If I'm not in surgery."

His conciliatory tone meant that whether he was in surgery or not, he wasn't answering his damn phone. Because he didn't like being expected to do things, especially by me.

"Fine." I hung up without a goodbye. It was hard to be civil with so much anger coursing through my mind and body. It'd be easier if I could understand how a guy who wanted a big family was suddenly willing to sever all ties with that family. But then, he'd never had any of the responsibility. I'd done all the heavy lifting.

Henry had better not ruin football for Landon.

Landon talked nonstop about football and his coaches —Coach Barron and Coach B. Cousins, he'd said. Coach Barron was the head coach, and Coach B was the assistant. I hadn't met them. Landon was done with practice and had walked home before my shift was over.

Avery was in the bleachers with the two other girls, waiting for me. Mom had to cover at the seed co-op for a few hours, and I hadn't wanted them around when I called their father.

I pushed my phone into my hoodie. The morning was cool, but with the sun arching overhead, the temperature was going to climb. It'd be a beautiful early September day. I had a T-shirt on beneath my hoodie, and my black yoga pants had become a second uniform outside of scrubs.

"Number eight," I muttered to myself as I pivoted to look at the bleachers. I'd look for Landon after I sat.

Avery had taken Afton and Riley to the far edge of the

bleachers. Smart girl. Learning too fast as she'd taken over more minor babysitting duties. The spot would cage in Riley, but we weren't too far away from the bathrooms. I could watch Afton run to the potty, or Avery or I could take her.

"Landon's over there." Avery pointed to the gaggle of kids. The group all wore blue jerseys and black football pants and had their helmets on. They surrounded the coaches, who were both squatting, their backs to the crowd. I'd have to find Landon when I could see his number.

When I'd told one of my new coworkers at the clinic that Landon was in football, she brightened. "Oh, Stetson coaches that. He'll take care of your boy. Don't worry."

Lyric's words had comforted me more than she could know. I didn't need another man in Landon's life letting him down.

I dug out snacks for Riley. She crawled onto my lap and daintily ate her Goldfish crackers one by one.

"It's starting," Afton said, her voice filled with excitement. I found myself smiling despite the constant stream of *shit I had to do today* running through my head.

But unpacking and sorting and hauling trash to the dump could all wait. We were doing something fun. Together. We hadn't done much of that since Riley had been born.

The boys lined up. I glanced at the coaches. Both big men, one a little taller and broader with inky black hair. He was the one facing the stands as he talked to the boys. A navy-blue Coal Haven Drillers ball cap was tucked low on his head. I couldn't hear his exact words, but he was direct without yelling. He interspersed his directions with encouragement that contrasted his hard appearance.

Lyric was correct. He seemed like a good coach. She was not correct in joking that I might want Stetson to do more than coach me. She'd labeled him the county's most eligible bachelor. I wasn't sure why she wasn't dating him, but I wasn't interested.

My eye kept getting drawn to the other coach. He kneeled in the line of kids, his back to the stands. He also wore a cap, but his hair seemed a few shades lighter than Coach Barron's. He wore a blue T-shirt with Coach written on the back. He was hunched like he was curled around a clipboard or something, but the pose plastered his shirt to the muscles of his back.

I ripped my gaze off him. I didn't need to be noticing a man right now. That was what the other night had been for. And look how it haunted my dreams. Some nights I woke up after dreaming I had given in and tucked myself against Holden's side as if the message about vomiting didn't happen.

But when I woke, I reminded myself that a hot cowboy wasn't going to be interested in a woman with relationship baggage and four kids.

The game started. Riley squirmed on my lap. Afton had to run to the bathroom before the second down.

I juggled snacks and drinks, trying to keep the kids from irritating the parents around us. When the stands erupted in cheers, Riley hugged me tightly, burying her face in my chest.

"It's okay," I murmured.

Landon was in as the running back. I perked up. The play started and he ran, getting open. The kid had his dad's speed.

The quarterback threw the ball, using his whole body to get some distance. The football wobbled in the air.

My breath caught as Landon paused, his little arms poised to catch it. He snatched the ball out of the air and fumbled it for a moment before tucking it into his side.

I hollered and clapped around Riley, Avery joining in with me. Eventually, Riley slapped her little hands together and grinned.

My smile froze when two other boys, both larger than Landon, charged him from each side. The three kids crashed, and Landon spun in the air before hitting the ground hard.

The stands went quiet. Landon didn't move.

Panic flared hot in my chest and all I thought was that I had to get down there.

"Mommy's gotta go real quick." I shoved Riley at Avery and sprinted down the bleacher stairs. My son had to be okay.

* * *

Holden

Shit, shit, shit.

I raced Stetson to Landon's side. The ref was already there, but he was a junior at the high school, another football player who did this as a side hustle. But he was pale and his eyes were wide.

So it wasn't my imagination. The kid had taken an unusually hard hit.

I got to Landon's side and crouched next to him. He started moving. My relief was only temporary.

"Was he unconscious?" I asked the ref as Stetson bent over Landon's head.

He blinked at me, then crouched on the other side of Landon.

"Knocked out?" I pressed again.

"N-no?" The young ref looked like he was going to pass out.

Landon groaned.

I touched his shoulder. "Hey, buddy. How you feeling?"

He scrunched his face up and groaned again. Another person arrived and muscled the high schooler aside until he was forced to stand and get out of the way or topple over.

I glanced at the newcomer and was about to slide my gaze away when I froze. "Em?"

She looked up, her face creased with worry. Her eyes flared and disbelief joined the concern in her emerald irises.

"Mom?"

Our attention was snatched away. Landon pressed a foot on the ground and arched his back, a little moan leaving him.

"Where do you hurt?" she asked as she bent over him.

Mom? She hadn't mentioned kids. But then she hadn't mentioned much of anything. I couldn't dwell on why it bothered me she hadn't mentioned her kids.

"My arm," Landon said and held it up.

Everything looked straight. Em palpated his arm and moved it through a range of motion.

Right. She was a nurse. I knew that much. She'd said she was divorced. And apparently she was a mom.

Did she legitimately have to leave that night? Why hadn't she said anything?

Would I have found a reason to quit talking to her if she had?

Her familiar voice, touched with warmth and support, brought me out of my head.

"I think you might've gotten it crunched against the ball." She leaned over him. "Do you remember everything, like getting knocked down?"

I glanced at Stetson to find him staring at me. He'd

caught the quick exchange between me and Em. Emery Halliwell.

A little girl a few years younger than Landon appeared next to her. "Is he okay, Mom?"

Two kids?

"He's fine, hon," Emery said without taking her eyes off Landon. She wasn't sure he was fine, but she was telling her little girl that.

Two kids. Why did that seem so much more significant than one kid? Other than it doubled what she didn't mention the night we were together.

She worked through Landon's extremities, inspecting him. After she was done, she nudged Stetson out of the way. Stetson was a big guy, but Emery acted like he would do what she wanted without question. And since her actions screamed competence, he moved.

We'd gone from *what the fuck do we do?* to being damn lucky the kid's mom was at the game and that she was a nurse.

"Let's get your helmet off, kiddo," she said softly. Nothing about her tone would alarm Landon. Hell, it was calming me.

I helped her as much as possible, and the little girl patted Landon's hand. Her hair was a medium brown, a shade between Landon's dark brown and her mom's light brown.

Another girl appeared, older this time, holding a toddler. She spoke to the girl. "Come on, Afton. Let's give Mom some space."

Three kids?

The toddler reached her arms toward Em. "Mama."

What the...

I lost the professional detachment I'd been striving for and gawked at Emery. "How many kids you got?"

Her guilty gaze met mine before it swept across her kids. All four of them.

Four. Kids.

Was she really divorced?

Landon picked that time to ask, "Where's Dad?"

Emery's features tightened. I didn't miss the blazing anger before she looked away. "He couldn't make it. You can try calling him later."

Aw, hell. The kid had been so excited about his dad seeing his first game. Emery's response told me a lot. Yes, she was most likely divorced. And she wasn't promising Landon that his dad would talk to him. So that clarified what was keeping Landon's dad away.

Henry Halliwell was a dick.

"Why don't we help you up and see if you can walk?" Emery braced her hands under Landon's shoulders. Stetson and I circled around him. Landon stood and tested out his weight on his feet. One arm hung at his side and the one he said hurt was curved into his belly, like it was tender but not excruciating.

"I think I'm good, Mom." He started to the edge of the field. His teammates and the families in the stands clapped for him. Landon ducked his head like he was embarrassed.

Stetson and I stood on either side of the pair, and the girls followed.

She patted his shoulder. "Okay, let's head to the parking lot."

Landon jerked his head up. His dark hair swirled around his head. "No, I don't want to leave."

"We should get that arm checked out," she said gently but firmly. "Make sure it's not fractured or anything."

"*Mom*. I don't want to go."

"Landon—"

"It's my first game!"

Based on Emery's expression, she wasn't budging. She was in full mom mode and a nurse on top of it. I agreed with her. I'd sleep better knowing the kid was okay, but I also knew how devastating and embarrassing it was to be the kid knocked out of the game. In seventh grade, I'd missed half the season thanks to a torn hamstring.

Stetson put a big hand on his back. "Why don't you check that arm out so you don't miss more games than you have to? You can't play when you're hurt."

Landon's eyes misted over. "I want to play."

I didn't know what made me say, "How about I go with?" but once it was out, I couldn't take it back. The tightness in my chest eased once I offered.

Stetson looked at me like I was speaking gibberish.

Emery's expression wasn't much different, but it was more guarded. "No, Holden, you don't have to do that."

It was the first time she acknowledged that she knew me. And the wrong time for the thrill I got hearing my name come from her pink lips.

"It's Coach B," Landon said.

Emery patted his shoulder again, but avoided looking at me. "I know."

We reached the sidelines. Stetson leaned down to speak to Landon. "I've gotta get back to the game, but you need to go take care of yourself. Don't feel bad about it. The team will be here when you get back."

Landon sniffled and nodded, but dejection hung heavy on his shoulders. He gazed up at me in a way that made me want to suspend the game and everyone here in some form of animation until he could come back. "Are you coming with?"

Emery spoke first. "I think Coach B—"

"Would love to help." I gave her a flat look. She'd been about to make an excuse for me. But I'd offered to go, dammit. Unlike the kid's dad, if I said I'd be there, I was going to show.

Besides, it couldn't be easy to juggle one kid at the doctor with three more in the wings. And I really needed to know Landon was okay. I wouldn't be much good to the game with my mind on the kid.

What if it was worse than we all thought? What if he hit his head and—?

Fuck. This was why I was no good around kids. Worst-case scenario was almost as bad as wondering how life would be if things had turned out wonderfully instead of dreadfully.

Emery was staring at me. Her kids stared at me. All four of them. "We'll be fine. You don't have to."

"I'd be worried the whole time if I stayed here," I said honestly.

Something about that statement swayed her. Her features softened. "All right."

She took the toddler from the oldest girl, and I followed them to her car. The kids flanked Emery. She tucked the littlest on her hip, and as soon as one hand was free, the next youngest snagged it. The oldest walked ahead like she was leading, when it was her mom in charge, and Landon kept his head down but stuck to Emery's side, as if he'd hold her other hand if it was free.

She stopped at a gray Traverse. If I had seen what she drove when we were at the bar, would I have known she was a single mom? Would it have made a difference? It wasn't like I hadn't been with single moms before. I had just made it extra clear I wasn't interested in fostering relationships with her or her kid.

She opened the driver's side back door. "Avery, can you get in the far back instead of Landon this time?"

"Fine." The girl had the same exasperated tone as her mother.

My pickup was a few rows away, but my feet weren't moving. The gentleman in me wanted to offer her a hand, but I would be clueless about how to help.

Before Landon climbed in, Emery assisted him out of his jersey. Seeing something I was useful at, I stepped in to help him out of his shoulder pads without jostling his sore arm.

When we were done, Landon asked, "Coach B, are you riding with us to the clinic?"

Emery's gaze jumped to mine but she shuttered the alarm, putting her calm mom mask in place. The woman I'd met at the bar had left that mask behind that night. "You can if you want."

I was going to the clinic anyway, but the cheer of the crowd behind me reminded all of us, especially Landon, that the game was still going without him. I couldn't heap more disappointment on him. "Sure. Thanks."

Avery, a tiny version of her mother but with dark-brown hair like her brother's, and the other little girl, Afton, crawled into the back. Avery dropped a booster seat on the middle seat and Emery handed her the shoulder pads to throw in the far back. I helped Landon into the booster as Emery buckled the youngest into a car seat.

The little girl—I was shit with ages—stared at me with big eyes that weren't completely brown. A green, much darker than the green of Emery's eyes, was woven through the girl's irises.

Memories surfaced. Big baby eyes. A dark blue. Nurses said her eyes would be a darker color, like brown.

I shook the memory away and focused. The floor of the Traverse was filled with toys and a couple of toddler cups. A few sweaters were scattered around, and what looked like crackers were crushed into the floor liner.

The mess eased the pressure in my lungs. What a mess. My pickup was immaculate, but that was because I could run a vacuum through it once a week. My work kept me busy, but some days, I felt like I had nothing but time.

"Cleaning's not the priority it used to be," Emery said, as if she was preempting a comment.

I snapped my gaze up. She was adjusting the straps around the girl but had caught me eyeing the mess. Of course she'd take it the wrong way when I'd been dangerously close to pondering what it would've been like to have to clean crumbs off my seats.

"You have more important things to worry about," I said gruffly.

I got into the passenger seat. Emery slid in and went to toss the bulky bag on the seat I was in. She paused, a small frown on her pretty lips—lips I'd tasted and had wanted more of for the last two weeks.

I held my hands out. She gave me a tight smile and handed me the bag. The zipper was open. The bag was filled with snacks and diapers and clothes. A few bottles of water. Armageddon could happen on the way to the clinic and we'd be fine for a while.

She fired up the engine and pulled away. I adjusted the bag and tried to evaluate Emery out of the corner of my eye. She drove with her gaze constantly darting to the rearview mirror. A worried mom.

"Think it's a sprain?" I asked more to break the ice.

"Probably."

I didn't know what else to say. We had a hell of a history, but it was a blink in the grand scheme of life. Then the new girl at the bar turned out to be one of the moms on the football team. It shouldn't have come as such a shock. "How did

I not know you were his mom for the last two weeks of practice?"

Her startled gaze jerked to the rearview mirror again. Was she afraid her kids would figure out how we knew each other?

A thought settled like a lemon sour in my belly. Had she realized I was helping coach and had avoided me?

"I work until five most days," she said. "He walks home after practice."

He'd finally gotten me his address. He lived only a couple blocks away from where we practiced at the school.

"You know Coach B, Mom?" Landon asked from the back. The weight was back on my lungs. This was territory I'd avoided for so long.

Emery ran her lower lip through her teeth. I wasn't the only one wondering how we'd explain how we knew each other. "We've...met."

Yeah, we had. We'd met hard. "What a coincidence, huh?"

"It's something, all right." She spared me a glance that, despite the gravity and the awkwardness, held faint amusement. "I really did have to go. Riley had a sour tummy and was throwing up."

That shouldn't have been the relief it was. "Yup."

The rest of the trip was filled with silence.

Four

Emery

The walk-in was the same clinic I worked in, only with minimal staff as a couple of the doctors in town rotated through their weekends. The physician I worked for didn't work weekends or holidays, but I could pick up extra hours if I wanted. Maybe someday, but I hadn't moved so I could work more.

The young nurse assistant running the registration desk recognized me, and Landon was the only patient. "You can go right into exam room three."

"Thanks." I ushered Landon to the door. "You guys hang out here with, uh, with Coach B."

Holden. My lungs squeezed the air out of my chest.

Were small towns really so small that I couldn't avoid experiencing the rejection I thought I had escaped?

The older girls made noncommittal noises, and Riley was attached to Avery, so she would be fine. I glanced at

Holden and paused at the door. He was staring at the wall with a stricken expression.

Was he all right? "Just holler if you need me, Holden."

He blinked back into focus, but I wanted to make sure he was okay. I pointed at each girl as I said their names. "Avery, Afton, and Riley."

He silently mouthed their names, but his gaze was guarded. He wasn't the type to get in their faces and ooze friendliness. Which was fine, but I couldn't shake the feeling that he was covering deeper emotions.

As if he knew I wasn't comfortable leaving him alone when he seemed off, he gave me the same smile that hooked me at the bar. "Avery, Afton, and Riley. Got it."

I wanted to reassure him, but I wasn't sure about what. I was the one leaving him with my kids.

"Mom?" Landon waited for me on the other side of the door.

"Right." I let the door to the waiting room shut behind me. "I mean, go to the left. It'll have a three on the door."

The nurse who came in had been with the clinic for a few decades. She was no nonsense but also no drama. "Emery, hi. I thought I recognized the last name."

"Hi, Gale."

She leaned forward to speak to Landon. "Have I got an NFL player in the house?"

Landon's bony shoulders sagged. "No. I had to miss my first game."

I rubbed his uninjured arm. Today hadn't gone how either of us hoped it would. I was mostly sure Landon hadn't broken his arm, but I wasn't going to risk ignoring a break in a growing kid.

They went through the litany of entry questions, then Gale stood. "Nisha will be here to get him for an X-ray in a few minutes. Then the doctor will be in."

"Thanks."

Gale left us, and I closed my eyes, willing myself to forget that my one-night stand was in the waiting room with three of my kids. I hadn't even told him I had one. It wasn't that I was ashamed. I wouldn't have talked about my ex either, if Holden hadn't noticed the line from my ring. I was fiercely protective of my life and that of my kids.

That was why we'd moved to Coal Haven. It was why I'd driven to Crocus Valley to have a drink. I'd wanted the privacy.

It was one instance. One impulsive decision, and it'd been *fantastic*. And then it'd been done and I was back to being responsible me.

There was a light knock on the door. Nisha popped her head in. She grinned at Landon. "You get to come with me and take some pictures. Mom, are you coming along?"

"Do you want me to?" One of my big goals was to be chill when it came to the clinic and what happened inside. I tried not to make a big deal out of strep throat swabs, wellness visits, shots, and the occasional X-ray, but I also didn't shove them out the door, telling them to sink or swim.

"It's just pictures?" he asked, his voice pitched higher as he tried to be brave.

"With a big camera," Nisha said. I hadn't had a chance to talk to her, but I liked how she was with patients. "And I even have a special vest for you to wear. It's made of lead. Wanna see?"

Landon's curiosity got the better of him. "I'll be right back."

Pride swelled in my chest. I'd go with him in a heartbeat if he needed me, but I also needed a moment.

I braced my elbows on my knees and sank my head into my hands. What the hell?

Holden was my kid's coach. I wasn't just going to see

him today, die a slow death, and never have to see him again. Every Saturday game for the next six weeks, I'd be torn between watching my son and his coach.

He lived in Coal Haven? Why hadn't that come up when we talked?

I snorted softly. As if I hadn't been avoiding every scrap of personal information I could. And it wasn't like we had talked for long before I was leaving the bar with him.

How many kids you got?

His incredulous question continued to ring through my head. "Good one, Emery," I whispered.

Was I going to have to grin and bear it when I went to get milk and saw Holden with a new girl on his arm? Seeing my husband with the other woman for the first time was a painful, surreal experience, but those emotions had developed a nice callus. Nothing about Holden living his life should bother me. But how many women would I have to see him with before the thought didn't bother me?

Did the other coach know? Weren't they cousins?

I had wanted a fresh start. No drama. I'd left plenty behind. I hadn't even been in town a month and I'd slept with my son's coach.

Was it possible to cringe to death?

I straightened. It wouldn't do any good for Landon to come back while I looked like I was having a breakdown. He was a kid; he'd think it was about him or his dad. He'd seen me cry too often when I'd first learned Henry was cheating.

I stared at the door. I didn't have to wonder what I was going to do. It didn't matter how many women I saw Holden with. My circumstances didn't change. I would do what I'd been doing since my divorce. I'd take care of me and my kids.

* * *

Holden

I roamed the waiting room like a caged animal. Em and Landon had been gone nearly half an hour. The players' parents signed waivers, but I'd feel shitty if Emery was left with a huge medical bill.

Avery was in the corner with Afton, coloring in the books offered. Riley marched around with her no-spill dish of crackers and her cup.

Anxiety clawed through my stomach as I took a half-hearted sip from the lukewarm waiting room coffee. All I had to do was be a responsible adult and make sure they didn't go out the door.

Shit. Could the little one choke on something?

I had no experience with this, and wasn't that what I hated dwelling on?

I rolled my neck. Goddammit, I could do this. Hanging out in a room with three kids wasn't a big ask, but I'd psyched myself out so badly over the years. I was stronger than this. I inhaled slowly and exhaled slower.

Riley dropped a cracker, jabbered, and picked it up. She probably shouldn't eat off the clinic floor. But before I could decide the cracker was a no-go, she'd popped it into her mouth and happily chewed.

My breath froze as I waited for the world to implode. What could she get sick from? Kids were so fucking fragile. So much could go wrong. But she took a swig from her sippy cup like it was her fifth beer pounder and sidestepped to the next chair.

They were cute kids. I could see Em in them and come up with an idea of what her ex must look like. The underlying solemnness in their expressions was all her, but they must get their curly mahogany hair and doe-brown eyes from their father. Except Riley. Flecks of green made her eyes twinkle, just like her mother's.

Riley tried to climb onto a chair with her hands still full of her items. Her chubby little legs pedaled for a few seconds before she gave up and tottered around the waiting room. I hovered. I didn't need another injured kid on my watch.

I finished the coffee and winced. I'd tasted worse, but not by much. After throwing away the cup, I stuffed my hands in my pockets. A woman in purple scrubs popped out of the back room to speak to the young guy working registration.

I did a double take, then resisted the urge to squat behind Riley as if she could hide me.

The nurse glanced up. "Holden?"

I wanted to groan like Landon had on the field. "Krystal, hey."

Krystal and Stetson had been hot and heavy. Then she'd gotten possessive and demanding, leaving Stetson with an ultimatum: marry me, or I'm leaving.

I didn't for the life of me know why she thought Stetson was a long-term guy. He was a couple of years older than me and still single. His parents were equal parts revered and feared around town. They were my aunt and uncle, and I could see why Stetson didn't want to risk a tumultuous marriage like theirs.

"Hi." She looked from me to the computer the registration guy was planted in front of. "Are you here to be seen?"

"Ah, no. I'm helping a friend." Did that come off as clumsy as it felt? I didn't want to make small talk with her, but I didn't know what else to do. "You're back in town."

She pulled her attention away. "Yeah. But they already filled my position, so I'm working part-time." Her gaze strayed to the exam rooms, and I filled in the blanks. Krystal had abruptly quit a couple of months ago. The job had probably been advertised. It would've taken a couple more weeks for interviews, and the new hire was in an exam room.

Emery had gotten Krystal's old job.

Awkward.

"Who's your friend?" Krystal was still scrutinizing the computer screen. "We only have one patient in the back."

I'd never liked her nosiness. She'd pried into Stetson's life until I joked that he should check his pickup and phone for trackers. "I'm here with Emery." As Krystal's brow ticked up, I rushed to add, "Landon is on Stetson's—my— football team." Ah, fuck. I didn't mean to mention Stetson.

Krystal's attention zeroed in on me. The avid interest in her eyes left me nauseated. "How's he doing?"

"Good, I hope. Emery thinks he just sprained his arm."

Krystal shook her head with a wry smile. "No. Stetson. How is he?"

Didn't she care about the kid at all? Or did her disinterest mean Landon was fine?

"Good." Jaded as hell about relationships, as if he hadn't been before Krystal.

Emery opened the door to the waiting room, herding Landon out. His arm was in a sling. ACE bandages circled his wrist, but no cast that I could see. I was more thrilled to see he hadn't broken a bone than I was to have my conversation with Krystal interrupted.

"Thanks, Krystal," Emery said.

"You bet." Krystal's reply was generically automatic, like she'd already forgotten they existed. "Tell Stetson hi for me, okay, Holden?"

I'd warn him. "Sure."

Emery was already gathering her kids. My little drama of how to avoid getting between Stetson and his ex was way off her radar.

I waited at the end of the row of chairs while she packed

the sippy cup and the snack dish. The two older girls were folding their coloring pages to bring with them. Landon looked as dejected as he had when he walked off the field.

I was all about distracting oneself from the shittier feelings inside. "How's the arm?" I asked him.

He lifted his good shoulder and blinked like he was fighting tears.

"Not broken, but bruised." Emery sounded relieved as she picked Goldfish crackers off the floor and tossed them into the trash.

Landon sighed, looking like the doctor took his puppy and all his action figures away from him. "I have to miss a week of football."

"Sorry, kid. That stinks."

Emery stood and handed the monster diaper bag to Avery. She picked up Riley and glanced around like she was counting her duckies. Being a mom was built into everything she did. The night we'd had together was her getting away from the minutiae of her day, which clearly revolved around everyone but herself. I held the doors open for them as they trailed out of the clinic.

The temperature had caught up with the blazing sun. It was going to be a hot afternoon, but my mom wanted to fix fence. Working with my mom was more like doing a job with a cranky uncle. Only, my uncle Bruce wasn't as cranky as Mom.

At the Traverse, Avery waited for Landon to get in. "Get in the back," she ordered.

Landon didn't budge. "Mom said I could sit in the middle."

"You're fine," Avery snapped. "It's not broken."

I watched the exchange, unsure how to help, until Emery's flustered tone broke through. "Avery, can Landon just sit in the middle so he doesn't wrench his arm?"

"Ugh. Fine."

The age gap between my sister, Nora, and me was more like Avery and the toddler. There were almost ten years between us, and we hadn't gone through this bickering stage.

The drive to the parking lot went faster than I wanted. When Emery parked by my pickup, her cheeks took on a pretty pink hue. I didn't have to ask if she remembered what had happened in the back seat two weeks ago.

I didn't fucking forget.

"Thanks," she said, her hands gripping the steering wheel. "For helping with the kids."

"I don't know how I helped."

"Keeping them in the room is sometimes enough."

I had expected her to be more worked up about leaving three kids with a near stranger.

I didn't feel like a stranger to Emery. There was so much I wanted to know about her. Why four kids? What had happened between her and her husband? Why had she moved away from their dad? Why Coal Haven?

None of those answers were my business, though, and she wasn't acting like she wanted to chat. I opened the door and got out, but turned back, my arms braced on the doorframe. "Call if you need anything. My number should be on the sheet Landon brought home on the first day."

"Oh, okay. Thanks."

She nodded. I nodded.

Okay. So. That was all there was between us. I shut the door and waved as she drove off, like I wasn't steeped in confusion about why I wanted to get to know Emery more after a quickie in my back seat when she was giving off zero vibes about wanting more.

I knew when a woman was done with me. I didn't need to relive the pain from nine years ago.

Five

Emery

The pace at the clinic was so different from the hospital where I'd worked. I stayed busy, but I was mostly rooming patients, fielding calls, and returning messages. I wasn't hanging IVs, cleaning drainage tubes, or ordering transfusion products like before.

Dr. Abdallah was a demanding doctor, but after working in ICU and being married to Henry, I found her refreshingly ego-free. I would've taken this position no matter what, but knowing she was also a mom and had practices and games to get to eased my worry that not being able to give 110 percent to my job at all times might be held against me.

I finished recording notes about the patient I'd just given a B12 shot and logged out for lunch. In the break room, Lyric was taking a bite out of an apple and reading a thriller I'd seen on the grocery store shelves. She gave me a little wave since her mouth was full, then went back to her book.

Before my divorce, I'd hated chatting during breaks, if I had time to take any. They were often the only part of the day I could be alone with my thoughts and read a chapter before I had to return to work.

After my divorce, I rarely got any adult interaction other than recording patient vitals. I wouldn't mind visiting. I liked Lyric. She was a med tech in the lab, several years younger than me, and an odd combination of optimistic and cynical. But I wouldn't interrupt her reading.

I heated up leftover lasagna. The microwave dinged just as Krystal barged in. I didn't vibe as well with her as with my other coworkers. She liked to loudly correct mistakes and throw other departments under the bus in front of patients. I'd seen Dr. Abdallah roll her eyes once when she thought no one could see after Krystal loomed over me to lecture me on how often to charge the blood pressure machines. It'd taken the sting off the new-girl embarrassment I'd had.

Krystal sniffed and wrinkled her nose like she was draining a stinky catheter. "What's that smell?"

"Garlic, probably." I smiled apologetically as I carried my food to the table Lyric was at. I sat across from her, but a couple of chairs down.

"Better have some gum before patients complain." She opened the fridge and stood with it open, her back to us.

Krystal was one of those. I'd come across her abrasive personality in the workplace before. The best thing to do would be to not take it personally. And interact as little as possible. Lyric didn't look at Krystal, but I caught her rolling her eyes. There were a lot of like-minded people when it came to Krystal.

Krystal had been talking to Holden at the clinic, but he'd worn a similar expression to Lyric's current one when I'd walked into the waiting room with Landon.

She continued to hold the fridge door open. I bit my

tongue. She wasn't my kid. I didn't need to tell her to shut the door. But seriously. The open door with cool air rolling out fueled my anxiety. A byproduct of being the major income earner for a family of five.

Krystal peered in further. "Hasn't anyone been stocking our pop stash?"

"Not since you left," Lyric said without taking her eyes off her book.

Krystal shot me a pointed look and let the door fall shut. "I guess that job falls to you now too."

Right. Because I didn't have enough to do.

Lyric turned a page. "If someone really wants it, they can take over the pop fund. Making the new girl do it isn't fair."

"I was able to get it done."

Krystal never failed to remind me that I had her old position. I wasn't sure about the story behind why she moved, but Dr. Abdallah refused to shift my position to float nurse, which Krystal now was. I had already been hired, and I got to keep the position I was hired for.

Krystal sauntered closer to our table. She tucked her hands into the pockets of her scrub top. "Hear from Stetson?"

Hadn't she mentioned Stetson when I'd brought Landon in?

Lyric didn't look up from her book. "Nope. I'm Isla's best friend, not his."

"But you see him a lot."

"Not really."

Krystal wasn't daunted by a topic Lyric clearly didn't want to engage in. "I should probably call him."

Lyric turned another page and didn't respond. I dug into my lasagna. This interaction helped me remember why I was better off giving up those late-night fantasies about Holden. Concentrating on Krystal's infatuation with

Stetson helped me forget the appalled expression on Holden's face when he'd counted how many kids I had and how quickly he'd bailed out of my car after Landon was done at the clinic.

"Well, if you see him, tell him I need to talk to him," Krystal said.

"Sure," Lyric said in a way that told me she would tell Stetson no such thing.

Krystal rounded on me. Wasn't she supposed to be covering lunch breaks for me and the other nurses? "That was nice of Holden to go to the clinic with you."

I didn't rush chewing my Stouffer's masterpiece. Technically, she shouldn't be talking about my son's visit to the clinic in front of Lyric, but I didn't mind. Okay, I did. I didn't need the clinic to make any connection between me and Holden other than that he was one of Landon's coaches. "Yes, Landon's one of his players and he was worried, and I needed an extra hand."

"Weird he'd be willing to do that. He hates kids."

My fork froze in the layers of cheese and noodles. Holden hated kids?

Lyric answered first, her tone chiding. "Hating kids and being uncomfortable around them are two different things."

He seemed relaxed enough around them. I agreed with Lyric. I wouldn't have left a man who acted like he hated kids to watch three of mine. A guy who hated kids wouldn't coach. Krystal wanted to spread rumors. I'd known more people like her in my life than like Holden.

Holden made me want to lower my defenses, not padlock them like Krystal did.

"He steers clear of women with kids," Krystal said. "Stetson said he'll never get into a relationship with a single mom."

My appetite vanished. I had been so looking forward to leftovers too.

Lyric's gaze flickered to me before going back to her book. "Holden doesn't get into any relationships."

Krystal snorted. "True." She breezed out the door, and it was like fresh air got pumped back in.

Lyric took a deep breath and closed her book. "She's *a lot*."

I chuckled, but I was aware I was the new girl. I wasn't going to get involved in anyone else's conflict.

"How's your son?" Lyric asked with genuine concern.

"Good. Upset he has to miss practice this week. You were right, though. Stetson and Holden seem to be really good coaches."

"Yeah, they're good guys. Not good boyfriends, but good guys."

Uncomfortable around kids. Commitment-phobe. Good thing I hadn't been looking for more. "Krystal doesn't seem daunted."

Lyric shook her head and her blue-tinted bun bounced on top of her head. "Stetson's attracted to women who like to play games. It's not like Krystal keeps how she is a secret." She shrugged like she was saying whatever happened was his own fault.

"It's like that, huh?" I said wryly. A tale as old as time— one partner was willfully clueless, the other was toxic. I thought I had escaped that type of relationship. But I'd been unwittingly clueless.

"It's so like that." She opened her book again, then paused. "And for the love of God, don't worry about the pop fund. It was nothing but people leaving notes on the fridge to quit being an asshole and stealing the pop."

I laughed and went back to eating. I dug out my phone just to have something to look at, but I didn't see the screen.

I couldn't quit thinking about what had been said about Holden, and I couldn't figure out why I was disappointed I'd found the one guy other than my ex-husband who would never want to be with me.

* * *

Holden

I parked in front of the little two-story house. A buddy from high school used to live next door. The neighborhood looked the same now as it had fifteen years ago. Different cars lined the street, that was all.

What the hell was I doing here?

Landon hadn't been at practice, as was expected. But the entire hour, I'd been thinking about how crestfallen he'd been. Was he sitting at home, all dejected? He'd been so damn excited last week. Then he'd gotten hurt. And I couldn't forget his face when he'd asked where his dad was.

I knew that feeling. I hadn't been as old as Landon before I'd given up on my dad showing up for anything. The kinship I felt with the kid was a surprise and probably part of why I'd come here after practice. I wouldn't consider the other reason.

I got out of my pickup and trotted to the door. I knocked a couple of times.

Yelling came from inside. "Mom! Someone's at the door!" A pause. "Okay!"

Everything went quiet. Prickles ran over my skin as if I were being watched.

I peered at the living room window. Two faces peered out. I gave Avery a casual wave, but she only ducked down.

Landon appeared, and his face brightened. Reading lips had never been so easy. "Coach B!"

His reaction helped ease my anxiety. He was excited to see me. The door opened. Emery was in purple scrubs, the standard color for the clinic according to what Stetson's ex had told us once, and they were baggy around her legs, but snug at the hips and breasts. As if I needed my nights disrupted by more images of Emery being sexy just being herself.

"Holden, hi." Surprise registered in her expression, and she looked behind me as if she assumed I'd come with Stetson.

Landon danced behind her, trying to see me.

"I wanted to see how Landon was doing and let him know what Coach Barron worked on today."

Was I imagining the disappointment in her eyes? She hadn't given me the impression she cared if I ever talked to her again.

But I wanted to.

She pushed the door open wider and told Landon, "You can talk to him on the front step." Before I could be disappointed I wasn't invited inside, she gestured behind her. "I just got home. I'll run and get changed."

Landon came out, and we sat on the front step.

"How ya doing?" I asked.

He flexed and twisted his arm. "Still hurts, but the doctor said I don't have to wear the sling anymore. Mom got this cool ice pack that wraps around my whole arm."

He described the ice pack in great detail. I wouldn't be surprised if he grew up and entered the medical field like his mom if an ice pack thrilled him this much.

I ran through the drills we'd covered in practice, using pebbles to show him where players would be situated. Basic stuff. The kids were still learning the rules and which direction to run. Landon nodded, his face serious like money was on the line at the next game.

The screen door opened behind us. Emery stepped out in black leggings and a green-and-white UND T-shirt. Her familiar peaches scent wafted over me, slamming me with a memory of the night we were together.

"We were just finishing up," I said gruffly, making no move to leave even though I knew I should before her scent gave my dick the bright idea of making this moment uncomfortable.

"Thanks for stopping by." She patted Landon's shoulder, but he also made no move to leave. "Head inside. Wash your hands and help set the table."

Landon's big brown eyes turned on me. "You staying for supper, Coach B?"

I should have been insulted at the flare of Emery's eyes and the way she shifted her weight on her stockinged feet. "Oh, I'm sure Coach B has plans."

"I don't," I answered too quickly for a guy who didn't pursue relationships with women who had kids. A guy who'd told himself for years that he was better off without the heartbreak.

Discomfort and indecision played across her face. I'd been inside her, but inviting me into her house was too much.

"Cool!" Landon wasn't deterred by my half-answer. He ripped inside, yelling, "Coach B's staying for supper!"

She rolled her lips in and stared at me like she couldn't believe I wasn't already running to my pickup to get out of a meal with a single mom and a lot of kids.

I couldn't believe I wanted to stay either, but what I'd seen at the clinic had been fascinating. She was the eye of a storm that should be raging but was functioning like a well-oiled machine. I hadn't witnessed the chaos, but I didn't believe Emery would disappoint. I thought she'd calmly carry herself and her kids through to the other side. And that was something I hadn't gotten when I was growing up, nor was it something I'd had when I needed it the most. I wanted to witness an involved mother.

But I couldn't be selfish. If she didn't want me around, I wouldn't use her kids to get close to her. "Sorry. If it's a problem, I can go."

Annoyance crossed her face. "No, you got his hopes up. He doesn't need them shattered after the way his dad no-showed last weekend."

I should've shot Landon down when he'd asked, but I didn't want to be another adult sliding out of his life. "Shit, I'm sorry. I'll eat and run so I don't interfere with your family time."

She rubbed her temples. "No, I'm sorry. It's not your fault. It's just..."

"I had a piece-of-shit dad." I stuffed my hands in my sweats. Why had I said that? I never talked to anyone about my dad. "I take that back. He was only a crap dad to me."

The fading sun highlighted the green in her eyes as she considered me. "I'm afraid that's what's happening here. Henry has become— He's always been selfish, but I could understand after I met his parents. Anyway, I just didn't think it'd play out like this."

Afton appeared on the other side of the screen door. She was in a princess dress I doubted she wore to school, but what did I know about kids' fashions? "Mom, Landon said I have to set the forks, but it's my day to do napkins."

"It's Monday. Who does forks on Mondays?"

"Landon."

"Okay, then Landon can set the forks."

Landon stuck his head out from what must be the kitchen. "But I already did napkins!"

Emery looked between them as if she was running football plays through her head. This was the chaos I'd anticipated, and like expected, Emery didn't shy away. "Afton, can you set the forks today? Landon made a mistake."

Afton's expression was scandalized. "But—"

"Please." Emery's tone said Afton was setting the damn forks no matter what.

Afton stomped away, and Emery lifted her eyes to the sky. "Come on in. Hope you like shredded chicken."

I followed her into the house and was wrapped in homey warmth. It was the time of year when it was too cool to have the AC on and too warm to turn on the heat. Her place was on the warm side, probably a solid five degrees hotter than I kept my house.

But the aroma of barbecue chicken hit my nose, and my stomach rumbled.

The lived-in home. Home-cooked food. I didn't get this unless I was the one cooking and inviting people over.

Emery looked over her shoulder, and for the first time since the night at the bar, she smiled, and it punched straight to my gut. The woman from the bar and the woman in front of me were one and the same. "Hungry?"

"I'm always hungry." That was the truth, but if there weren't so many kids around, I might've meant something else.

We rounded the corner and entered the kitchen, and four pairs of eyes stared at me. Riley was wiggling on what looked like the top of a high chair strapped to a metal dining chair. The other three kids were lined up on a bench from biggest to smallest, and there was an open seat at the head of the table. The table itself was a good size. The room wasn't. How'd she fit that thing through the door?

"Pick a seat." Emery went to a cupboard and dug out buns.

"Can I grab anything?" I wasn't used to being the one entertained. Mom wasn't a cook. I had made meals for me and Nora. Mom usually grabbed something in town. If she invited a guy over, she picked up something in town, or we grilled. Ranchers weren't short of meat, and Mom was good at the grill. The oven could go fuck itself in her opinion.

Emery shoved the buns into my hands and opened a drawer behind her. She lifted out a spoon, and I took that too. Grateful to have something to do while four kids tracked me through their house, I made it to the table.

Choosing a seat was familiar territory. I was aware of the pitfalls of choosing poorly. Growing up, my grandparents used to have me and my cousins over and we had fought over where we sat. But I sat next to Riley, and none of the kids objected. I'd chosen correctly.

Emery was right behind me with the Crock-Pot. She left the table again, and my heart rate kicked up. Avery opened the buns, took one, and flung the bag to Landon. He did the same to Afton. She was nicer when she handed it off to me. I took a bun and found Riley watching me expectantly.

Fuck, this was so far out of my norm. I stalled, not knowing what to do. I had some knowledge of the baby stage, but not older babies. Or was Riley a toddler?

"I've got her." Emery dropped a bag of spinach and one of baby carrots on the table in front of the older kids and took over making a plate for Riley. She separated small chunks of shredded chicken and spooned cooked carrots out of a jar of baby food.

Afton ignored her food and stared at me. "Coach B, do you play football all day?"

"No, I have a cattle ranch." All eyes were on me again, but I had Emery's interest, and I was way too keen on that. "I work with my mom, actually. And we have a hired guy, Colt. We...ranch..."

Could it be any more obvious I had no clue what to do or say? Put me in a bar with a woman I'd never met or in the diner with old farmers, and I would talk about what I did all day, crop prices, how much I could get per head for cattle, and of course, the weather. Did kids care that the summer drought drove hay prices through the roof?

Afton grinned and wiggled on the bench. "Like with horses?"

I nodded. "And cows. Lots of cows."

Avery's high-pitched squeal would make a pack of dogs come running. "Can we ride the horses?"

Emery had the same expression as when Landon had asked me over for supper. "Avery, we don't invite ourselves over."

"Here's the thing," I said, knowing how to save us both. I had no idea how to handle four kids charging my horses, and I could be the bad guy instead. "My horses aren't familiar with kids."

Avery put her shredded chicken sandwich down. "But they could become familiar with us. Right?"

"I don't know," I answered honestly, hating to disappoint her. "There are a lot of factors. Mostly, the personality of the horse, their age and experience, and how the kids act around them."

"We'd be good." Avery's gaze was pleading. This girl had pretended I didn't exist Saturday at the clinic. But give a guy a horse and he was suddenly worth her time?

I liked her standards.

I exchanged a glance with Emery. Her expression was apologetic.

Avery doubled down on her effort. "Dad said he was going to look for a place where I could take lessons in Bismarck, but that's not going to happen anymore."

The amount of bitterness in a kid Avery's age was startling. Landon wasn't the only kid affected by their dad's absence.

Emery was shaking her head, getting ready to shoot down Avery, but something about Avery's request broke down my determination to keep my distance.

She was giving up hope for something she'd been told could be possible. She was old enough to know that they lived too far away to make it happen, and the person who was supposed to make her dreams come true wasn't going to try again.

I knew that feeling. I also knew what it was like when a dream you planned went to shit. When my world tanked and I was left rudderless and alone, I'd been an adult.

I could be more than the fun guy around kids. "Maybe I can talk to your mom?"

Incredulity entered Emery's eyes. "Holden, no. You've already done so much."

I hadn't done anything but show up. I knew this was my chance to turn back, but I forged ahead with no idea why. "No promises. Just talk."

Emery wasn't appeased, but she said, "After dinner."

Avery smiled and did an excited wiggle with Afton. I chuckled, but I knew the discussion wasn't over. It would be a hard sell, and if Emery said no, I wasn't out anything. I wouldn't have to figure out the logistics. When would I teach a kid how to ride? How would I teach a kid to ride? I'd taught Nora and had helped my cousin Isla out when Stetson was teaching her, but that was when I was a teen. I had to be a mature adult and plan, *if* we were going to do this.

All I knew was that I'd be disappointed if Emery said no.

Six

Emery

What was his angle?

Holden offered to help clean up the kitchen. I shamelessly took advantage of it so I could get the kids ready for bed. Mostly, I needed a moment to myself. Holden did that to me.

He was in my house. My one-night stand was wiping down my table. The guy I thought I would never see again —and then when I did, I'd assumed I had thoroughly scared him off—had eaten supper with us.

And he hadn't ditched as soon as he'd eaten the last bite. What did that mean?

I was perched on the toilet lid while Afton toweled off and Riley splashed in the bathtub.

"Can we see Coach B's horses?" Afton asked as she shrugged into her nightgown.

"Probably not, honey."

"Why not?"

Because Holden was supposed to be uncomfortable around kids. He was supposed to be a commitment-phobe. He was supposed to be a one-night stand I wasn't going to see again.

He was in my house.

Why had I been so naive about hookups that I thought we wouldn't cross paths? Crocus Valley wasn't far enough away. I should've driven to South Dakota. Or Canada.

It was hard to argue it wasn't worth it, though.

"I don't know, Afton. I'll talk to him." But not about what I really wanted to know.

Like, what was he doing here? He'd checked on Landon. He'd stayed for supper. And now he might do riding lessons.

He was too good to be true. I didn't trust it.

Afton slipped out of the bathroom, and I pondered the big man in my house. I wasn't delusional. I wasn't that good of a lay that a guy would jump through those hoops to get me again. We'd had a frenzied fuck in the back seat, undressing only as much as necessary. For him, that was completely dressed with his fly open. For me, that was my pants pulled down far enough for him to spin me around and thrust in behind me.

It was like he'd surrounded me that night. What could've been impersonal had been hot and erotic, and his hands had been all around me, down my pants, up my shirt with his mouth at my neck—

I wiped off my brow. Was the furnace on?

The room wasn't hot; I was. The libido I had thought had been destroyed by work and kids and a cheating ex hadn't left. And it hadn't been a one-time flare-up that night at the bar.

Or maybe it was just Holden.

Riley tried to stand up. A little reminder that I couldn't lose my head over a guy like I had with Henry.

"No, honey. Sit until I get the towel."

I helped her out, dried her off, and dressed her in her pajamas. I'd cooled off by the time I ushered her into the living room.

Holden's voice drifted out from the kitchen, bringing back the flush all over again. "Appaloosas are the spotted horses."

"Are there Oreo horses?" Avery was all in on the horses. I should go save him. But it'd been months since I'd seen her avidly interested in a subject. She was at the precipice of outgrowing toys, but no new interests had cropped up.

"I guess a black horse with white markings could look like an Oreo. There's a special kind of beef cattle that looks like it's got a white belt going all the way around, but sometimes you see a Holstein look like an Oreo cow."

"What are Holsteins?"

I wandered in with Riley on my hip as Holden replied, "The big cow statue you see off the interstate at New Salem."

"Salem Sue?"

I heard only Avery's excited tone. I couldn't take my eyes off Holden. This place didn't have a dishwasher. Instead, I had Holden, with his biceps flexing as he held the bowl for the Crock-Pot with one hand and dried it with the other. His ass looked so firm in his sweatpants, I pictured flicking a quarter off it and watching the coin bounce across the kitchen.

How could a newly divorced mom of four look at this guy and think, *I'd have his babies; I'd have his babies so hard*?

I gave myself a mental shake and was nearly undone again when he gave Avery his easy lopsided grin. "You been to Salem Sue?"

Avery nodded, thrilled to have someone to talk to other

than her siblings and a perpetually distracted mom. "Mom took us there during one of our moving trips."

As Avery rattled off the story of how she chased Afton around all four legs of the giant cow statue on a tall hill and how cool it was to see so much of the land spread out around them, Holden met my gaze as if he knew I'd been watching him the whole time.

I had been cooling off, but heat seeped back into my bones. I wished Henry had taken my hormones with him when he left. I'd thought he had. Until Holden had slid onto a stool next to me and his scent wrapped itself around me. Whatever he wore for cologne or aftershave was nothing like Henry's expensive cologne.

Holden's smell was like a mix of Irish Spring and aged whiskey barrel. I wasn't a drinker, but I would happily over-imbibe everything Holden.

He dragged his gaze back to Avery. He might've been looking at me, but I had a feeling he'd heard everything she said. "My sister, Nora, used to be scared of Salem Sue. And the big buffalo in Jamestown."

That set Avery off about visiting the big buffalo earlier this summer. Jamestown was only an hour and a half from Bismarck, and it made a quick day trip. The kids were at the age where giant animal statues were cool. We could make memories for less than a tank of gas while Henry flew his girlfriend to St. Martin.

Easy to do when he'd saddled me with half of his student loans and gotten out of paying much child support because of his half of the debt. But I wasn't going to dwell on my ex right now.

I hated to interrupt, but Riley was starting to squirm. I set her down, and she ran to the living room. Afton was probably playing with her dolls, and I hoped she'd be in the mood to let her tiny sister play. "Avery, can you read Riley and Afton a couple of books while I talk to Holden? Landon's going to shower."

"Sure." Avery's shoulders drooped. She was enjoying being the center of someone's attention. The girl had been a rock through the whole divorce. I knew it'd affect her, I just didn't know how yet, and I hoped I wouldn't see the fallout in her teenage years.

With just Holden and me in the kitchen, the room grew infinitely smaller. His body took up more space than was fair.

"Mind if we go outside?" As I twisted, the wet splotches on my shirt were cold against my skin. Classy. At least I wasn't wearing supper.

Holden's gaze dropped to the wet patches and brushed over my boobs on the way back up to my eyes. "No problem."

What an unexpected moment to feel sexy. I stuffed the feeling away. Nothing about tonight would tell Holden I was looking for a hookup again. I had to learn to quit wanting what I couldn't have.

He followed me out, and I dropped onto the front step where he'd sat with Landon. He settled next to me, his hands draped loosely over his knees and a shoulder brushing mine. His shoulder was the perfect height to lean my head against, but I resisted.

"You don't have to teach Avery how to ride," I said.

"She seemed really excited. I taught my sister to ride, and that seems so long ago, but she's almost done with college. So, I'm not completely inexperienced, but I'd have to figure out how I'd work with Avery."

"Henry... God, he made so many promises he flaked on." I guess it wasn't realistic to keep Henry out of my thoughts. He was the father of my kids, and I wouldn't stop wishing he was different with them. Instead, he was turning into his parents. I should've seen it coming. He'd been raised by two selfish individuals, and he'd turned into one too.

He'd been that way since I met him, and I'd ignored it.

Holden was looking at me, but I stared at the house across the street. It was just as old as this one, a little more run down. Studying the peeling siding was easier than seeing that chiseled jaw and counting the deep-brown flecks in Holden's amber eyes.

"For Avery, it's horses. She's been asking to learn to ride since she was four, and Henry kept telling her that after Riley was born, they'd check into it." Holden could figure out the rest. Riley was born, and instead of horses, Avery cried while Henry packed his belongings to move out.

"How old is she?"

"Eleven." I twisted my hands. The story spilled out. I should've expected it. Holden being easy to talk to had made me forget a lot of things. "I met Henry in college. He was premed; I was nursing. We got pregnant with Avery before I graduated, but I graduated. Then we got married, and I hit the road running with a new kid and a new husband. He got into med school in Grand Forks and we talked about more kids. Neither of us had siblings and liked the idea of a big family. He really seemed to love them. I mean, he does love them, but he liked the idea of them more than the responsibility." I chuckled quietly. "It's like being a surgeon takes all he has, and when he walks out of the hospital, he acts only for himself."

"I won't expect to see him at any games, then?" He sounded disappointed for my kids. But he'd mentioned his dad, so he probably understood more than I first assumed a single guy like him would.

"Who knows? He took a vacation with his new girl-friend, the twenty-three-year-old nurse he cheated on me with. I was training her. That's how they met."

Holden let out a low whistle. "That's low."

"That's apparently Henry. I was foolish for not seeing it."

"Nah. Assuming a man who wanted to be a husband and a dad would be good to you shouldn't be considered a fault."

"Thanks." I wanted to lean into him. A wall of strength and understanding. But I stayed still. My mom had heard all this, but it was good to talk to someone else about it. I didn't have anyone other than her. I had work friends, but they were in Bismarck. I'd gotten to know some other moms at the kids' activities, but no one I'd split a bottle of wine and rage about Henry with.

"I have a horse that I think would be good for teaching a kid to ride. Bring Avery by this weekend."

"No, I can't..." What if he didn't follow through? What about the other kids?

"I won't flake." He looked over his shoulder toward the door. "I know what it's like."

"Your parents are divorced?" As much as I wanted to take him at his word, I barely knew him.

"No. Mom would have to get married to get divorced, and she's anti-vows. My dad might've wanted a family with her, but when she wouldn't settle, he left us and settled somewhere else. He didn't want to deal with me or Mom. Nora's dad was about the same. It's not like either of us were planned. I'm more like Mom's business partner than her son."

The traces of bitterness in his tone were for both of his parents.

"I'm sorry."

"It is what it is. But whenever Dad bailed on me, I had my cousins to hang out with. I had horses to ride. Chores to do. Friends. I still go for a ride if I've had a shitty day. I doubt Avery wants to spread manure, and I get it. It's not like she can walk out the door and jump on a horse, but when she's an adult... I dunno. That shit's easier to learn as a kid."

"Like skiing?" I asked. "I tried once a few years ago. Wished I'd learned as a kid."

His eyes twinkled. "Ride in the summer, ski in the winter."

He wasn't even trying to turn on the charm, and awareness tingled through my body.

I didn't think he was using my kids to get to me. That would be a lot of work for a guy who'd already had me. But I wanted to clear up what this arrangement would be. If only for my sanity. "Holden, I'm not looking for—"

"A relationship?" The twinkle vanished. "Yeah, I gathered that."

"I mean, you aren't either, right?" I pressed my fingertips against my forehead. I could tell a forty-five-year-old married man that he had gonorrhea and counsel him to notify his wife and the woman he'd had an affair with so they could get tested, but I shouldn't be spilling gossip I'd heard to the guy at the center of it. "Sorry. I worked with Krystal today."

His jaw muscles flexed. "I wouldn't believe everything she has to say."

"She said you hate kids and you shun relationships." I winced. I didn't want to hurt his feelings over what someone I didn't care for said. "I'm really sorry I brought that up. I don't know you."

"I don't hate kids," he said quietly.

"I know. You're really good with them." He looked at me like I'd said something ridiculous. I shrugged. "Not everyone who's good with kids dances around and acts like a character on *Sesame Street*. Sometimes, just talking with them like the small people they are is enough. Actually hearing what they have to say is more than they often get."

"I avoid relationships. That part's true." He glanced away. "I don't want to avoid you, though."

His confession filled me with equal parts dismay and satisfaction. I bit my lower lip. "What does that mean?"

"I don't know. But I know it doesn't mean you have to be afraid to bring Avery over to learn to ride or that we can't talk or that—" His gaze dropped to my mouth. "Goddammit, I really want to kiss you."

My lips parted, and the only thing I knew right then was that I wanted the same thing. Desperately. I wanted it even more knowing he did too. It was a surreal dream I thought I'd only get while asleep. But there were more reasons why it was a bad idea. The kids might see. The neighborhood might see. And dating would add too many complications to a life I was trying to simplify. "Holden..."

He tore his gaze away. "I know."

Did he? Because I didn't know what I was going to say.

"Just bring her over this weekend. Sunday's a good time." The heat from moments ago was gone from his tone. Had I imagined it? No, not after what he'd said. "With football Saturday morning, I have to catch up on work Saturday afternoon."

I liked everything about that statement. He carved football into his day. Work wasn't his excuse to get out of life.

My job's stressful, Emery. You're not helping with the nagging.

I shook off Henry's old arguments. Avery would be disappointed if Holden backed out, but I'd also have to deal with her disappointment if I flat out refused. So... Let's do this, I figured. As long as allowing Avery to have lessons had nothing to do with me wanting to see Holden again. It didn't. It couldn't. "Sunday would work. My mom can help watch the other three."

"Probably best until we know whether or not this will work."

I was tempted to ask him to specify. Whether we knew if Avery would be interested after getting on a horse? Whether he would decide to cut out on us? Whether I would bail because I couldn't handle him right now?

But it was best to keep my mouth shut. I didn't know if he'd live up to his end of the arrangement in the first place.

* * *

Holden

Stetson's pickup rolled down my drive. Shit. It was Sunday, and I was grabbing a quick bite of lunch before Emery arrived with Avery.

I took another bite of my leftover-roast sandwich. Nora had made me some rendition of her gluten-free bread. It wasn't terrible, but I wouldn't be eating it if she hadn't made it. Her health kick was important to her, so I didn't give a fuck if she was following trends or if gluten shredded her insides like glass. Mom gave her enough shit for the both of us.

Stetson parked next to my pickup and got out. Tension traced across my shoulders. He'd asked me about Emery and her kids at the game, but I'd managed to evade his probing questions. We had been surrounded by kids or had gotten interrupted each time, and I hadn't tracked back to address a damn thing.

"Enjoying a Sunday off?" Stetson asked as he swaggered toward me. My yellow Lab, Sally, beelined for him, her tail wagging so hard she could knock someone out. Stetson's boots hit the zero-entry porch, and he leaned against the railing next to me.

"Just enjoying some of Nora's gluten-free bread."

Stetson blanched and scooted a couple of inches farther away. "Her shit tastes awful."

"Not all of it."

"Not when she actually uses butter and sugar."

"She has food sensitivities."

"So do I," Stetson grumbled. "To all her food." I was ignoring him and polishing off the rest of my crumbly sandwich when he said, "Finally gonna tell me what the thing with Emery is all about?"

I coughed around my food. The fucker would pick that moment to ask about her. He swatted me on the back and nearly sent me spilling over the railing.

"That's what I thought," he said and leaned on his elbows again. "She's the one that bailed on you."

I swallowed and took a swig of my apple cider, also made by Nora. The cider was better than the bread, but not yet as good as the stuff sweetened with real sugar. "Yup. One of her kids was sick. That's why she had to go so suddenly."

"Does that change anything?"

It changed everything, but I wasn't sure how. "Krystal told her that I hate kids."

Stetson grunted. Krystal was the type of woman both Stetson and I steered clear of. If drama didn't follow her, she started it. I doubted she'd been in love with Stetson. She'd been in love with his family name, the big truck, the money, and the sex. And I doubted Stetson had been in love with her either, but he'd pretended he was. That part I couldn't figure out.

"Krystal doesn't know about you and her though?"

"Krystal doesn't care about anyone other than herself.

What'd you tell her?" I trusted Stetson, but his ex had a weird hold on him.

"Nothing. Just said you aren't settling down anytime soon and that you didn't want to deal with kids."

It sounded heartless, but it was the truth, and the rest of the town didn't need to know the details, which would've happened had he told Krystal what I'd gone through. Grateful he continued to keep my secrets, I just nodded.

Stetson's jaw tensed. "Look, I haven't told a soul. No one knows why you don't like kids."

I scowled. The other rumors I didn't care about. "I don't dislike kids."

"No one thinks that. You know how Krystal is." He gazed into the distance. "Don't think I haven't seen how you are with Liam's boys."

I lifted a brow. I could count on one hand how often he mentioned his half brother. Whether it was to keep the peace with his parents or to keep the town from exploding with chatter, he gave Liam a wide berth. "They're older. Makes it easier."

"I know. Just like I knew why the age of the kids we're coaching bothered you. It's why I didn't quit bugging you." He gave me a steady look. "Avoiding shit doesn't make it easier."

Sounded like he was speaking more for himself, but he was still right when it came to me. It hadn't made it easier. Lonelier, maybe.

"Landon said you went to visit him the other night."

I'd heard Landon tell him I had checked in. It was why it wasn't a surprise Stetson hunted me down. Might as well spill the rest since we were digging deeper than we normally did. "I'm teaching his older sister to ride a horse today."

"No fucking way." He straightened and faced me. "Are you telling me you're into a woman with four kids?"

I adjusted my ball cap. It shouldn't have been a shock, but it wasn't as if I'd given him a reason to think otherwise. "I don't know. She's pissed at her ex. Her kids are in a new town and have daddy issues. There are so many red flags."

"That's why she intrigues you."

Emery did more than intrigue me. She was cute. Sexy as hell in an understated way. And I liked being around her. "She's not like anyone I've met."

He snorted. "That's because she's been working and raising kids. She's lived an entire life that makes you and me look like we're fucking around without a care in the world. Add in the fact that she had zero problems walking away from you and that magic dick girls talk about, and she's like a damn drug you can't quit."

No, it was more than that. *I* was more than that. "I haven't done anything more with her since that night. We've barely touched."

"Exactly. You're huffing the fumes and can't get enough. If I didn't know you, I'd think you had it bad. As it is, I think you're curious."

"I'm not curious." I wanted to know everything about Emery, but that wasn't what Stetson was saying.

"You're something. Got any more coffee?"

"Make some more if you take the rest."

Stetson grunted as he walked inside. I stayed on the porch, facing the drive, waiting for a gray Traverse to head my way.

* * *

Emery

. . .

Holden's big dog, Sally, kept me company as I leaned against the fence around the practice riding arena. Avery had been excited to ride, but Holden had warned her that today would be a lot of learning and less riding.

He had shooed Sally out of the pen like he'd shooed Stetson out of his house when we'd arrived. My vehicle had looked tiny sitting next to their pickups. Stetson had given me a shameless grin as he'd ambled to his pickup.

Safe to say he knew about my history with Holden. It wasn't a secret, but that hadn't stopped the embarrassment from flaming across my cheeks. The blush hadn't improved when I'd caught a glimpse of Holden.

He was in jeans and a gray Coal Haven Drillers hoodie. This was the second time I'd seen him in worn cowboy boots. The first night at the bar, he'd been wearing the same pair. It changed the way he walked. He went from stalking to swaggering, and I couldn't pick which one I liked the most.

I shouldn't have been thinking about it in the first place.

I absentmindedly scratched Sally's head. She hadn't looked like a big dog when she'd been trotting next to Holden, but I didn't have to bend to pet her. And she made sure to be in petting reach at all times.

Her tail thumped the grass and we both watched the action. Avery had been introduced to Holden's oldest horse, Poppy. My daughter learned how to approach a horse, and Holden let her pet Poppy for a while. Then they went over gear, and he walked her through putting it on.

I hadn't seen my daughter this excited since well before the divorce. I hadn't noticed how the dullness had set into her eyes and become permanent. This girl used to play soccer. She used to be on the dance team. Then I'd become a single mom who couldn't get her to practices, and I'd needed her help.

I chewed the inside of my cheek to keep tears from springing into my eyes. Holden had a hold of the lead rope and was leading Poppy, with Avery on her back, around the pen. Avery's smile could take over her face.

When Holden handed her the reins and she got to maneuver Poppy, her laugh made the stress of the move worth it.

He let her ride for several minutes, had her stop and switch directions, before he walked up to lead Poppy to the side. Avery dismounted and turned to me, mouthing *did you see that?* and discreetly pumping her fists.

I grinned in return. Holden would never know how much this meant. If Avery never touched a horse again, this memory would carry her through some hard times. This was worth the tears when I told the kids I could only bring Avery. I had shamelessly bribed them with Nana's candy to distract them so Avery and I could leave. My mom had still promised a trip to the park to keep them from following me to the car.

Holden showed her how to take the saddle off and store the tack. She helped him lead Poppy back to the pasture, where the mare joined three other horses munching on grass with their tails swishing.

"Mom! Did you see that? I turned her." Avery slammed into me, her arms squeezing the air out of me.

"You did great."

"Ohmigod, that was so exciting." She whispered, "I have to pee."

Holden was approaching. I suppressed a shiver—because *damn* he was fine—and smiled at him over her head. "Can Avery use your bathroom?"

"Of course. Run on in."

She hesitated and glanced at me. She was scared to go into someone else's house alone. "It's fine." I wondered if I should go with her or if that would be intrusive for Holden.

"It's a big house, but you'll find the bathroom easy enough. You can peek in every room if you want." He lifted his hands in a mock surrender. "My place is usually the hangout for my family. I promise it's clean. But don't let Tabby in. She'll hang out by the back door and convince you she's a house cat."

Avery suppressed a squeal. "Can I pet the cat?"

"Yes, she's overly friendly. It's all part of her long game to get access to the house." Avery sprinted off. Holden gave me the lazy smile that had gotten me in the back of his pickup. Good thing I was here with Avery. "You might want to check the back of your car before you go. Avery might sneak a cat or two away."

"The way she smothered Sally, I wasn't sure she'd be distracted enough by the horse. Thank you."

He shrugged. "No problem."

"No, it's a big deal for her. And it helped me realize that she hasn't been getting to be much of a kid lately."

"Why don't you come again next weekend?" His tone was casual, but sincere.

I wanted to jump on the offer, but this place didn't run itself. I wasn't sure what farmers and ranchers did all day, but Holden's and Stetson's pickups looked used. They were nice, but they weren't for show. "I can't keep taking your time, and I can't pay for riding lessons."

"Good thing I'm not charging. Seriously, it's okay." He hooked his thumbs in his pockets. "Listen, I'm not going to lie, I'm interested in you. I know you're not looking for anything and neither am I, but the football and the horse riding—that's not about us. She wants to ride next weekend, she can ride next weekend."

Was that a fear I was harboring? That he was using my

kids to get to me?

No. The consideration had run through my mind, but he had a reputation of avoiding children. I'd seen hints of his discomfort around my kids. Yet, this gorgeous, generous, successful man told me he was interested in me. He could have anyone he wanted.

He wasn't exactly pursuing me, but he wasn't not pursuing me either. And either way, I was relieved. But I couldn't let go of what he'd said.

"Why?" I asked. "Why are you interested in me?"

He drew closer and pitched his voice low. "I still remember how you called my name when you came."

I drew in a sharp breath as a shiver traced down my spine. I remembered too. Everything. How he felt. How strong he was. How it'd been so damn good for such a cramped, quick interaction.

"I want more of that, and I want it from you."

His screen door slammed and I jumped away. Avery was running around to the back of his house, probably to find the cat.

"I want..." I couldn't bring myself to look at him. I didn't want to believe him, but I was tired of avoiding my reaction to him. "I want more of that too." I chanced a peek at him, only to see him grinning.

"So we do more and don't worry about the rest?"

I chewed my lower lip. "It's not that I don't want to. It's just not that easy for me."

"Then we won't." He was supportive, but dejected. And the flash of panic in my stomach had me reaching for his hand.

"I've never done this, Holden." I released him in case Avery ditched the cat and found me holding hands with a guy. "I wasn't lying that night. I don't have experience with casual. I had a couple of high school boyfriends and only one was serious. Then I met Henry. You were the first since the divorce and…" Ugh. This was awkward. "How do people decide to just…you know?"

He thought for a moment. "Stetson and I usually meet for a drink on the weekends. Want to meet us Friday? No pressure to do anything, just get out first without expectations. You know Stetson, so there'll be another friendly face."

That was how he normally did casual. Just like when we met. He went out. Struck up conversation. Maybe had some sex. It worked for him.

Wouldn't people talk?

Did I care? How would it affect me otherwise? There were worse things than being linked to an attractive man who seemed well liked in the community. Besides, my last attempt at getting out for adult time had been cut short. This was just visiting. I didn't get much of a chance to be social.

I could see whether Mom would watch the kids Friday night. "Okay, it's a date." Mortification swamped me. "I mean, it's not— I know we're not—"

"It's okay." Holden laughed, unfazed. "Call me if Friday doesn't work out. You can meet us there." His grin widened, and it wasn't his typical slow grin. This one had dimples. As if he wasn't perfect before. "I'll even park under a streetlight."

My cheeks flamed hotter than the sun. Avery saved me by appearing around the house with a cat in her arms and a triumphant grin.

A boldness I hadn't experienced since the night Holden flirted with me erupted. "I might park in a dark corner," I said as I started for her.

Holden made a sound between a cough and a choke, and I sauntered away, grinning.

Seven

Holden

I got to Rattler's earlier than I told Emery that Stetson and I would arrive. I didn't want her to wander around looking for us, or worse, think I'd ditched her.

The week had crawled by slowly. I hadn't seen her after practice. Landon was back to normal, but getting him over his fear of running with the ball again would take a few more practices. I didn't blame him. That'd been a hard hit.

I nodded toward the teenage hostess who was used to seeing us and had started saving the big round table in the back if no large parties came in. Stetson and I attracted a crowd. Between the women and the relatives, the owners of Rattler's that we were buddies with, and the guy that worked for my mom, we liked to have extra seats around.

On my way through the restaurant, I caught sight of another cousin. Archer had an arm slung over the booth, looking like he'd been born and raised in town instead of being a recent transplant from Texas. His wife, Laney, was across from him. Archer moved here for her after some marriage turmoil.

He saw me and grinned. "Holden, how's it going?"

"Good," I said. "Date night?"

Archer winked at his wife. "Every night's a date night."

Laney nodded. "Especially the night we were chasing a fox away from the hen coop. You want an egg drop next week?"

I nodded. She got special feed from the co-op, and her chickens laid the richest eggs. "I'll leave the money in the box."

"Want to join us?" Archer tipped his head to the spot next to him.

"Nah, man. I'm meeting Stetson and another friend."

Archer might have been new to town, but he knew everyone who walked into Rattler's on a Friday night. If I didn't specify the friend's name, then both he and Laney knew that friend was a woman and that my thoughts toward her weren't merely friendly. But they each gave me knowing nods and wished me a good night.

Stetson was already parked in his usual spot, casually chatting with Remington. Remington's ball cap was backward, and he must've ditched his apron while he was in the dining room, but that didn't mean he wasn't working. He'd talk to us, then he'd make his rounds.

I'd been to Rattler's enough to know that he and the other owner, Shawn, took turns being visible, asking everyone how their meal was, making sure that if there were issues, they were resolved quickly. It was part of their business plan. Remington mentioned once that if they kept workers and customers happy, they kept their doors open. That was critical in any size town, but especially a community as small as Coal Haven.

"There he is," Remington said, but I didn't trust the sly look in his eye. "Did you come early to beat your date?"

"It's not a date."

Both guys shot me dubious looks.

I dropped into a seat. "Don't be weird, all right? It's just drinks."

Remington stroked the dark scruff on his face. "I was at the clinic earlier this week to cater lunch. She's cute."

I glanced at Stetson, but he remained cool. He might've told Remington about Emery, but he didn't tell him I'd already hooked up with her. "You hit on her?" Of course he did. It's Remington. He flirted with all the nurses from twenty-four to sixty-four.

He barked out a laugh. "I got more approachable vibes from Ethel Blackwood in the waiting room, and she's ninety-five. I know because she said she's still 'got it going on.' Her words."

"She should," Stetson said. "She outlived three husbands."

"Said she's working on her fourth and she wants someone younger. I don't think she was joking." Remington righted himself and put his elbows on the table. "Want an appetizer for when she gets here? On the house. I can do a dessert too."

I scowled. "What the fuck? I'm not taking her to prom. What's the big deal?"

This time he exchanged a look with Stetson as if they were wondering what wasn't the big deal. "Nothing. Just being hospitable. I mean, if she likes the place, that's five more customers."

"Six, with her mom."

Both the guys leaned over the table. Remington's tone was incredulous when he asked, "You've met her mother?"

"No, I was just saying. I don't know if her mom's eaten here or not."

"Well, bring 'em by. I'll spoil them all." His gaze strayed behind me. "You're on, bro."

I stood like I had been raised by a mother who cared about manners. Emery was at the door, scanning the place for me. I stole a second to soak her in. This woman was here for me, and that was a thought I hadn't experienced for a long time.

I ditched the guys and went to her. When she saw me, relief filled her features and she started toward me. I'd seen her in yoga pants and leggings, then there were her scrubs, but tonight she was in jeans that hugged her curves and ankle boots. She wore the same fleece jacket from the other night with a simple striped top underneath. Tonight was the first night I'd seen her hair down in smooth waves just below her shoulders. She was casual, but classy.

I liked it.

What the hell was wrong with her ex? I had disliked him for what he was putting her through, and I couldn't understand how a guy could ditch four kids, but tonight I could see he was just plain an idiot.

"You look good." I almost—almost—pressed a kiss to her cheek. I wanted to, but neither of us was ready for that. Tonight was going to get the town talking as it was.

"Thanks. Uh, you too."

"Oh, this old thang?" I said with a twang.

She laughed. I was dressed the same as I was the night we first met. In fact, I was wearing the same damn clothes. Not that I was superstitious. But it couldn't hurt.

I led her through the restaurant, my hand hovering over the small of her back, and nodded at Archer and Laney, not missing the way they exchanged glances that said *I knew it*.

I even pulled out her seat. It was something I hadn't

done in forever, a throwback from the one real relationship I'd been in. The outcome of it had put a damper on my mood. I pushed it out of my mind. Tonight wasn't about the past for either of us. "You know Stetson. Remington is one of the owners of Rattler's and also the chef."

"Right. The chicken parm you brought to the clinic was amazing."

Remington's grin was full of confidence. He knew he was a good chef, but he never acted tired of the compliments. "Thanks."

"Ready for the game tomorrow?" she asked Stetson as soon as she sat.

We talked about the upcoming game and how practices were going. Remington excused himself so he could help in the kitchen. I was enjoying the night. This was meant to be an easing into whatever was between me and Emery. It was a way to get me to slow down and take a hard look at what I was doing.

I liked her. I'd already fucked her. Usually, that would be the end of it, unless both me and the woman wanted nothing but another release later. Not quite friends with benefits, but not exactly fuck buddies. Neither felt appropriate when it came to Emery.

I had built a good life after the devastation I'd been through years ago. Was I willing to get more serious, and would it be with a woman with kids?

A shadow towered over us. "Ya eat yet?" Colt grunted. He yanked a chair out and dropped into it.

Emery's eyes flared. Colt usually got that reaction. Rough around the edges was an understatement. Colt didn't waste words, and he didn't waste energy on speaking. Combine that with being tall and built like he could throw round bales instead of the small square ones, and he either terrified the ladies or intrigued them so much their clothes fell off as soon as he was alone with them.

He always kept a beard of some sort. He'd worked for Mom long enough that I knew his beard care routine. Shorter and trimmed in the summer. Longer, with an unkempt fuck-it look, in the winter. He was a little older than Stetson, old enough that when I moved home and met him, I thought he'd be just another boyfriend that would stomp out of my life after Mom pissed him off. But I'd never gotten the vibe there was anything more between the two other than mutual respect, which kept my life cringe-free.

"Are you hungry?" I asked Emery. She'd had one Bud Light and that was it. This wasn't supposed to be a date, but I didn't want her to leave hungry.

"Mind if I look at the menu?"

I slid it over. "Anything Alfredo is amazing. One of the owners, Shawn, makes the best you'll ever taste."

"Sounds like I need to try it and find out. It'll be nice to have something I didn't make or that doesn't come out of a drive-through. Chicken or steak?" Her eyes twinkled when she looked at me. "I probably don't need to ask the beef farmer that."

I chuckled. "As long as it's meat, I'm not picky, but the steak here is second to none. If I couldn't grill, I'd be here every night to have it."

Her smile was pleased. "I don't grill, so steak it is."

Colt arched a dark brow as he looked between us. My body was angled toward Emery and I was helping her decide what to eat. He'd been with me plenty of times, here, at the other bar in town, and in Crocus Valley. This wasn't how I picked up women. Usually, I didn't pick them up, and if they asked me what they should order, I made some comments. I wasn't bent over the menu, helping them fucking decide.

Colt exchanged a look with Stetson as if they couldn't believe what they saw. I straightened in my chair and scowled at my beer.

If I wasn't careful, I'd be chasing this divorced mother of four who didn't want a relationship and it'd end in my heartbreak. It'd end with me wondering how the hell else I thought this would turn out. It'd just plain end, and that had devastated me before, had ended so badly that I had written relationships off.

This was moving too fast, and it was my fault.

* * *

Emery

After the scary guy joined us, Holden grew noticeably quieter, but I didn't think it had to do with Colt. Our food arrived, and my steak Alfredo was everything he'd said it would be. I had found my new favorite dish in the world, and it was one I didn't have to cook. When I told him that, I barely got a grunt in return.

My excitement from earlier had faded, leaving a dull ache in my chest. The reason for his change was me. Had he realized there's nothing special about me? That there was no reason to waste his time maneuvering around my many obstacles?

I dug into my food and let myself drown in their conversation. Hurt feelings weren't going to stop me from enjoying a meal out, especially when I was paying for it.

A couple of women sidled up to the table. Holden visibly tensed as one of them rested a proprietary hand on the back of his chair as she greeted everyone. I took a drink of water to force down the jealousy that had no place in this night. This wasn't a date, and I was old enough to know that Holden was a single guy in a small town. Our pickup interlude wasn't an isolated event, and this woman he called Holls was gorgeous in her western jeans and nice boots. She had more in common with Holden than I did.

The other woman, who Stetson greeted as Sienna, took an empty chair by him, and *Holls* took the open spot next to Holden. There were two open seats between me and Colt, but he must not be the one either woman was after.

Was this a thing? These guys sat at this big table and the women just came to them?

I was so far out of my element. I dug back into my food, an ear on the conversation I could've tuned totally out. None of it had to do with me, and no one was going out of their way to include me.

I should have felt more upset, a little righteous even. But with each uninterrupted bite, I swallowed more relief.

My hands had shaken with nerves as I got ready for tonight. I'd argued with myself about how I shouldn't be anxious, this wasn't a date, but also why didn't I have something nicer to wear? I hadn't dated since college. Henry was the last guy who'd taken me on a date, and look how that turned out.

As I'd driven here, nerves had cramped my stomach so hard I thought I'd have to stop on the side of the road and do some Lamaze breathing to get through the rest of the three-minute trip.

Walking into the restaurant had been the ultimate test of my nerves. I'd bagged patients to keep air flowing into their lungs until the doctor could intubate and ventilate them. I'd talked families through end-of-life procedures, and I'd pumped on chests during code blues in the hospital when it was all hands on deck to get a patient's heart restarted. But walking into Rattler's to meet Holden had almost made me run.

And for what?

A guy who was chatting with another woman, someone he'd probably slept with. A guy who'd made me wish this was a real date and immediately reminded me of the reasons why I shouldn't date.

I polished off my food, wishing I could bring the kids here as a treat. I'd taken a giant pay cut at the clinic in exchange for no shift work and a less intense work atmosphere. I might not have to pay for day care, thanks to Mom's help and the size of the town, but I'd gotten financially screwed in the marriage and in the divorce.

I took two twenties out, enough to cover the meal and my drink and leave a nice tip. I didn't want to ask for the check and then wait and wonder if the server knew to split the tab. I placed the money by my plate.

When I glanced up, Colt was watching me. He was a quiet person. His presence alone was intimidating. But once I looked into his fathomless eyes, I knew he was an observer. He'd seen the one-eighty Holden pulled, and he knew I was withdrawing my stakes from this game. It was the approval in his eyes that bolstered my confidence.

I gave him a small smile. "It was nice to meet you," I said quietly.

As I rose, Holden turned toward me. "Are you leaving?"

I squashed the flare of anger and bit back my sarcastic *Ya think?* He was the one who'd invited me and then promptly forgotten me. But I managed a light "Yes. Have a good night."

I tipped my head toward Stetson. His half grin was reminiscent of the approving gleam in Colt's gaze.

From their reactions, I guessed women didn't ditch Holden too often, and I'd done it twice.

I breezed out of the restaurant. I was looking forward to getting into pajama pants and watching a show with Avery. It was getting late, but tomorrow was Saturday. I might let her make popcorn too.

I was sifting through my keys when footsteps approached. Holden slowed next to me. "Em?"

He hadn't called me Em since that night. I didn't bother to look at him. "See you at the game tomorrow." My car was only a few steps ahead.

"Wait."

The anger I thought I had quashed roared back. I spun. "For what, Holden? So I can watch you flirt with someone else?"

He had the audacity to look confused. "What do you mean? I wasn't flirting with Holly."

I held up my hands, my keys dangling from one, and inhaled slowly to calm myself. "You can flirt with who you want. I get that we're not dating. But it was kind of rude. You know why? I'd like to go out and meet friends, but if I'm just going to be on the fringes while everyone else hooks up, no, thanks. I have four little people at home and my mom who actually like to hang out with me."

He shifted his stance, but his brow was still furrowed. "I like to hang out with you."

I shoved a finger in the direction of the restaurant. "Until someone better comes along. Look, I've been there, done that. I don't need to actively witness it this time."

Regret shone in his eyes. "Em—"

"No, you know what? This just shows me I'm not ready to do more. I'm not going to trust easily. And I'm not ready to be just casual. And I guess that was the ultimate goal of this night." Tonight wasn't a date, but it had been a test. A surprise quiz neither of us had acknowledged. But I had my answer. "Mission accomplished." I backed up a step. My car was so close. I could dive in and be done with this mortifying conversation.

"You scared me."

I paused. That wasn't an apology, but I needed to hear more.

"I'm doing things with you that I swore I wouldn't do with anyone ever again. I swore I wouldn't be put in a place I could easily go with you." He shoved a hand through his hair. It was dark and he wore a long-sleeved shirt, but that didn't hide the flex of his muscles.

Fatigue swamped me. Pajama pants and a movie were all I wanted. "Then go see if Holly wants to join you in the back of your pickup. It seems like you two have a history, and you don't have the same reservations about her."

"I don't want to fuck Holly." He spat the words out. "Yes, we've been together, but it was just something to do. I don't mean any more to her than she means to me."

"And I'm tired of men and their bullshit." With that, I strode to my car and got in. I thought I'd make a clean getaway, but I couldn't shut the door.

He leaned in, one hand braced on the frame and the other on the door. "I'm really sorry."

"Yeah, you said that." I didn't look at him, but stared out the windshield. I'd heard it before.

I'm sorry. I can't help how I feel.

I'm sorry, but I don't love you anymore.

I'm sorry, but she's the one I want to spend my life with. You and I just grew apart.

"Em." He let his head hang. "I don't want to get my heart broken again any more than you do."

It was the again that got me to finally look at him, to let my gaze stroke over his shadowed face under the streetlights.

He sighed. "It seems superficial when I look at what you've been through, but there was a time I thought I'd be the happily married guy with four kids by now. In the end, we went through a difficult time and didn't make it. I was alone and hurt and swore I'd never be there again."

The sadness etched into his features was startling. I dropped my gaze. "Yeah, that sounds familiar."

"I was being an ass. Holly showed up and I knew she wouldn't tie me up in knots because I'm not interested in her. I wasn't going to do anything with her, just normal small-talk shit. But I shouldn't have ignored you. It was immature."

How sad was it that I got more of an apology from Holden than I had from Henry? "How old were you?"

"I'm thirty-one."

That wasn't what I'd meant. I shook my head, then froze. Frowning, I asked, "You're thirty-one?"

"Yeah." Confusion wrinkled his brow. "Why?"

"I'm thirty-two, almost thirty-three, and I feel like such a cougar. But no, how old were you when you almost got married?"

His jaw tightened, and I worried I'd asked too prying of a question, but the pain in his eyes was like a glimpse into his past. "Things went to hell nine years ago. I moved back shortly after that. And..." He looked over his shoulder at Rattler's. "No one really knows anything about it. Only Stetson knows the details."

A hard feat for a small town. It must've been devastating; I wouldn't press further. He would've been around twenty-two. I had gotten married a year younger than that when Henry and I found out we were expecting. I'd given birth to Avery and juggled my internship and studied for my nursing boards with a newborn while Henry was in his first year of medical school.

It hadn't been easy. Every time I thought the stress would let up, Henry wanted another kid and I relented. Like a part of me was afraid that if Henry didn't get his way, he'd leave.

What would it have been like if I hadn't gotten pregnant and I'd had the awful breakup with Henry then? I was so much younger. Less resilient. I'd had a normal childhood. My dad had died when I was a teen, and that was what had led me to nursing. But my work experiences in the hospital built the foundation I survived my divorce on; they really shaped me into a person who wasn't going to stand for Henry's shit.

I didn't know what Holden meant by *went to hell*, but it sounded like he'd been alone when it had happened. Or he'd felt alone. I'd had Mom, but I knew the feeling.

"Thank you for explaining." I ran a key through my fingers, noting the dips and the cool touch of the metal. I'd been so intent on leaving but my keys weren't even in the ignition. "See you at the game."

"What are you doing now?"

I might be dressed to be out, but I wasn't feeling it anymore. I'd gone from flying to sinking low. "I'm going home to watch a movie."

He didn't back away. "Sounds nice."

I waited for him to tell me good night, to go back into the restaurant and keep the night going with Holly. But he didn't. And I didn't want him to. "Avery's probably still up. Mom might stay and visit for a little. We don't get much time to talk without constant interruption."

"What movie?"

I studied him. What was he getting at? He wasn't asking me to stay. I wouldn't go back into Rattler's tonight. Another night, maybe, when it wouldn't be *a thing* after the way I'd breezed out. "I don't know. Avery's eleven, so it opens up a few more options for us." He wasn't making a move to go. It was like he wanted to stay with me. "Do you want to watch it with us?" I asked out of curiosity, but it came out sounding like an invitation.

"You mind?" His expression turned hopeful.

"What?"

"If I watch a movie with you?"

The smothering excitement from earlier threatened to return, but I couldn't handle it again. Topping off that peak hurt. I gave him another chance to back out. "With my daughter and maybe my mom?"

"I'm not doing anything else tonight. I'd just go home once you leave otherwise."

He was ditching Rattler's and his buddies and the girls no matter what? He'd chased me out of the restaurant when he could've called. He'd messed up and immediately owned up to it. That was new for me. "O-okay. Just let me warn my mom."

"What's her name?"

"Lynnie."

He gave me a quick smile and straightened to close the door. "I'll meet you there."

He closed me into the car, but it was a full minute before I put the key in the ignition. How had the night flip-flopped like that?

Eight

Holden

I had fucked up. Even though Emery scared the shit out of me and I'd had a moment of panic, my rudeness was uncalled for. I wasn't interested in Holly or Sienna. Emery was right. Holly might've been willing, but I wasn't.

The force of my panic when Emery had walked out was nothing like the blip from earlier. It'd been all I could do to keep from running through the restaurant after her.

How could someone so much shorter than me walk that fast? Was it a nurse thing?

I parked in front of her house. I almost needed a moment, like getting ready before a big game. But she was at her front door, waiting for me before she went inside when she would've been justified to tell me to fuck right off.

There was a little red sedan in front of where I parked at the curb. I was meeting her fucking mother. I hadn't met a date's mother since Teagan and I started dating in college. At least I was dressed decently.

Emery didn't open the front door until I reached her. "You ready?"

No. I had another urge to run. Then I recalled having to chase her down in the parking lot. I was doing this. "Let's do it."

We went inside. Her house was warm compared to the crisp late evening air. Lynnie was on the couch with Avery and both of them stared at me. Recognition flared in Lynnie's eyes and her mouth dropped open. I'd seen her around town, but here I was, with her daughter. I hadn't met a date's parent in *years*, and the last time I had, I'd been easy enough for them to cut out of their life.

"What's he doing here?" Avery asked with blunt curiosity.

Her question snapped me out of the past. "I heard you're watching a show and I wanted to crash girls' night."

Her eyes lit up as she directed her gaze to Emery. "I get to watch a show with you?"

Emery nodded. "Why don't you go pop a couple bags of popcorn while I check on the others?"

Avery let out a squeak and scrambled off the couch.

"Mom, you know Holden Barron?"

Her mom dipped her head, but questions simmered in her gaze. "Nice seeing you outside the co-op."

"Nice to officially meet you, Lynnie."

"I'll be right back." Emery disappeared up the stairs, leaving me alone with her mother.

Awkwardness descended. My last name could be intimidating to those who didn't know my family well—and to those who did. I struggled to find something to talk about. "You work at the seed co-op?"

Lynnie looked surprised I recognized her. "Yes, I'm their office manager. I moved to town when Emery was in college."

Ten years was long enough to hear all the same things about my family that everyone else had. I kept saying I didn't care what was said about me, but the anxiety chewing away in my stomach said otherwise. "Laney gets the co-op's seed for her chickens. Best damn eggs I've ever tasted."

Lynnie chuckled. "I was happy to hear she's going to keep the egg business alive. Have a seat, Holden."

Relieved the ice was broken, I took the rocker-glider. Emery came down the stairs, but turned down the hallway. It was like she couldn't do anything else until she checked on the other three. So much different from how Nora and I had grown up.

A cacophony of pops emanated from the kitchen. The microwave door opened and shut and started again. I remembered nuking popcorn for me and Nora when Mom was on a date. It'd been the shit. We hardly went to the movies, so microwave popcorn was the next best thing.

Emery appeared at the edge of the hallway. She had changed into plaid flannel pants and a loose white T-shirt, but she'd kept her hair down. Cute as hell. "Want anything to drink? We've got juice and water. Maybe some mineral water if Avery and Landon haven't drunk it all."

"Water's fine. Need a hand?" I was the entertainer in the family. It was weird just sitting.

"No, you're fine." She vanished again, and it was me and Lynnie. I launched into small talk with her, mostly asking if she watched Landon's football games and how she liked Coal Haven.

She'd moved to Coal Haven for the job, and she loved it here, but it was even better now that Emery and the kids were in town.

Emery reappeared with Avery, carrying bowls of popcorn and glasses of water. I got my own bowl and water while they shared a big bowl on the couch with Avery tucked between Emery and her grandma.

"What should we watch?" Emery asked Avery.

Her daughter launched into a list full of titles I didn't recognize. Emery settled on a Disney movie that was a villain origin story.

I relaxed into the movie. I hadn't done this in...years. When I'd been with Teagan, we'd been finishing college and working part-time. At times, our relationship seemed more like we were roommates. Maybe that was why it hadn't withstood what we'd gone through.

Emery's relationship with Henry had to have been that way. They were going to school and having kids. And their relationship hadn't lasted.

Why wasn't this enough for Henry? I'd spent the last nine years mourning that I didn't get this. I'd been going to the bars with Stetson for almost a decade, and it got old. Once every couple of years I asked him if that was it for us, as if each of us was only the wingman for the other but we'd be willing to quit in a heartbeat if the other was. All he'd say was *we'll see* and we'd keep doing what we'd been doing.

Halfway through the movie, Lynnie scooted off the couch. "If I'm going to Landon's game tomorrow, I should go home and get some sleep. Nice to officially meet you, Holden. I've heard a lot about you."

I grinned. "I wish I could say none of it was true."

She chortled and patted my shoulder as she walked past.

My mom wasn't affectionate like that. I had no idea how she'd react if Nora brought a date home, but that could be why Nora had never brought a guy home. She and Mom were like apples and pineapples. Nora was the polished apple that was sweet but also a little tart. Mom was prickly with a tough core.

The movie wrapped up, and Emery nudged Avery. "Bedtime."

Avery had other plans. "Are you giving me more horse lessons on Sunday?"

I glanced at Emery. We had discussed it, but after how I acted tonight, I didn't know how much she wanted me around. She invited me here. Had I read too much into it?

Her jaw tightened but she met my gaze. "I don't know. Are you up for it?"

"I'm still game, and you can bring all the kids." I couldn't believe I had offered—all the kids?

She tilted her head like she hadn't heard correctly. "All of them?"

"They can at least pet a horse from the other side of the fence. And when Avery's riding, you all can wait in the house."

When I was younger, I'd assumed I'd grow up and farm and ranch and that my place would have a bunch of kids running around, just like my cousins and I did at each of our homes while we were growing up. Then that fantasy had taken a hell of a hit, and I didn't recover. Each year that passed, I thought work would make up my life. That I was more like my mom than I feared.

Being around kids used to remind me of when my life imploded. Of when I found myself alone, with no one in my corner. Stetson had been the only person I talked to because he'd been the only one I trusted to tell.

But around Emery's kids, I wasn't reminded of memories I'd been avoiding for nine years. I reflected on that time of my life with less wincing, less regret that I didn't do enough, and began thinking that maybe I'd stuffed everything inside myself so securely that it was causing more issues. And that maybe I could start looking over my tightly packed baggage without the hurt devastating me again.

Avery tried to keep her squeal quiet. "Landon will be sooo excited."

Emery touched the tip of Avery's nose. "Then you should go to bed and rest up."

Avery rolled her eyes, but she trudged upstairs.

Finally, it was me and Emery, alone.

"So..." She rose and straightened the blankets on the couch. "Riley's going to get up early."

Oh. That was my cue to leave. "I don't want to keep you up." I did, but I wouldn't.

"I know you invited all the kids, but are you sure it's okay?"

"Yeah, why?"

"You got a little—" She fluttered her fingers in front of her face.

Pale? Panicked? She didn't know the huge step I'd taken in that moment. I came up with a valid reason for why I might have looked like I was going to pass out. "I realize it's a big responsibility to have kids around horses. My horses aren't used to small kids. My cousin Liam's kids have been over a couple of times. They know how to behave around horses, but they're still six."

"Gotcha. I'll give them a good lecture on the drive out."

"Look forward to it." I grinned and rose. "The visit, not the lecture."

"I bet you got a few in your day."

"You haven't met my mom. She wasn't patient enough for a lecture. But I've given a few to my little sister. Nora's ten years younger than me."

She chuckled. "I can picture Landon being a bossy big brother to Riley. He tries with Afton."

I could picture it too. My chest tightened. I was getting to know them. Not just Emery, but everything that was important to her.

She walked me to the door. I didn't want to move too fast. Tonight was supposed to be about her getting to know me. I was prepared to take this slow. Trying to kiss her might be a setback. But I lightly put my fingers under her chin. I didn't miss the way she stiffened, but she let me tilt her head up. A wide, green gaze met mine.

"May I kiss you?" I asked, terrified she'd turn me down. "I promise I won't go too far."

She didn't give me a hesitant nod or twist away from my touch. She stood on her tiptoes and slid a hand up my chest. I lowered my head enough that our lips met.

This was nothing like the wild clash of our bodies our first night together. This was a tentative touch of our lips. I didn't open my mouth. I wanted to sweep my tongue inside, to taste her again. I knew she'd open for me. But I restrained. I kept my kiss light and pulled back.

Her eyes were dreamy, but when she focused, disappointment infused her expression.

I hated to leave her wanting, but—she wanted me. My ego surged. "See you at the game, Em."

"Have a good night, Holden," she said, her voice breathy.

I left, knowing I'd get a shitty night's sleep as I replayed our first night together while I was alone in bed.

Nine

Emery

I was less nervous going to see Holden today than I had been the other night. At the game yesterday, he'd high-fived Landon and coached like normal while I replayed the sweet kiss he'd left me with. Every time my life gave me a moment to myself, that kiss was on my mind.

I had sat with my mom, and the other three kids kept me plenty distracted. No one got hurt, and after the game, we all went our separate ways. The kids and I worked on the house and homework and planned meals for the weekend. The day had gone by so slowly.

I had a restless night's sleep, anticipating today. Which was ridiculous. I'd be making sure Riley didn't get away from me and run under a horse. Same with Afton, and probably Landon, depending on how excited he was.

He was pretty excited.

"Mom, is that his place?" Landon was staring out the window at a giant white-and-red shop.

"No, that's his mom's place."

"Holden's house looks like a log cabin," Avery said, sounding like the all-knowing one. "It's cool."

It was cool. Like an alpine ski lodge in the middle of a pasture. He'd built off the road with three rows of young trees planted between him and the gravel county road. A ground-level porch ran across the front of his house, and it looked like there was a second-level loft. The house had no basement, so there were no egress windows or a basement foundation. I'd been surprised by how small it was. It was big, but with no upper or lower level, my rental house probably had more square footage.

It was like he'd built it planning to be a bachelor all his adult life. Or at the very least, to not have kids.

I was reading too much into his home. I had to stop.

Landon strained against his seat belt. "Is that it?"

"Yes."

"There're the horses!" Afton hollered from the back seat.

"Ho'ses!" Riley echoed.

Avery had already told them all about the dog, Sally.

"Please take it easy on her," I warned. We'd had the lecture I told Holden about, but reminders didn't hurt. "She's an old dog."

"I want to pet Sally first!" Afton was going to vibrate out of her seat.

I was grinning despite my underlying stress when I pulled in. After I parked, the kids spilled out of the car. I unbuckled Riley from her car seat and carried her to keep her from running off.

She struggled against me until she saw Holden, then she stared. I knew the feeling. I couldn't take my eyes off him for a different reason. He was just so much. He was sexy at the restaurant and sitting in my recliner in the living room, but in his space, wearing his dirty boots and jeans that moved with him like they knew how to best show off his form and his muscles, he was a work of art.

The other three kids piled against the fence around the riding pen. "Don't climb over that," I called.

He put his hands in the pockets of his jeans. "I just took Pittance out instead of Poppy. He's been around Liam's twins a few times."

I shifted Riley to my other hip. "Who's Liam?" The name was familiar.

Holden lifted his chin toward the road. "He lives on the other side of Coal Haven. He's my cousin. There's history there I'm sure you'll hear soon enough." He flashed a smile. "When kids aren't around."

"I'll keep my ears open."

Avery ran over to take Riley. She set Riley down and held her hand all the way to the edge of the pen.

"She's a protective big sister," Holden said.

"She's been such a huge help. That's why I'm so grateful you can help with the horse lessons. She's had to mature a little more than I would've liked at her age."

"I know the feeling."

His statement resonated with knowing. The comment he'd made the other night about his mom added some context. "You were in charge of your sister a lot?"

He lifted a shoulder. "Sometimes, it felt like I was all she had." He grinned, wiping all heaviness from his eyes. "Want to pet Pittance?"

"How'd he get his name?"

"When I picked him out, Mom said it was a pity I didn't want a better horse. I was all of fifteen with an ornery streak, so I named him Pittance."

"She would've chosen a different horse?"

"Only different from what I wanted, depending on her mood."

I didn't know how to respond to that. I'd had two loving and supportive parents. Mom had been my rock before, during, and after the divorce, never questioning whether I should leave Henry. She had questioned whether I should've married him, and looking back with twenty-twenty hindsight, I realized I should've paused and listened. Mom had never asked me to stop and think about anything I'd done before or after.

"I'll bring him around so they can pet him and feed him treats. Then you and the others can hang out while I let Avery ride."

Pittance was already saddled. To me, he looked similar to Poppy. Holden hopped the fence, and my belly tightened. All because he jumped a fence. Henry wasn't the fence-jumping type. He liked to run while decked out in head-to-toe moisture-wicking fabric and the most expensive shoes on the market. His weekend hobbies aligned with what his fellow surgeons did on the weekend. Golf trips and boating. He would probably get a pontoon now that I had half his med school loans dumped on me.

Don't worry, baby. When I'm a surgeon, we'll pay those off in no time. I'll probably get a signing bonus.

He had. And he'd pumped it into a new, bigger house in the million-dollar-house neighborhood where he'd heard other doctors lived. So then we'd had a giant mortgage along with his student loans.

I'd paid most of mine, using my signing bonus and taking extra shifts when Mom could help with the kids.

But those were thoughts for another day. They were worse today only because I'd had to pay bills last night.

Fucking Henry.

I helped referee the kids as Holden let them come in one

at a time to pet Pittance and give him a carrot. Since Avery had ridden before, I had them go by age. He put Landon in the saddle and led Pittance around. Riley squealed and my heart stopped, but Pittance only tossed his head.

Next was Afton. She was so nervous, she didn't move once she was in the saddle. She looked like she'd been hit with a freeze ray the entire time.

"Next is Riley's turn," Avery said, leaning against the fence like a seasoned cowgirl. All she needed was a blade of broom grass sticking out of her mouth.

I went through the gate and approached Pittance. I let him snuffle around her. Breath puffed out of his nostrils as he turned his head to sniff her. She patted him and twisted her hands in his coarse mane.

I didn't realize how much I was grinning until Pittance lifted his head to smell me, his big nostrils flared in his velvet nose. "Are you going to get on and hold her?" I asked Holden.

His gaze landed on Riley. For a single heartbeat, stark pain flitted through his amber eyes.

Whatever had caused it, I wasn't going to add to it.

"She's too young," he said with a slight waver in his voice.

I didn't know where his fear was rooted, but there was more to him than just being uncomfortable around kids, and the younger they were, the easier it was to see. Riley was going to throw a fit if she didn't get on a horse like she'd seen the others do, but I could carry her to the house so she didn't upset the horses. "Sorry, I wasn't thinking."

I took a step back, but Riley swung her body toward the horse.

His normal affable look was back in place. "Maybe you can go to the other side and hold her up? I'll stay on this side."

I was only average height, but I knew I'd be able to set her in the saddle, and it would prevent a tantrum. I wasn't scared of horses, but I didn't know enough to be comfortable around them.

"Okay, hold on right here," I told Riley after we'd walked around in front of Pittance, giving the horse a wide berth. She wrapped her chubby hands around the saddle horn.

"Ready?" Holden asked. He led Pittance slowly around the arena for a full lap.

When she was supposed to get off, she held her arms out to him. He blanched, and like earlier, he covered it with his trademark grin, but I was already lifting Riley down.

"Come here, hon." She reached her hands behind me and strained for Pittance. "No, baby. It's Avery's turn. Should we find some kitties?" Tabby would be the perfect distraction if she was as friendly as Holden said.

"Kit-ty?"

"Yeah, kitty."

Afton's eyes grew wide. "A cat?"

I gave Holden a reassuring smile as he helped Avery into the saddle. Was it babies that bothered him? It was a mystery that wasn't mine to solve.

Landon spotted a cat and took off with Sally on his heels. I didn't know if that cat was Tabby, but Afton followed. I put Riley down and she toddled after them. We spent the next twenty minutes searching the barn and around the house for the cat. At the back of the house, we found Tabby. She preened and stretched and sauntered toward Landon. He dropped to sit on the concrete. Afton did the same.

This was such a nice place. A person could get lost in nature. Dogs, cats, horses, cows, and acres to explore. My old house had all the space in the world and a yard the size of half a football field, but it hadn't been welcoming. The house I rented in town was small, but it fit us and had a small fenced-in backyard. The kids could play, but I missed being able to let them run.

Riley sat on my lap and I helped her pet the cat without tearing out its fur. Avery rounded the corner, excitement flushing her face, and she dropped to her knees to hug Tabby.

If there was a cat that loved the attention more, I'd be surprised.

Several minutes later, Holden found us and grinned at the cat. "She's in heaven."

I held Riley as she tipped forward to pick a pebble from the concrete pad. "I can't believe she's so friendly."

He squatted down and scratched behind her ears. "She's an indoor cat in a barn cat's body. She's always been that way. It's not like I socialize them, but I try to make sure they're not feral. I find mama cat and give her some attention and let the kittens get used to being handled. Tabby even cuddles with Sally."

I grinned as I watched the cat happily twine around all the kids, going from person to person and loving the adoration. "She's so good with kids too."

Landon ran his hand down Tabby's length to the tip of her striped tail. "Do you have kids, Holden?"

I was about to shake my head, but I realized I didn't know. It seemed like something he'd have mentioned. When I glanced at him, my heart dropped. Oh, no.

He'd gone still, his face draining of color. He swallowed hard. I didn't know what the story was, but I knew it wasn't our business.

I was about to say something, but stalled. How should I respond? How could I respond in a way that wouldn't make the kids ask even nosier questions? I was used to difficult conversations, but I wasn't in the work environment where I was accustomed to them and better prepared.

"Oh, Landon..." I began.

Holden gave himself a shake and rose out of his crouch. "It's fine. Uh, I'm going to go check on..." He spun on a boot heel and vanished around his house.

Whatever had happened might not have been my business, but that didn't mean he had to hurt alone. "Avery, do you mind making sure everyone sticks around the patio while I see if Holden needs help with anything?"

She nodded, thankfully not questioning what had just happened. Grateful that kids' minds moved from subject to subject so quickly, I went in search of Holden.

Ten

~∽~

Holden

I was on the front porch, my hands braced on the railing, my boots braced on the wood flooring. My jaw was clenched so hard I wasn't sure I could pry my lips open. My heart thudded, recovering from the beats it had skipped when Landon asked his question.

Emery slowly approached. "Are you all right?"

I gave a curt nod, forcing my jaw to loosen. "I haven't been asked that before." I let out a soft, humorless laugh. "I had no idea what to say. Isn't that something?"

She stopped next to me and leaned her butt on the railing, facing the house, as if she knew it would make it easier to talk. I could continue to stare at the ground while she studied my siding.

"No one knows," I finally said. "Isn't that fucked up? I haven't told anyone. I didn't tell anyone about, fuck, any of it."

She laid a hand on my arm. Could she feel the tremors

racking my body? So many years, and sometimes the memories still clotheslined me. "It's not as uncommon as you'd think."

"I had a kid and kept her a secret." I dragged in a breath and let it out slowly. "We knew from the beginning we were going to lose her."

Her fingers tightened around my forearm. "I'm sorry," she whispered.

"Teagan and I were getting serious, and then right after college graduation we learned she was pregnant. Mom didn't like Teagan, mostly because Teagan had no plans to settle in Coal Haven and Mom wanted me to run the farm and ranch. So, Teagan didn't come home with me often and not many people knew about her. It wasn't like Mom to tell anyone about our business anyway."

I fell quiet for a moment, then turned around and planted my ass against the railing like I needed to be propped up. The truth was out, and it was something I never talked about, but suddenly, I couldn't stop.

"When we first found out she was expecting, Teagan wanted to wait to tell people about the baby. She said, three months and then we'll share the news. But by three months, there were concerns, and then we learned...well...we learned that we were just waiting to say goodbye."

"Oh, Holden."

I dropped my head back. "So many ultrasounds. So many tests. Still, we prayed for a miracle. She told her family, but I didn't tell mine. My dad's an asshole that never wanted anything to do with me, and Mom's...cold. Nora was in middle school and I wasn't going to put her through the worry." My throat grew thick, but I'd come this far. The details were painful, but they weren't as debilitating as they used to be. "Our daughter was stillborn at eight months. Faye, named after Teagan's grandma."

"That's a beautiful name." Tears shone in her eyes. "Only Stetson knows?"

"Yeah." I tipped my head forward. Krystal had said I hated kids, but the opposite was true. I thought they hung the moon and stars, but I also knew what it was like to be crushed by grief when something happened to them. "She was the last baby I ever held. The last baby I ever dared to hold. I just never got over it. Months of fear. Afraid to hope. I didn't know how I was ever going to face that again. But Teagan? She's married, with two kids now." I didn't mean to sound bitter. I was happy for her. Both of us didn't need to be miserable, but...I didn't know how not to be.

She rubbed my back. "She had a support system, and you didn't."

"I guess." Those two words said a lot, like asking how Teagan could move on when I hadn't. Two words that said I thought life wasn't fair. And they said I hurt and was tired of holding it in.

"Holden, you did nothing wrong. They don't give us textbooks about how patients are supposed to appropriately grieve. Some people are fortified and plow through life like a boss. Some people bury it so deep that it festers until they explode. Some people are devastated and struggle to find their way out of the pain. Others coast until their need for something different outweighs the hurt of moving on. There's no time line, and there aren't any rules."

The pain in my chest dulled, if only a little. "Given that talk a few times?"

"Usually, it's a more abbreviated version." She continued to stroke my back. "Does it help to know you aren't alone? The perk of being both a nurse and a mom is that members of each group speak frankly and share freely. What you went through with your daughter and the dissolution of your relationship afterward isn't limited to you."

I was quiet for a moment. "It does help. That feels a little fucked up."

"That's common too."

The corner of my mouth tipped up, but the ghost of a smile faded. "That's the first time I told that story. After Teagan moved out of our apartment, I came home and went to work the next day. I doubt that's recommended."

"Maybe not, but it's done."

Her words continued to ease my tension. Was this what it would be like if I'd had someone to talk to? Teagan had visited a counselor, and she'd spent a lot of time with her parents. It had seemed like she talked to everyone but me. Perhaps it had been me not talking to her. "You're something, you know that?"

"I'm pretty average."

I turned to her. "You're so far above average, Em." I brushed the backs of my fingers down her cheek, seeking as much comfort as possible.

"Mom!" Avery called before she rounded the side of the house.

Emery gasped and jumped back.

I yanked my hand away, but hurt flickered through my stomach. Yearning. I'd shared my deepest secret and I'd wanted a moment with Emery. To soak in the comfort she offered. But this wasn't the time or the place.

"I'm sorry," she whispered as she faced Avery. "What's up, hon?"

"Another cat let us pet her."

I tucked all my emotions back in the box I'd kept them in. Only this time, I didn't lock the lid. I stepped around her, and we were back to acting like nothing had happened. "That would be Downy. I call her that because she keeps mice away better than the fabric softener sheets."

"Those keep mice away?" Avery asked, her tone incredulous.

I grinned. "I don't know, but that's why I have so many barn cats."

Avery darted away, yelling the cat's name to the others. I started to follow her.

"Holden. It's just that—"

I hoped my reassuring smile didn't come across as forced, but I was still raw. "I get it, Emery. Just because my dad was a piece of shit didn't mean that I wasn't a shitty kid when Mom dated other guys. You want to keep your kids from that. I get it."

She pressed closer to me. "You can talk to me. Any time. Okay? I need you to know that I'm not going to shut you out."

I briefly tangled my fingers with hers. "I know."

Telling her about my past had been like turning myself inside out and thwapping myself against the ground a few times for good measure. But as I went in search of Downy and Avery and the kids, my steps were lighter, like a perpetual dark cloud had been released to float away, if only for a little while.

And now it was about the kids. The pivot should have made my head spin, but I'd told Emery I understood and I did. I was like Avery once. I had been like Landon and Afton too. It didn't matter the age. Mom would bring a guy home, or I'd wake up to him in the kitchen. Sometimes he'd be really nice to me, like I was the way to win Mom's cold, brittle heart. Other times, he'd ignore me. I preferred that.

I didn't want to be one of those men, but the way Emery had reacted, I found myself in that category. Did I want to be the annoying new guy, the one the kids didn't want around?

I had tried so hard not to be. I didn't go home with my

dates if I knew they had kids. I wasn't going to be that strange guy at the fridge looking for eggs. The line in the sand was crystal clear and permanent. Until Emery.

She had shit going on with Henry, and that was where I had to be a better man. I had to get over my pride. Emery was trying to protect the kids from the way their suddenly absent dad made them feel. She shouldn't have to worry about my reaction to her doing what she thought was best. But when I'd reassured her that I understood, my sincerity had been lacking.

I should talk to her. Before I got to the patio, I turned to talk to Emery and froze.

Her brows lifted and she waited, but my gaze was on the road. A large F-250 was turning off the highway.

Shit.

Mom wasn't the warm, welcoming type. Before Teagan, I'd had a couple of other long-term girlfriends. One in high school, and then one the year before I met Teagan.

Mom had hated all of them. She didn't come out and say it, but I suspected she supported my playboy lifestyle. Less hands in the Barron pie. Mom could deal with me, she could barely tolerate Nora, and she definitely didn't care to deal with another person who thought they had a say in her business. If I got serious about someone, that would shit all over Mom's day.

So nine years of fucking off all over town and she was going to have questions about Emery and her kids.

"My mom's coming," I said as if I was warning about an F5 tornado bearing down on the property.

"Oh." Emery twisted and squinted toward the road. "I can gather up the kids and go."

"You don't have to." If I thought my earlier comment was missing reassurance, this was empty. I didn't want her to go, but I wanted what was best for her, and that wasn't meeting my mother.

She lifted a brow. "No, it's fine."

I stuffed a hand through my hair. Things were going so well. We had obstacles yet to face, but I wanted the chance to deal with them. Mom could obliterate all that with one caustic comment. "Em, I don't want you to go. I wanted to talk to you more, but my mom is like walking across coals barefoot on a good day."

"No, it's no problem." She went to the corner of the house and called to the kids. "Hey, guys. We've gotta get going."

There was a chorus of disappointed sounds that, no shit, made me feel good. They liked it here. It was more about the animals than me, but I'd made this place into my haven from all things shitty. My family was the only exception, but they weren't crappy all the time.

"You want to bring them by next weekend?" I asked.

She wrinkled her nose. "It's supposed to be Henry's weekend. We'll see if he actually goes through with it."

I hoped he did, but I'd miss having them out again. "Okay." I toed my boot in the dirt. I'd miss the kids, but Emery wouldn't be at Henry's. "You want to go out with me, then?"

"Holden, are you asking me on a real date?" Interest sparked in her eyes.

I was about to say *hell yes* when Landon appeared with Riley. "I think she ate a rock."

My pulse kicked up. "Is she okay? Do I need to call for help?"

Emery patted my arm. "She's fine. If it's small enough for her to swallow, it's usually small enough to pass through to the other end." Her mouth twisted in a wry smile. "Usually. But it wouldn't be the oddest thing one of my kids has eaten. Don't worry."

Relief rushed through my veins. Her confident, nonplussed tone was everything I needed. "Okay. Good."

Mom rolled down the drive. Her chin jutted out as she glanced from Emery's Traverse to where I stood talking with Emery and the kids.

I ground my teeth as I worried for a moment whether she'd block Emery's vehicle in. Mom could be petty like that. But she parked next to it, with the bed of her pickup sticking far past the back end of the Traverse.

Emery could drive over the grass; I didn't care. But Mom had made it more inconvenient for her to back out.

I walked Emery and the kids to their car, my anxiety ramping up. I hadn't thought about what I'd tell Mom about Emery. It wasn't her business, but she'd make it hers.

"Are we coming again next weekend?" Avery asked.

All four sets of eyes landed on me, even little Riley's, the girl I'd nearly passed out over when Emery had asked if I wanted to lift her up.

It seemed silly now.

I'd been so bitter about Teagan, but Emery had nailed it. Teagan had built herself a support system that I had made mine too. So when she was gone, I was left with no safety net.

"You'll be with your dad," Emery answered like she wasn't questioning whether Henry would live up to his end of the custody arrangement.

Landon's face lit. "Dad's picking us up after school Friday?"

Emery finished buckling Riley in. "That's the plan."

She closed the back door. "Thanks." Her gaze strayed to the side where Mom was, thankfully, walking to the house.

"She's not one for introductions. I have a long-lost

cousin from Texas. When he first chased his wife up here—long story—Mom and my uncle Cameron antagonized the shit out of him until he quit talking to them. That's what she does to family. You don't need to deal with her."

"That's so isolating."

If I told someone else that, their response would be closer to "that's fucked up" and I would agree. But not bighearted Emery. She saw immediately why I withdrew into myself after losing my daughter. It was what my mom had done all my life.

How could Emery think she was nothing special? "Call you later?"

She hadn't answered me about a date yet, but now wasn't the time to cement the details. "Yes. Thank you for everything."

"No problem." I waited for her to pull away before I gave one last wave and wandered to the house.

I steeled myself to face my mother. I found her inside, a boot kicked up on my end table, reading one of the magazines about ranching published out of Bismarck. Not a dyed-brown hair out of place for a woman who worked outside for a living. Both of her brothers, Cameron and Bruce, had a healthy dose of gray that they didn't hide. I hadn't met Archer's dad to know whether he was the same. Mom never let her gray show. I wasn't sure if that was a woman thing or a Mom thing. If people might think gray was a weakness, she'd smother it.

She was dressed similarly to me. She used to wear my clothes and boots until I grew a good few inches taller than her. I doubt she borrowed from Nora. Too "girly."

"What's up?" I asked, testing the water. I wasn't offering information if she didn't ask for it. That was how our relationship worked.

"We've got to talk about moving cattle."

More like she was driving by and saw an unfamiliar vehicle and came up with a reason to stop in. "Is there something new I don't know about?"

Mom scowled deeper than normal. "You have that football thing."

Mom had always hated sports. She'd tried to forbid me to participate, but Uncle Cameron was more about the community than her. He'd talked to her about how good it would be for the school to have the Barron boys involved. How well it would reflect on them since they had a hard time earning a lot of the goodwill themselves. I doubt he'd said the last part; I just filled in the details.

"Stetson's been coaching for years, and he's still been able to help move and work cattle."

She hmphed and paged through the magazine. Deceptively out of my business. Until she said, "Who was that?"

"Emery. She's new to town, and her daughter's always wanted to learn to ride."

"And you let her bring all her kids out here?" Her voice was filled with more disappointment than disbelief.

"I invited them all."

Mom frowned. "You like her or something?"

Yeah, I liked her or something. "Is that so wrong?"

"She's a city girl. You can tell."

"It's Coal Haven. We're all a little country."

Her eyes narrowed. She always had a good bullshit detector. I just wished she called herself on her own. "Is it serious?"

"I met her only a few weeks ago, Mom. Besides, what's wrong if it ended up serious?" I knew what would be wrong. The ranch was everything to Mom. And something that shifted my priority from it scared her.

Mom pursed her lips and set the magazine down. "People who don't grow up like us don't understand the life. They hear about the oil money, call us rich farmers or rich ranchers. Wealthy cowboys. You can't trust 'em, Holden."

"She's divorced. I don't think I'd be the only one dealing with trust issues."

"Yeah, but you're not dealing with money issues and she probably is."

I sighed. Mom was most likely right, but it wasn't my business. "Is it so hard to believe that maybe someone will like me for more than my last name? You realize it doesn't mean a damn thing outside of the county, and Emery wasn't raised here."

Mom snorted. "Money talks everywhere, Holden. And it often talks louder when we profess our love." Her boots were heavy on the hardwood as she crossed to the front door. "Make sure that football thing of yours doesn't fuck with our schedule."

She pushed out and let the screen door slam behind her.

"Thanks for the pep talk, Mom."

I might not have had a support system, but I never regretted not telling Mom what had happened. If I had waited so many years just to tell the right person so I could heal the way I needed to, then that said a lot more about Emery than Mom would ever know.

Eleven

Emery

I shut down the computer for the night. I was the last nurse left. Dr. Klevin was in his office with the door shut, catching up on his dictation. Dr. Abdallah had left at noon, but I'd stayed and fielded phone calls and helped the other nurses.

The nurses' desk faced out. We could see all the exam rooms and the patients as they walked by. Lyric breezed down the hall, her white lab coat softly rustling. She'd secured her hair in a bouncy loop on top of her head, and her purple scrubs matched mine.

"Anyone left?" She stopped and leaned her elbows on the higher ledge of the desk where Dr. Abdallah often stood with her laptop or tablet to jot down notes or give me instructions.

"No, sorry. Krystal was supposed to tell you when the last patient left." One of the other med techs swept by at the end of the day to make sure it was safe to close down the lab and leave. I had hoped to save them a trip.

Lyric rolled her eyes. "She probably wanted to go hunt down Stetson as soon as possible."

I almost mentioned that I didn't see Krystal last week when I met Holden and Stetson at the bar. But that'd encourage questions I didn't want to answer. "Sounds like she burned that bridge."

Lyric shook her head. "She thought she was *the one* but she doesn't know him or she'd know better. Honestly, as much as I dislike her, I feel bad. She's only going to get hurt again. She needs to move on." She waved her hand like she was shooing the topic away. "Anyway. Any plans for the weekend?"

I wasn't sure what to say. I opened my mouth and closed it again. I did have plans—ones I didn't want to think too hard about. I'd get too excited, too nervous, and if Henry bailed, I'd be too disappointed.

Lyric chuckled. "That good? Or that bad?"

"No." I smiled. I'd grown to trust Lyric. She didn't say anything behind anyone's back she wouldn't say to their face, and she also didn't lash out for her own benefit. She was pragmatic. "I'm going to Holden's. He's grilling and having some cousins over."

Lyric stared at me and her eyes widened. "Ohmigod. You're the one Laney was talking about."

The name was familiar. Wasn't she the wife of one of the cousins Holden had said would be there tonight? And people were talking about me? I had thought I might be fuel for the talk around town, but experiencing it was another thing. "I don't know."

"Holden, like, chased you out of Rattler's." She leaned over the counter and hissed. "Holly was so pissed."

"I don't know—"

She waved her hand again, and it was like a magic spell to shut me up. "Holly moved on, don't worry. I think she was more surprised and that's what upset her—she doesn't want to be attached to anyone either. So don't worry. It won't be another Krystal scenario."

"Okay?" This was how it was in Coal Haven. People already knew my business before I told them. That was my trade-off for a slower-paced life.

"You and Holden, huh?"

Nerves fluttered in my belly. "I'm not sure. Maybe? I'm not really looking for a relationship. Before I go to his place, I have to make sure my kids are packed for a weekend at their dad's. Then we're all going to sit and wait and wonder if Henry will actually show."

She grimaced. "That sucks. I never thought of Holden as relationship material, but he's a good guy." She pushed off the desk. "I'm gonna go shut down. Have a good weekend."

Holden would be excellent relationship material.

I mentally shook that thought out of my head. He'd confided in me, but that didn't mean he was a decent boyfriend. He might be out of practice. I was out of practice, and I wasn't looking to get into the game.

But he was magnetic. I couldn't quit wanting to be around him, and I liked the way he made me feel. Henry had acted like I was special when he'd wanted his way. Holden enjoyed treating me right, and I wasn't scared there were strings attached.

I gathered my things and let Dr. Klevin know I was leaving.

My tension rose with each block closer to home. Mom's car was in front of the house. She'd offered to pick up Riley and meet the kids at home to help them all pack. I'd asked her to get them a snack too. Henry might be an intelligent surgeon, but he was clueless about what to feed hungry kids.

I parked in the driveway and trotted inside. I went

through the rounds of greetings and kisses before popping into my room to change into jeans and a hoodie. This wasn't what I was wearing tonight. Or maybe it was, if Henry didn't show.

Overnight bags and the diaper bag were stacked by the front door, and the kids were at the table eating apple slices and caramel.

"Nana thinks of the best desserts," I said as I dipped an apple slice into the caramel and loaded it with as much as would fit.

I had just shoved it into my mouth when the doorbell rang.

Mom slid out of her chair. "I'll get it. Finish chewing."

I was midcrunch when I heard more than one voice. A hot pit formed in my stomach. I'd been diligent about Holden and what the kids knew about him and me. But Henry obviously didn't have the same worries.

I swallowed without choking on my indignation. "Finish up, kids. Your dad is waiting."

I swept into the living room and found Mom handing the luggage to Jenni. Her blonde hair had been blown out, and aviator glasses were perched on her head. The kids had had no warning that Jenni was now part of their weekend. Couldn't Henry put them first for once?

I knew they were living together, but Henry hadn't talked about it. I naively assumed they had come up with an arrangement that wasn't "Here's another mommy. Surprise!"

"Hi, Emery," Jenni said quietly, like she wanted to sink into the worn carpet. Henry hadn't put her first either.

"Hi," I said flatly, holding my irritation in check. I aimed my annoyed gaze at Henry. He fixed his challenging stare on me, daring me to say something about her. So, it was like that.

"The kids are coming" was all I said. I hated to say he looked good. He wasn't blatantly sexy like Holden. Not as tall or as muscular. His expression was frozen on the arrogant side. But his inky-black hair was combed into submission, and he glowed from his recent vacation. They both did.

Meanwhile, I fought chapped hands from washing and sanitizing them so much, and my hair hadn't seen a stylist since before Riley was born.

"Tell them to hurry." Impatience dripped off his tone.

I rolled my lips together and did no such thing. He was their father. He could do it himself.

He huffed and called, "Come on, guys. We gotta go."

"I'll take these bags to the car." Jenni jogged down the stairs, her perky, perfect ass apparent in her skinny jeans.

I needed to find something nicer to wear tonight.

The kids piled out of the kitchen.

Henry's face twisted. "Can you at least wipe off Riley's face? Good God, Em. I drove out here, can you at least—"

I cut a hand through the air. "If you want to start with the 'can you at least,' I would bet my list is longer than yours. So, if you wanna go ahead and finish that statement, just be prepared."

He shook his head. "Hmph. Never mind. We've wasted this much time already. We'll stop at the gas station."

Avery grabbed Riley's hand. "I'll do it," she said softly and led Riley away. Mom rushed after her.

I gave Henry a *can you be less of an asshole* look, but he was ushering the other two out the door. Jenni greeted them with a big smile and exuberant energy and led them to a Suburban I'd never seen before. This one was red.

Henry rounded on me. "Was that called for, Em?"

"Was bringing your girlfriend to my house called for?" I shot back.

His disapproving frown grated on my nerves. "Em—"

"Emery. Only people close to me call me Em."

"You're being childish."

Mom's sharp inhale resounded between us. Henry had the grace to look abashed, and he dropped his gaze to his daughters. "Let's go load up, girls."

Riley let out a squeal and toddled for Henry. Moments like that were why I needed to watch how I talked about him and around him. They needed to form their own opinions of him, and I didn't want to quash a kid's excitement to see her dad.

With a stony expression, he scooped her up. He put his arm around Avery and led her out.

When the door shut behind him and Mom closed the main door, I groaned. "I forgot to give the kids a hug." I felt like I had a Bad Mom of the Year award to apply for. And after I mentally berated Henry for putting himself first, I let my anger distract me.

"I think it would've caused more of a scene." I didn't detect censure in her tone, but it was heavy with regret.

I scrubbed both hands down my face. "I went too far. I should've been the bigger person."

She patted my arm as she passed me on her way to the kitchen. "You also need to stand up for yourself." She paused at the entrance. "It's not a bad thing that your kids see you holding your own against him. You don't trash him in front of them no matter how much he deserves it, but you're also not letting him continue to be an ass to you."

I followed her in to help clean up the sticky mess. I wasn't big enough to keep from hoping caramel handprints got all over the inside of that new Suburban.

Mom rinsed out a rag. "You said only people close to you call you Em."

"I know, no one does but—"

"Holden calls you Em?"

I brushed it off. "That was how I first introduced myself to him."

"He seems nice."

"He is."

"And he's giving Avery riding lessons."

I swiped the back of my wrist across my forehead. "Mom, are you digging for something?"

"It's your business. I've heard a lot about him and his family over the years."

"I heard all the same rumors." About Holden anyway. I hadn't paid much attention to the rest other than what had been said about Stetson at the clinic.

"I just don't want you to get taken in by another Henry."

I was about to blow off her comment, but I paused. Holden was the way he was because of who'd raised him. He saw himself as a parental figure to his sister. His mom seemed unapproachable and unsupportive of anything that didn't serve her. Stetson was like a brother. He'd kept himself closed off to everyone because he'd been trying to heal a wound without giving it proper care.

But Henry wasn't an asshole for recreation. His parents treated their dog better than him. We'd had a running joke between us. How many more pictures of their Yorkie, Brutus, would be on their fridge than the kids?

It wasn't that his parents were outwardly abusive. They were uninvolved and oblivious. They'd had high expectations for Henry, but they hadn't praised him when he'd met their goals. He'd grown up feeling alone and unloved. It was why he'd wanted to keep having kids.

Then when I'd been busy with those kids and my own work, he'd gravitated toward those who noticed him and praised him. That was Jenni.

Mom's worries weren't unfounded. She'd been my confidant throughout my marriage. "I'm not looking to get taken in."

She tossed the rag on the table. "I've heard enough about him to know he doesn't watch movies at women's houses or invite them out to his place. That's a big thing about him, Emery. Do you know that? He doesn't take women to his place."

That would explain why we had sex in the back of his pickup. "Yeah," I mumbled. "I've heard similar rumors."

"So what if he really likes you?"

I exhaled. "I just like hanging out with him, Mom. I know what point you're trying to make, but he's a single guy. I have four kids, and my baggage is supposed to come around with his girlfriend every other weekend. He's going to be disenchanted soon enough."

She hummed doubtfully before saying, "Well, go, have fun."

"I need to change."

"Why? You look fine. Isn't he just grilling?"

"Yeah, but there's going to be other people there."

"Who?"

She was so sweetly curious that I had to answer. Mom had been here long enough to know these people.

I racked my brain. I worked with names all day. I recalled Lyric talking about her friend. "Laney?"

"Oh, and Archer?"

I nodded, hoping I was right.

"She gets her chicken seed from us. Archer's dad moved to Texas before Archer was born." She pulled out a chair and I fought a smile. My mother was filling me in on the gossip. "I guess he met Laney in Texas and they got married when she was on the outs with her family. Then she came up here for a family emergency and left Archer. I don't know what happened, but he eventually followed her up. You should've heard the town ripple with excitement when they learned she married one of the mysterious Barron kids."

I relaxed the more Mom talked. I wasn't the only one showing up with a salacious past. "I think the other couple is Kennedy and Liam? Did I get that right?"

Mom nodded. "I don't know them personally, but Liam is Cameron's son."

"Stetson has a brother?"

"They don't associate. Liam was from an affair. Quite the scandal. Stetson and his sister don't talk to Liam."

Right, the Liam story he couldn't tell me. "That must be why Stetson's not coming." I had thought to ask but had decided not to question it. I wasn't planning the get-together.

"It'd be quite the deal. I've heard nothing but good things about Kennedy and Liam. I guess Liam was a little wild as a kid, but I would doubt his behavior is that much different from a lot of the kids running around now. He just had a spotlight on him."

"I think Holden mentioned his sister and maybe an Aspen."

"I don't know much about them. Aspen sounds familiar, and I haven't heard about his sister."

"Thanks for the heads-up on everyone else, Mom." If they were talking about me, at least I was going in having heard gossip about them.

"They're Coal Haven royalty. People like to talk about them."

And would I be added to those conversations? I wasn't royalty, so as long as the gossip didn't rebound on me or my kids, I wouldn't care.

* * *

Holden

Emery was the last to arrive, pulling in next to Liam's pickup. She'd messaged she was on her way, and I had let myself get excited about tonight. The night would've gone fine without her, but I wanted more than fine.

Aspen stood on her tiptoes next to Kennedy and whispered, "Is that her?"

"Who else would it be?" I sounded like a grump, but the buzz of excitement over Emery was nearly tangible, frolicking through my guests, and the worst was my sister.

What was I thinking by inviting Nora? She was sweet and innocent, and she'd think Emery was her new big sister. Nora might scare Emery away faster than the others and their stupid chittering.

I ditched my prep at the grill to stalk toward the line of vehicles along the side of my driveway.

Emery got out, that snug fleece jacket hugging her curves over a green print top that made her eyes impossibly lighter. She spotted me and smiled, but there was an underlying strain in her eyes.

"Are you nervous?" I asked.

"No." She closed her eyes and opened them. "I mean, yes. But it's not that. Henry picked the kids up and our exchange wasn't terrible, but it wasn't the best."

"What'd he do?"

She gave me a thin smile. "He brought Jenni."

"That's kind of a dick move, right?" She'd treaded carefully with us, but Henry had stomped over her efforts.

"I thought so. I mean, they're still together, so there's that. But it seemed too soon, you know? And I think it made him extra defensive." She wrinkled her nose. "Anyway, he's ruined enough of the night, but it helped take my mind off meeting everyone."

"Just think of it as accelerated introductions. You'd be seeing them around town eventually." I didn't know whether to take her hand or throw an arm around her.

She saved me by moving on her own toward the house. She was used to kids grabbing her hands when they wanted. I'd have to be on the ball if I wanted to do something as simple as that.

"We're on the back patio as long as the wind stays down and the temperature stays up." As we got closer, I put a hand on the small of her back. I didn't have to guide her, but that was the excuse I used to touch her. She didn't speed up or ask me to stop touching her.

The group didn't stare as we rounded the back of the house, I'd give them that. Except Nora. Shit—what had my sister heard about me?

I ran Emery through the introductions, then offered to grab her a drink. "I have Bud Light."

Her cheeks flushed with pink dots that had nothing to do with the cool air and everything to do with how I knew she drank Bud Light. It was what she'd ordered when we first met in Crocus Valley.

"That'll be fine," she said almost shyly.

I had to go into the house for the beer. I hated leaving her alone in the crowd, but when I returned a minute later, Aspen had engaged her in conversation about her work at the clinic and Aspen's friend Lyric.

I handed her the beer and started grilling. I'd started the potatoes and vegetables earlier. I'd hosted enough of these that I had my time line down.

When I was a kid, our house had been activity central. I'd had friends obnoxiously revving their engines up and down our driveway. Whatever guy Mom was dating would be coming and going. She had never dated anyone with kids either. Nora had even had a few of her friends over sometimes. When someone was over, Mom would lay off her. I didn't have the family-filled house I thought I'd have by my thirties, but I wasn't a hermit.

The rest of the night passed quickly, with good food and good friends. Aspen left first with Nora. Then Kennedy and Liam left to pick the kids up from Liam's grandma. Laney and Archer were the last to leave. Laney had been grilling Emery about the three doctors at the clinic and which one would be best for a pregnant mom.

Kennedy and Liam were expecting a baby at the end of March, and I wouldn't have been surprised if Laney and Archer had one soon after.

A tightness pulled at my chest. I rubbed a spot between my pecs. I hadn't consciously been planning to avoid the new Barron arrivals, but I'd been doing it anyway. I had feigned happiness when Liam told me Kennedy was expecting, but I'd had an inner recoil. The one where I expected my world to turn dark and swallow me up again.

After my talk with Emery, I hoped that wasn't the case with Archer and Laney. I wanted the ever-present tension to be gone when they had news to share.

I didn't realize I had spaced out until Emery gently nudged me with an elbow. "Whatcha thinking about?"

I shook my head, but I answered anyway. "How nice it'll be when Barron kids fill up Coal Haven again."

"Family is nice to have around. When everyone gets along. I always hope my kids are close as adults."

"With you in their lives, they will be. But I guess Nora and I are kind of close because Mom was the opposite of you and our dads weren't around."

She tilted her head. "Your dad's not in Coal Haven?"

"No, he used to be. After he finished law school, he

came here and opened an office. Technically, I guess he worked for a company in Bismarck that wanted a presence in town. After the fallout with Mom, he moved back to the Bismarck office and now he's in Billings." It had gotten easier for me to deal with Dad's neglect when he moved farther away. My brain had latched onto the excuse.

I went to the patio and started gathering the garbage. There wasn't much cleanup, but I wanted to get it done before morning or it'd attract critters that would piss Tabby off. Emery jumped in to help.

I kept talking about Dad. Like with my daughter, I never talked about him to anyone other than Stetson. "I went to see him once for some legal help. I was going to propose to Teagan and knew that Mom would have a fit over ownership of the ranch. I thought maybe he could draw up a basic prenup to appease Mom. Teagan didn't give a shit about my land or the oil money I'd get when I was twenty-five. But Mom's really militant about keeping it in the family. Something about Naomi sticking way too much of her nose in it."

"Naomi is an aunt?"

"My uncle Cameron's wife. Stetson and Isla's mom. She makes my mom look warm and cuddly." I set the garbage bag by the sliding door.

The corner of her mouth ticked up as she gathered beer bottles. "I didn't get a close look at your mom, but she did look tough. I take it the meeting with your dad went horribly."

"He told me that Mom would make sure she ruined my engagement before I said I do and that since she'd raised me, I'd probably do a good job of fucking the whole thing up before that anyway."

Emery's mouth fell open. "He did not."

"He also said that for a kid who wanted nothing to do

with him, I had a lot of balls for coming to him." I'd had a lot of optimism that had been shattered. Looking back, I know I wasn't wrong to expect him to help me. My only regret was that I hadn't pressed him more, made him answer for his treatment of me, instead of blaming Mom. But perhaps it was one of the many signs that Teagan and I weren't as committed as we should've been.

She dumped the bottles into the bucket I used for recycling. "That's awful."

I lifted a shoulder and shook out the grill cover. I had heard my dad was a good lawyer and that he was ruthless, but I didn't think he'd turn on me. That he had no urge to make some sort of amends or help in a small way the son he'd abandoned and ignored.

I had put myself in a vulnerable spot by going to him. And I'd learned my lesson. "It wasn't like I knew any other lawyers. But I shouldn't have gone to him, and now there is nothing that could make me talk to him again." I was done with him.

"He's completely out of your life?"

I nodded and lifted the garbage bag I had left by the door. "I'll put this in the trash bin. Go on inside."

"Sure." She wiped her hands on the back of her jeans. They weren't dirty, but it was like she needed to do something.

Grinning, I put the garbage in the bin in the garage that would keep raccoons and barn cats out of it. I trotted to the house.

Emery was at the sink in the kitchen. I couldn't get too poetic about what seeing her in my house did to me. I liked her there. That was enough to admit for tonight.

"You don't have to do my dishes." I came up behind her. I couldn't help myself. Her ass in those jeans was a firm peach ready for the squeezing. She hadn't taken off her fleece jacket, but I smoothed my hands under the hem and cupped her butt cheeks.

She gasped and spun. Her sudsy hands sprayed water over my shirt. "I'm sorry." She giggled. "You startled me."

"No, I'm sorry." I chuckled, and when she looked around for a rag, I cupped her damp hands. "Don't worry about it."

Her gaze dipped to my mouth and jumped back up to my eyes. "I wasn't expecting...this." She took a fortified breath. "I'm so nervous." A strained laugh escaped her. "Weird, right? Like I jumped right into your back seat after knowing you for what? An hour?"

I brushed her hair off her face. "I'm nervous too. It's easier when you think you'll never see someone again." I traced a finger down her cheek. "Easier when you know it's an arrangement. And a whole lot easier when the man leading you out of the bar is the best-looking guy you've ever seen."

She laughed, tossing her head back. That same rich laugh from the night we met. Uninhibited and real. She hadn't been trying to strike up anything with me then, and she wasn't flirting.

"That is true." Her smile was radiant. "You are the best-looking guy I've ever seen—and I didn't think I'd see you again."

Her honest admission shredded the last of my weak restraint. I kissed her, and this wasn't a practiced invitation that told her I wanted more. She'd be able to tell as soon as I pulled her close.

The wet spots on my shirt were momentarily cold as she pressed against me. Heat ignited between us and chased the chill away. I slid my hands over her ass again. I loved her butt in jeans.

I loved her butt all the time.

But I wanted to touch skin. Our one time together had been as clothed as possible thanks to being in the back of my pickup. Crocus Valley was a small town that was quiet on the weekends, but it wasn't private.

I'd been left wanting more then, and she was right here.

I stroked my hands up, tunneling under her shirt and jacket. As soon as my fingers touched her bare skin, she moaned. Her skin was blistering hot, matching the fire inside me. Together, we were going to burn my house down.

I splayed one hand over her back. With my other hand flattened against her, I got between her waistband and jeans. She rocked against me, but I didn't want to make her uncomfortable with my hand shoved down zipped and buttoned pants.

So, I remedied that. I unbuttoned and unzipped her pants and skimmed underneath her waistband to cup her butt, skin to skin.

It wasn't enough. I wanted to feel more of her. I reversed the direction and found her hot and wet and ready.

My erection throbbed behind the fly of my pants, and the exquisite pain worsened when she rubbed her hand against it.

I groaned and ripped my mouth off hers to kiss my way down her neck. "I remember how fucking wet and soft you were that night." She bucked against my hand. I slid two fingers through her folds and pushed inside her. Fuck, the grip of her body was heaven. I hit her clit with my thumb and settled into a steady pace, thrusting my fingers in and out of her, matching it to my strokes over her clit.

"Oh my God." She nearly climbed my body but stayed on her tiptoes, her backside pressed into the counter. She angled one knee out like she was trying to give me more room. "I can't believe—" She cut off with a moan.

I whispered in her ear. "What don't you believe, baby?"

I kept my rhythm, and she tightened around me. Her walls clenched and milked my fingers, and her arms hugged tight around my shoulders.

She let out a small cry. "That you can get me off so easily."

My ego exploded as fast as my dick wanted to. She was fucking right I could get her off. Not like that selfish ex of hers. Because she was fucking mine.

"Oh, God, Holden."

My head was next to hers, her gasps ringing in my ears until they turned into moans and a final cry as she came.

I held her as she shuddered, and I tightened my embrace. I couldn't wait to spread her out beneath me. To touch and taste every inch of her lush body.

I couldn't wait to bury myself deep inside her. I could fuck her here. I could strip her down in her postorgasmic bliss and wrap her legs around me. But I didn't want another fast, frantic coupling.

I withdrew my hand out of the heaven it'd been buried in and pulled back. Her eyes were dreamy and her face flushed.

"Let's go to my bedroom," I said, my voice rough with desire.

Her eyelids fluttered and the tiniest of frowns made an appearance. "You don't bring women to your bedroom."

Talk of other women was a firehose of cold water blasted into my face. I hadn't expected the rumors going around town to be so specific. I had to stop and think. I'd built the house four years ago. Well after my years with Teagan, and there'd been no one serious.

I hooked up in my dates' homes, in cars and motels. If I invited anyone to my place, they were either relatives or platonic friends who weren't ever alone with me.

"I haven't before, no." Inviting a date to my home was a

line that was crossed when a relationship reached a certain point, and I'd made sure none of mine had after Teagan. How could the entire town know my sex habits? Fuck. I hadn't prepared for my past to ruin something that could be really good for my future.

She put her hands on both sides of my face. "I didn't mean to blurt that out. People shouldn't be talking about you like that, but it still means something."

The gentleness in her voice clued me in to why it was an issue. The emptiness inside me yawned open. "And you still want me to be the guy you might never see again."

She dropped her hands to my chest. "I want to see you again, but I don't know if I'm ready for that responsibility. What if you've finally found yourself ready for a relationship when I'm so done with them?"

"I don't know, Em." Her hands fisted in my shirt. I didn't mind. I wanted her anchored to me. Maybe it'd keep the night from ending. "I just know that I don't want to find just anyone to hang out with. I like being with you. I like making you come." Her blush returned with a vengeance. "Can that be enough for now?"

"It can, but maybe not tonight?"

Not in my house was what she meant. The nosy townsfolk had spooked her.

Had they really, though? I was ready for more; she wasn't. Having sex in my bed might fuck with my mind as much as with hers. I was willing to be patient. "Fair enough."

Twelve

Emery

I couldn't be more furious with myself about last night. I'd been so close to paradise. Spending the night alone with Holden in his house. Coming as loud as I wanted to. Seeing all of him. Allllll of him.

Had I tried to win the masochist award?

I'd apologized to him for leaving him unresolved. His hard-on had obviously flagged with the topic of discussion, but when I apologized—because I felt like I should still be profusely apologizing—he'd given me a kiss. *I'm a grown man, Em. I can handle an erection.*

Em.

I liked when he called me Em. When Henry had said it yesterday, I'd had an immediate urge to wash his mouth out with soap.

I pushed the vacuum through the house like I was being timed and the prize was that someone else would dust.

Before I left my job at the hospital, divorced friends told

me to use the time without the kids to treat myself. They said that I'd need it after the rat race of working full-time with four kids and no full-time partner. I could understand that, but it was also a treat to clean with music blasting and not have to splinter myself into a cleaner, a babysitter, a delegate, and an entertainer.

My downtime joy was cleaning. How fucked up was that?

Mostly it burned off the anxious energy that'd been gathering since I'd left Holden's.

What had I been thinking?

Like I could be the one to break his heart? That I was so special and he'd be so devastated when I told him I didn't want to get married and have to juggle how my kids would adapt to a stepdad.

The poor guy...

I shut the vacuum off. Pushing hair from my face, I glanced at my phone. Dammit, it wasn't even noon yet. I'd have plenty of time for self-care.

Was this how my weekends alone would go?

I missed my kids, but they needed to be with their dad when he was willing to be involved in their lives.

I jumped when my phone rang. It was Holden.

I was staring at the screen like I was waiting for the letters to rearrange into another name when it rang again. Shit. I answered. "Hello?"

"Hey, Em." There it was again. "I just wanted to make sure everything's all right. Landon wasn't at the game."

I closed my eyes. Henry had the school schedule and sports schedule. "That asshole probably didn't want to bring him back to town and go back again." His time was so precious.

"Oh, good. Okay. I just wanted to make sure."

I'd left this guy with a set of blue balls and told him

rumors that had filled his eyes with a stunned hurt that broke my heart, and he was checking in about my son. "Are you still in town?"

"Yeah, the game got done. I was going to grab a bite and head home."

"Want to come over here?"

He paused, and I was certain he'd turn me down. Why would he want to see me after I ditched him the way I had?

"Sure. You want anything to eat?"

"No, I was just—" I bit down on my lower lip, but the words spilled out anyway. "I was just thinking that I was worried your place signified too much but my house is just some rental..."

I squeezed my eyes shut. Oh, God, that was bad.

"Be right there."

I stared at the phone long after he hung up.

Within minutes, there was a knock at the door. I opened it to find Holden, looking all sporty hot in his black sweats and hoodie. How'd he get here so fast? "Did you get something to eat?"

He pushed inside, toed his athletic shoes off. "I haven't waited as long for food as I've waited for you."

My pulse stuttered. His hungry gaze landed on me a beat before he started stalking toward me. "Where's your bedroom?"

"Straight back." I sounded breathless, like I'd run a few miles instead of vacuuming a small house. I still had on the same pajama bottoms and T-shirt from the night we'd watched movies.

The way his gaze raked my body could burn the flannel right off.

He picked me up. Startled, I wrapped my arms and legs around him and laughed. "Holden, what are you doing?"

"You'll find out soon enough."

My stomach flipped and my thighs tightened around him. I wanted to find out.

He beelined into my bedroom, not bothering to shut the door. The advantage of having the house to ourselves.

He laid me on the bed and stepped back to yank his hoodie off. He had on a plain white shirt underneath. I thought it looked pretty damn fine on him until he pulled it over his head and dropped it next to the hoodie.

"That's what you look like?" I sat up and hugged my knees to myself. My desire was frozen in place, like it was afraid to peek out from behind a snowbank and get incinerated by his abs. I was faced with acres of muscle. Pecs, biceps, whatever's in the shoulders—my education was failing me. Those diagrams in the textbooks were nothing like Holden.

He gave me a lopsided grin as he rolled down his sweats. I was helpless to look away. More muscle was revealed. Powerful thighs. I couldn't see his ass, but I saw enough to know that it had to be as spectacular as the front.

Then he lost the underwear and I just couldn't anymore. That erection was not like the textbooks. It was not like any of the past men in my life. Someone needed to make a song about that thing. Tall and proud, encased in tight skin that showed veins, it jutted unabashedly in the air.

I hadn't known what his cock looked like, but I knew what it felt like. Frenzied back seat sex wasn't going to be like this, though. This was going to be a long, hard fucking. That thing between his legs would make sure of it.

He was a fine specimen from head to toe. A statue come to life.

Stifling self-consciousness paralyzed me. I swallowed hard. He was getting a condom out of his wallet—and I was glad he was prepared. I wasn't ready for this.

He noticed my wide-eyed expression. "Something's wrong."

It wasn't a question. "I mean, you're all..." I wiggled my fingers at him. "I've had four kids, Holden. Stretch marks. Pooches. Parts that don't defy gravity like they used to. You look like you're fresh from the factory, and I look—"

"Sexy." He tossed the condom on the covers. "Beautiful." He crawled onto the bed, pushing me back until I was forced to straighten my legs. "Perfect."

When I'd had the bright idea of asking him over here to finish what we started last night, I hadn't thought about daylight. How it was merely dim in my room, and with the door open, there were fewer shadows.

"I'll show you how much I like your body." He drew my shirt over my head.

I groaned when I remembered I'd thrown on my everyday bra. The plain white one with no underwire that I wore when I didn't plan to leave the house but needed the support.

I nursed all my kids for at least a few months each. The details varied depending on time, whether I could actually pump at work, and how close I was to buckling under the pressure since I had little help or support.

"These are not my pre-baby boobs," I warned him. I was giving him every chance to back out. It was a compulsion. I'd been passed over for the younger, perkier model of me once already.

"All I want is your boobs..." He held my gaze as he reached behind me to unhook my bra. He didn't fumble. My bra was falling free in seconds. "...as they are now."

"You're really good at that," I breathed.

Only then did he pause. "Does that bother you?"

Damn, I almost ruined the moment between us with my

mouth. "No. If both of us were as nervous as me, we wouldn't get anywhere."

The corner of his mouth kicked up. "Oh, I'm nervous, Em. But my dick isn't going to forgive me if I mess this up again."

"You didn't mess it up before." I took his hands and laid them over my breasts.

Heat flamed in his eyes, and he massaged the flesh. I relaxed as his work-worn hands roamed over my skin. And I had to admit that it was a giant turn-on to see my boobs spilling out the sides of his grip.

"Just like I thought. Perfect." He dipped his head to close his mouth over a nipple.

I groaned and stretched out. That mouth on my boob? How could it feel so good? I stuffed my hands into his hair and enjoyed the sensation.

I arched into him, and he switched sides. I could do this for a while. My shirt was off. Daylight streamed through the thin window curtains. But he made me feel comfortable.

Until he began to draw my pants down.

I stiffened, but he lifted his gaze to mine. The promise in his dark eyes kept me from moving, from asking him if we could wait until dark.

My pajama pants and underwear slid down my hips. I lifted myself enough for Holden to tug them down to my thighs and the rest of the way off. Only then did his gaze leave mine.

The intensity around him grew as his gaze swept over the stretch marks that graced my hips and circled my bikini line. I kept my knees together, my breathing shallow. This was so much harder than having my shirt off.

I couldn't breathe when he started kissing and tracing each stretch mark with his tongue. My ex-husband had given them nothing more than a clinical review. Beyond that, he ignored them. The year before I got pregnant with Riley, he said we could set aside money if I ever wanted a boob job. I'd never mentioned it.

Fuck him.

I dragged in a ragged breath as Holden worked toward the other side. My legs relaxed, and he moved between my thighs.

My legs framed his powerful shoulders and nothing—nothing—I'd done sexually up to this point matched the hotness of that view. I didn't attract the attention of guys like Holden.

This was ridiculous.

But then he flicked his tongue over my clit, and I forgot everything. My world narrowed down to him and what he was doing to me.

The guy was a master. I'd never been the recipient of a partner who cared as much about my experience as his own.

He backed off but didn't quit tonguing me. He propped one of my legs over his shoulder. I was exposed. All of me. And he devoured me like he couldn't get enough. Then he increased the pressure and added a finger. Giving my body something to clamp onto while he drove me higher only sped up my trajectory.

My back bowed off the bed. I didn't think he meant to get me off this fast, but that was what happened.

I fisted my hands in the bedspread. The sound of stitches ripping barely registered before I called out his name.

And called out his name again.

I collapsed on the bed, but I didn't know how that was possible. I hadn't left it.

He crawled up my body. "Jesus, Em. That was beautiful."

I caught my breath while he kneeled and put the

condom on. And he watched—*he watched*—as he entered me, filling me in a way that told me, as if I didn't already know, that I'd been having the most vanilla sex ever.

I wasn't talking *extreme voyeuristic, exploring fetishes, BDSM, swinging, or any other type of non-missionary position* intercourse. I was talking the *watered-down, both partners just kind of going through the motions, so inside the box that the box shrank and couldn't hold anything significant* type of sex.

Because missionary with Holden was blowing all my past experiences out of the water. Just like back-seat sex had.

He had my legs spread, his big hands on my knees, and he was leisurely thrusting. His smug expression was all about where we were connected, as if watching himself stroke in and out of me was the pinnacle of satisfaction.

"You're so fucking wet, Em." He changed the angle and increased the force. Fireworks ignited inside my body, burning hotter until I thought I would explode with them. My breasts bounced, and I was about to try some sexy—I hoped—pose to cross my arms over them, but his hot gaze stuck on them. "I love your tits."

"I love your body." That sounded inane, but it was the truth. He was over me, in me, consuming me.

"I want to watch you come this time."

I was lost in him, but his request brought me closer to the surface. The other times I came, my back was to him or his face was buried in my hair. I wanted to give this to him, no matter how nerve-racking the thought was. "But I already came."

"You're coming again." He said it with so much confidence.

I almost laughed it off, but pressure was coiling inside me. Oh my God. I thought I could orgasm again.

He stopped so suddenly that I looked around. Was something wrong?

"You haven't come twice in one night before?"

I rose to my elbows, ignoring how my belly showed off its pooch. "No?"

"No, you don't remember, or no, you haven't?" He shook his head. "If you can't remember, then it hasn't happened."

"Logically, I know it's possible but—"

"Oh, it's possible. Just watch." He flicked his tongue over his thumb. I tracked his hand down to where we were connected, and he swiped his thumb over my clit.

"Oh!" I bucked and it acted like a thrust. The combination was gooood.

He kept the momentum going. His hand at my center, his cock stroking in and out of me, and his strong arm holding my leg increased that delicious pressure.

I kept ratcheting tighter and tighter until I was rocking my hips, encouraging all the parts of him that were touching me—and then I exploded.

I was sensitive from the last climax, and this one was more acute than before. I moaned and I hollered and I made a *scene*. And I kept going as he jacked against me, his back arching and his teeth clenching. He pulsed inside me, capping off my volcanic experience.

I sagged against the covers, breathing hard. He was spread out on top of me.

His solid body was over mine. A weight I didn't want to push off.

"You're right," I murmured. "I'm going to remember that."

He chuckled and rolled to the side. I missed him inside me, but curling into his side was nice. Really nice.

"Wait until I make you come a third time."

I lifted my head. "Seriously?"

His gaze said he was absolutely serious. "I'll give you a little time, and then I'll show you."

This was going to be an amazing self-care day—

The screen door banged open and Avery yelled, "Mom!"

* * *

Holden

Not since I was fucking around as a teenager had I been worried about being busted in a girl's bed.

"Wait! Don't come back here." Emery launched out of bed and dressed so quickly I didn't get a chance to admire the view. She tried straightening out her pants as she wrestled on her bra. Then the shirt was over her head, and she yanked her pants up and was gone in a flurry of cotton and flannel.

I covered myself with a corner of a blanket until it would be safe to get out of bed. My complete nudity kept me frozen in place.

"What are you doing back?" She sounded calm and collected. She had the awareness to close the door behind her.

With the protection of the door, I found a tissue box to wrap the condom in. There was a garbage can, but I grabbed two more tissues to fully encase the condom. Then I wrested into my shirt and sweats.

Voices drifted into the room as I got dressed. Panic welled inside of me, as if all the kids would stampede into the bedroom and demand to know what I was doing there. How would I explain this? I was fixing a window? I didn't relish lying to the kids, but were they even old enough to know what the truth was?

The kids' voices were hard to make out, all talking over each other. Landon was the loudest and most indignant.

"Slow down, slow down," Emery called over the din. "Henry?"

"Landon threw a fit about football." The defensive man must be Henry. "He wouldn't shut up and started hollering. Our new puppy got all worked up."

"So?" Emery's exasperated tone nearly made me smile. I liked puppies, but if my kid was upset, wouldn't they be a priority?

"Look, they've all been disrespectful and rude, and they can't act like that. Jenni doesn't deserve to be treated—"

"You're their father, Henry. It's your job to teach them how to act properly, not give up."

"Em—*Emery*." I really didn't like this guy's tone. "This isn't—"

"Kids," Emery said, "why don't you go upstairs— Oh, Riley, not in the kitchen. I don't have the gate to the basement up."

Then Landon asked, "Mom, is Coach B here?"

Silence descended from the living room. I died a little inside, came alive, only to wither again. Busted.

Shit.

"He, um, he had called to check on you...and..."

Poor Emery. She'd kept her head until she was busted with me. It was either hide that I was here and make weak excuses or walk out and pretend like it was all normal. Since the kids were used to seeing their dad with another woman, I chose the latter.

I straightened my clothes and opened the door. I'd faced angry bulls. I did it seasonally. I could do this. Heads turned my way.

A man a few inches taller than Emery but a few inches shorter than me went from astonished to pissed *the hell* off. His dark eyes sparked, and I half expected his immaculately gelled hair to straighten like he'd stuck a finger in an outlet. A woman who looked barely out of college stood by the door like she was going to sprint away as soon as someone gave her permission. Her eyes widened and her appreciative gaze dropped down my body only to take her time scanning back up. Disbelief filled her eyes.

She must be Jenni.

Landon smiled like me walking out of his mother's bedroom was an everyday occurrence. "Coach B!"

"Hey, buddy. We missed you today." Crap. Would that resurrect the argument? What else should I say?

His face fell. "Dad wouldn't let me go."

"Who the hell are you?" Henry planted his hands on his trim hips.

"Holden's teaching me to ride a horse." Avery's voice was full of oblivious excitement.

I didn't want to make this situation any tenser than it was. I crossed to him and stuck my hand out. "Holden Barron. Nice to meet you."

He eyed my hand but didn't take it. I glanced at Emery. Her cheeks had bright-pink spots, and I realized it was for the best Henry didn't shake. I hadn't been able to clean up.

I quirked a brow and shrugged. She bit the inside of her cheek like the bizarre unexpectedness of the situation was going to give her the giggles.

"I'm a surgeon," Henry said, his tone full of hubris. "I have to be careful where I put my hands."

My gaze flicked to the other woman, and I spoke loud enough for only the adults close to me to hear. "Are you, though?"

Henry sucked in a breath, and if he could slice me in

two with his glare, I'd be done for. Emery sputtered and coughed. The younger woman's eyes bugged out. I almost laughed, but I wasn't sure whether I'd overstepped.

Henry's nostrils flared. "We need to talk outside."

He wanted to get Emery alone to berate her when no one else could stand up to him. The woman saw her chance to leave and backed out of the door.

Emery glared at Henry. "If she's included, then Holden's coming out too."

I didn't care if I was used to make a point. That was how to deal with guys like Henry. He reminded me of a less suave version of my uncle Cameron. Used to being adored because of what he did for a living and pissed when he earned some consequences.

Henry made a disgusted noise and left.

I was game. This guy was going to lob all kinds of double standards on his ex-wife, and I was not here for it.

"Avery, can you watch the others?" Emery asked before she pushed out the door. I followed her.

As soon as the door closed behind us, Henry rounded on Emery. "His coach? You're fucking his coach?"

Of course he'd go there. I held my hands out in a *slow-down* motion. "Hey—"

"My intern? You're fucking my intern?" Emery hissed in a mocking tone. "Sound familiar?"

Henry's jaw clamped shut, and I bit back a grin. He wasn't used to a fired-up Emery. He had molded her into what he'd wanted; he didn't know the real her.

I did.

If he thought he was going to have time to think of a retort, Emery beat him to it. "Before you bitch about having a guy under the roof with your kids without you knowing, go look in a mirror. You didn't tell me when you moved Jenni in. You didn't tell me she would be coming with you to pick up the kids. You don't feel like you need to tell me what you're doing in your personal life, and I don't either." Her ex straightened with a chagrined expression. "And before you bitch about what I'm doing with the coach in the house, just go ahead and remember that I was supposed to be alone in that house until tomorrow."

Henry's hands turned into fists. "My boss got ahold of me, and I have to be on call the rest of the weekend, and Jenni starts her overnights tonight."

Wasn't it his job to find someone to take care of them like Emery did when she asked her mom? Why had it sounded like he was blaming the kids when he'd first arrived? The guy didn't like taking responsibility for himself.

Emery crossed her arms. "What kind of message does that send to them, Henry? You missed your last weekend. You've missed half your weekends for work."

"That I have a good work ethic."

She rolled her eyes. "Sure."

Henry flicked a finger between me and Emery. "So, is this a thing? Do I have to worry about a trail of men trooping by my kids?"

I was about to say something—no woman should be talked to like that—but Emery had it handled. "That is none of your business."

"The men who have access to my kids is my business."

"No, Henry. It's not. When you moved out and agreed to the most minimal partial custody possible, you were also saying that you trusted me and my decisions with the kids. So, you're going to have to trust me."

Pride puffed out my chest. She'd defended me.

Henry's nostrils flared again. This guy wasn't used to being questioned. He was used to issuing orders and having young nurses like Jenni look at him like he was a god among men. He was used to his patients fawning over him and watching him with awe.

He did not like his ex-wife standing up for herself.

Henry's eyes narrowed like he was coming to a conclusion. When resolution filled his gaze, his expression turned into a stern pout. "I'm going to say goodbye to them."

He didn't wait for a response, leaving me, Emery, and Jenni standing around.

Emery pretended Jenni didn't exist, and I did the same.

"You okay?" I asked.

"I will be." She ran her fingers through her hair. In her pajamas, with just-been-fucked hair, and righteously angry, she was a glorious sight.

A few minutes later, Henry stormed out of the house and past us without a word. Jenni got into the Suburban without being prompted as Henry got behind the wheel, and they drove off.

Emery shoved her hand through her hair again, tugging against tangles. She'd taken on her ex in front of his new girlfriend in bare feet and pajama pants.

This was what had attracted me to her. She was real. The other women I'd been with were real, too, of course, but I never got to see that side. The drawback of meeting someone at the bar was that I never knew which side of them I was seeing, and I never got to know them well enough to find out.

But after her unbridled laugh at my bad pickup line, I'd known it was the real her, and I'd known she couldn't be anything else.

"I'd better go make some lunch." She sighed. "I doubt they've eaten."

I shoved my hands into my pockets and clenched my stomach. I was not letting it growl around her. She had enough to worry about.

"I should get home and get to work too." I'd offer to stay, but I really did have shit to get done today.

"Okay." Her shoulders drooped. "Thanks for, um, stopping by." She winced.

I leaned in and dropped my voice. "Anytime."

Her blush returned, but she giggled. "Goodbye, Holden."

I didn't leave. "Can I bring pizza over after practice this week?"

She blinked, and her gaze grew guarded. I cursed my timing. Her ex had just been pissy about me. She had the kids to think about. "Can I let you know?"

"No problem. Can you tell the kids I'll see them later? I feel like if I go in after what happened—"

"It'll muddy an already messy morning? Yeah. It's one of those 'let's all sit on the couch and cuddle and talk about some feelings' moments."

"Thanks. You're a good mom." I'd have been told to suck it up and stay out of it.

She shrugged like it was nothing.

I wanted to give her a kiss before I left, but it was too soon for that. Not only might her kids see, but anyone in the neighborhood could. They all knew who I was. I walked to my pickup and hoped I'd hear from her about pizza. I wanted to be more to her than a good time.

Thirteen

Emery

I stayed on the sidewalk after he drove away. He'd asked me out again. Sort of. But he acted like he wanted to see me again. Not just me, but he was offering to bring pizza for everyone.

This wasn't supposed to be serious. The kids had been to their dad's and had to deal with a new woman in his life. I couldn't give them a tenuous *I don't know what this is* with Holden. When football was over and Holden had no reason to be around us, would he just move on? We'd had sex. The novelty was over.

Not for me. Not at all. It had been amazing, and my body had hummed through all the drama, undeterred by adrenaline. But I wasn't Holden.

How long would this last after football season? At Rattler's, I'd realized I couldn't arbitrarily fuck around even if it was with just one guy. But I wasn't sure I wanted to endure another breakup.

I'd been in love with Henry until I'd been betrayed by him. I'd looked forward to date nights and time together. Those rare mornings we were both home and the kids let us sleep an extra thirty minutes. I loved our family and the rat race that was working shifts and juggling day care.

He'd broken my heart.

That love was gone. I'd have liked to at least like my kids' dad, but until Henry treated both me and the kids better, that wasn't going to happen.

So a new relationship?

Holden might want to be a little more serious, but I wasn't a girl who could do short-term serious. Even worse, what happened in a year or two when things didn't work out?

Would I be sobbing into the covers of my bed so the kids wouldn't hear? I wanted those days to be over.

Coal Haven was so much smaller than Bismarck. I'd have to see Holden around town.

The coolness of the sidewalk seeped into my toes. I sighed and stared down at my bare feet. I'd been in the yard in my pajamas after arguing with my ex while his new girlfriend and the guy I'd just had sex with watched.

A laugh sputtered out of me.

Where did my life go?

I wouldn't get answers to my problems outside.

In the house, Landon and Afton were watching TV. It had probably been the best way for Avery to keep them from going outside. I found her feeding Riley some toast in the kitchen.

"Thank you for your help, Avery." I sat at the table on the other side of Riley.

"No problem. I started the oven to throw cheesy breadsticks in."

"Good idea. We all like those." Hot tears threatened to

gather in my eyes. She was an amazing little girl and I hated how much I needed her help. "What should we do today?"

Avery peered out of the kitchen window that faced the road. "Since we're home now, do we get to go riding at Holden's again?"

"Oh, uh...I don't think he's planning on it this weekend. He has to work."

Avery slumped in her chair. "Okay."

"We could still do something fun." I couldn't let them mope around. We could have fun on our own, dammit.

"There's nothing fun here, Mom."

The oven beeped that it was ready. I got up and dug the breadsticks out of the freezer and lined them up on a baking sheet. We hadn't moved for purely practical reasons. Okay, we had, but we'd moved to free us from the hamster wheel.

I tossed the pan into the oven and faced Avery. "Maybe it's time to explore our new town." A hint of interest dotted her gaze. I was on the right track. "We could go to the river. I think there're some recreation areas nearby."

She grinned. "We could camp!"

No. Absolutely not. Camping with just me? We only had the Traverse. I didn't own an RV or a camper. The days were nice this time of year, but the nights grew chilly for a tent.

"We're close to home."

"Mom!" Landon ran into the kitchen with my phone. "It's ringing."

No one had called, but I had a message from Holden. **You all can still come ride horses tomorrow.**

People liked to talk about Holden, but did they ever gossip about how considerate he was?

Avery rose and stretched. "Can I go play?"

"Of course." I took her chair and called Holden. It

seemed easier to call than to reply with a lengthy explanation.

After my misgivings about how and when this thing between us would end, I also missed him and wished he could've hung around. But I had the kids and he had his work.

He answered with "Is that a 'Yes, Holden. I'd love to come out and ride'?"

I laughed. "Why do you think I'm going to say no?" I hadn't thought that far ahead when I called.

"You'd have said 'see you tomorrow.'"

I would've. "Avery asked, but I told her I didn't think you had planned on it. But when I asked what she wanted to do and suggested we learn about our new hometown, she said she wanted to go camping."

"That would be fun."

"I'd have to keep the kids from getting lost in the wilderness, out of the river, and fishhook-free."

His chuckle made me smile. I was worried he'd brush off my concerns. I wanted to do this for the kids, but I'd been camping with my dad. He'd taught me to start a fire and put it out, but I'd never done it as an adult. Then there was the food.

"I don't want to let her down. But I'd have to get food, pack, figure out where to go, and—oh, crap—I'd have to find the fishing poles." I wiped off Riley's face.

"Do you have a tent?"

Surprisingly, that was one thing I didn't have to worry about. It was on a shelf in the garage. "Yes, we'd picked up a new one, planning to go, but then Riley came along."

"All right. I'll send you some directions. Just bring you, the kids, and a tent."

"What do you mean?" He couldn't mean camping. He couldn't mean now.

"Stetson has a lake cabin on Sakakawea. It won't fit everyone, and I'm sure the kids would want the tent anyway, but it's there for backup and a bathroom. I don't know if it's rained enough to do a fire, but we can rig up something for s'mores."

"I can't—"

"You won't. Let me make some calls. Maybe Stetson will come out. Nora's in town all weekend. She loves going to the lake—but don't eat her almond flour graham crackers. They'll ruin the taste of s'mores for the year. And don't tell her I said that."

"Are you giving me blackmail material?" I grinned as I helped Riley unbuckle from her booster and climb down. I watched her waddle-walk to the living room with the others.

"Yes. Nora is touchy about her concoctions. Some are good, but not her graham crackers."

I paused. Camping. With people I didn't know well. The kids would love it—and with other people to help watch my kids, I might have fun too. "Are you sure?"

"Absolutely."

"Just the kids and the tent? I can bring something."

"Bring whatever the kids need that a single guy like me wouldn't know about, and I'll bring everything else we need for camping and try to recruit enough adults that we'll have at least one watching each kid."

"You know how to sweet-talk a woman, Holden Barron."

His deep laugh made me briefly close my eyes. There was nothing about him that wasn't delicious. "Just follow the directions. See you in a few hours."

He hung up and I let out a dreamy sigh. That guy was just—

Hours. I jumped up. I was still in pajamas and the kids were packed for their dad's house.

I rushed into the living room. Four faces peered at me. Landon was driving race cars over the carpet while Riley watched and probably plotted to grab one. Avery was muscling Afton out of her dollhouse, but Afton had hoarded all the dolls on her side.

"After we eat," I announced, "we're going to get ready to go camping."

Avery jumped up and cheered, the doll war with her sister forgotten. Afton grinned and raced for her room, probably to start packing. Landon roared and raced for his bedroom. Riley paused to make sure the noise was happy sounds, then grinned and clapped.

I wished Holden was here right now. I could kiss him for this.

* * *

Holden

I was at the cabin before Stetson arrived. This place was little more than a hunting shack—a nice one—on two acres with a decent amount of shoreline. He hadn't taken his boat dock out of the water yet, so the kids had a safe place to fish. It was shallow, thanks to the dry summer, but it'd be fine for shore fishing. We'd all catch a lot of weeds.

The property had a firepit, and the outdoor patio furniture was still out. Next month, Stetson would call me and we'd come here to winterize the place. A shed nearly the size of the cabin functioned as a garage when there was bad weather, but it was mostly storage for the winter.

There were enough trees surrounding his place to give him some privacy, and he'd tilled a neat garden for Nora to grow her vegetables without Mom bitching at her.

Mom wasn't a gardener, and I had no clue why it irritated her that Nora grew more than the standard cucumbers and tomatoes that everyone planted. She grew a variety of cucumbers and tomatoes, but also all kinds of squashes, peppers, leafy greens, herbs, and anything she thought would taste good.

I suspected Nora asked Stetson for a little corner because she was afraid Mom would hit her produce with harsh chemicals when Nora was trying to keep everything organic.

Yeah, I could see Mom doing that.

Stetson pulled in with kayaks strapped to the bed of his pickup.

The perk of the summer drought was that it was a warm September with the temperature close to seventy. I'd put my sweats from the morning back on but left my hoodie in the truck.

Stetson got out and opened the back door of his pickup. He was wearing black sweats like me, but he had on an old Coal Haven Drillers shirt with the sleeves ripped off. His ball cap was on backward. "When's your girlfriend get here?"

I had yet to unload everything I'd brought, but I'd help Stetson first. "She'll be here in an hour. And maybe don't call her my girlfriend."

He snorted. "Right. Forgot who I was talking to."

"Jackass." I said it with more heat than I intended.

"Wait." He inspected me. "It's her you don't want to hear that?"

"She's got a lot going on."

Folding his arms, his biceps bulging, he faced me. A guy who hadn't grown up with him his entire life might be intimidated. "You want to be serious?"

"I am serious. But she's taking it slowish."

His eyes narrowed. "How do you take something slowish? Ohhh." He nodded. "Because you two already fucked and she hasn't opened the invitation again."

I didn't correct him about the best sex I'd ever had. "She's gun-shy. Her ex is a complete dick to her."

"They all say that." Stetson didn't avoid relationships like me. He dated everyone until they figured out he'd never ask them to marry him. We avoided two different types of commitment.

"I saw it. He flaked out on his weekend with the kids and was yelling at her and—"

"Holy shit." Stetson's deep laughter rang across his property. "You two are having sex, but it's the rest you want, and she won't give it."

I scowled. He could empty his own damn truck. I spun to my pickup. "It's new. For both of us."

He sobered. "And I'm happy for you, man. But...do you think you maybe picked the woman who had a lot of shit going on in her life so when she puts the kibosh on it for real, you can shrug and say 'knew it' then go back to fucking around?"

That behavior had gotten me through a tough time that I had let go on too long. I might be ready for a relationship, but not with just anyone. I wanted Emery. "I didn't 'pick' her. It's happening naturally, but slowly. Don't rush her and scare her off."

"The kids don't, you know...bother you? Not even the little one?" His question was full of concern.

"I talked to her."

Stetson's brows popped when he realized I didn't mean that I sat down and had a chat with Riley about my hang-ups, but that I had discussed my history with Emery. "Whoa."

"Yeah. And it helped a lot."

"Good." His expression softened like he finally realized I was serious. Emery was special; she wasn't a game.

Stetson wasn't just my cousin, he was my best friend,

but this talk was entering awkward territory and neither of us were gushy or huggers. "Thanks for coming out tonight."

He lifted a brawny shoulder. "Spreading manure on the fields will wait. And I saw Krystal's car at Rattler's when I passed. No way was I getting close to there tonight."

"You know you need to talk to her so she understands that you're done for good."

"I tried that three other times and I ended up back with her, even more miserable than before."

I rolled my eyes. "Don't take your clothes off when you talk to her."

"Nah, man. She's a tricky one. She has this way of making me feel like everything's my fault and I'm a horrible person, and next thing I know, I'm trying to prove her wrong, and the cycle starts again."

I gave him a look because it was obvious why he tumbled into her orbit each time.

"Yeah, asshole. I know who it sounds like. Now you know why I want to avoid her."

Stetson's mom was a master manipulator. Even my mom didn't mess with Naomi.

Krystal didn't have the subtlety of Stetson's mom, and maybe that was why he fell for her. He thought he knew what was coming and could handle her, but Krystal might be more like his mother than we all thought. And that was why he kept trying to break free.

He was a moth, and he thought that if he was going to get smoked, it might as well be with a familiar flame.

"You deserve better," I said because I didn't need another mopey Stetson when Krystal berated him for being himself. "You tell her that, and then tell her that 'better' will never be with her."

"That's a little harsh."

"Sometimes you've gotta be. No one's going to think

you're your dad by you telling Krystal to quit talking to you."

"No one thinks I'm my dad." He snorted. "Trust me."

I'd grown up with him. He'd made sure he was the amiable Barron, the one everyone liked, as if to balance out the wake of bad feelings his parents could leave behind. And when he turned to dig around in his pickup, that was my cue that he wasn't going to talk about it anymore.

He drew back with a duffel and a couple bags of groceries. "I feel like shit taking the cabin when she's in a tent with the kids."

"They're kids. Do you think we would've wanted to be in the cabin at their age?"

"True. But if she has trouble in the night, just holler. I can go home and sleep." He adjusted his black ball cap, turning it around. "Where are you sleeping?"

"I'll put my tent by hers so she doesn't feel like she's out here all alone."

The approach of an engine made us pause. Nora pulled in with Isla in the passenger seat of her Malibu and Lyric in the back.

They spilled out. Did the three of them coordinate? They all wore mirrored sunglasses with their hair secured back. Nora and Isla wore plain blue jeans, but Lyric's were more like her personality. Frayed around the edges with a lot of ink.

Lyric wasn't much older than Nora, but she'd gathered more than a few tattoos. I wasn't sure if Nora could name a tattoo parlor or even knew how to make an appointment.

I didn't have any either. Neither did Stetson, but years ago I'd heard our uncle Bruce comment about his oldest, our cousin Evander, treating his body like a coloring book. Probably one of the many reasons Evander quit coming home on leave. Isla wouldn't dare cross her mom about getting a tattoo. If she wanted any, she'd have to live vicariously through Lyric.

Isla peered around the yard. The sun brightened her hair, but her blonde locks looked different. Did she color her hair a pale lavender so light it was almost her flaxen color? Bold move for Isla. She was almost twenty-four, but what her mother demanded, Isla did, and since she still lived with her parents, Isla did what she was told.

Isla pushed back her almost purple hair. "Where do you want all the tents? Or do Emery and the kids get the cabin?"

I shook my head. "No, they want the tent experience."

Stetson pointed to the clearing across from the firepit but closer to the house. "Set up there. I want the kids to be close to the bathroom if they have to use it in the middle of the night."

The girls set up the tent they were sharing, and I set up mine. The task gave me a way to work off my nervous excitement. We had the place for Emery's tent all ready, making a loose triangle so that the entrances faced in.

Stetson hauled all of his supplies into the cabin.

I gathered bags from the back seat. When I turned, Nora was facing me, hands on her hips.

"So," she said.

"So," I said. I wasn't always sure how to act around her as an adult. She was graduating from college this year. A legit adult. I'd raised her. Mom had disciplined her. I wasn't her parent, but I'd had more responsibility than a brother for so long that I didn't know how to be just a brother. "How's school?"

She cocked a golden brow. Mom would kill to have Nora's natural glossy color. Sometimes I wondered if that was why Mom was so hard on her. Did she blame Nora for sapping her youth? Two boys might've been different. Mom hadn't known what to do with a girl.

"School's fine," she said and held her hands out for the grocery bags. There were more piled on the seat behind me. "Emery seems nice."

"She is."

"And you planned this weekend for her."

It wasn't a question, but I said, "Yep." Her expectant look didn't fade, and I sighed. She wasn't the younger sister I could shut down when I wanted. She was an adult. Someone I could have a real conversation with. "Don't tell me you've heard all the rumors?"

"Lyric keeps us apprised."

I snorted, more out of defeat than anything. No one was going to gossip around the Barron girls. The town was afraid of their mothers. But Lyric was open season. People hoped to get the dirt from her since she had a direct line to us through Isla.

Lyric was cool, and as far as I knew, she didn't talk shit about us. But did she have to pass on the nitty-gritty to my sister?

"Holden, I think I would've noticed that you haven't had a girlfriend since Mom pitched a fit over Teagan."

As long as Nora thought it was Mom that was the issue there. She'd be devastated to know that she'd lost a niece.

Except...if Nora had gone through the same thing and didn't tell me? Stomach acid ate its way up my throat.

I'd feel like I failed her. I'd wonder why she didn't think she could come to me. I'd regret not being able to support her.

"Are you afraid Mom's going to give Emery a hard time too?" she asked. "Is that why you haven't stayed with anyone since then?"

Dammit. She thought Mom derailed me and Teagan. Mom hadn't helped, but it didn't feel right to let Nora keep thinking Mom was to blame. I was her big brother. But she was an adult now.

I judged the time. I wanted to make sure I was around when Emery arrived, but I also needed to talk to my sister. I needed to build the support network I hadn't had when I'd been at my lowest. Emery wasn't going to show early if she had five people to get ready to camp.

"Hey, after we put these in the cabin, how about you and me take a walk? I've gotta talk to you."

Fourteen

Emery

The drive had been only forty-five minutes. I'd passed all kinds of pickups hauling boats, pontoons, and campers, but once I turned down the narrow road to Stetson's cabin, it'd been nothing but peaceful.

He owned this little piece of paradise. I sat on his private dock with him, Landon, and Holden. Boats floated or sped over the water in the distance, but it was almost like we had the lake to ourselves.

My heart clawed its way into my throat as Nora and Avery each rowed by in a kayak. Avery's life vest was the perfect size. The ones Stetson had brought were all adult sized, but Holden had stopped at the gas station before he'd come out. The place on the edge of town was more like a sporting goods shop than a convenience store.

His thoughtfulness warmed me down to my toes.

Nora hadn't let Avery kayak far from shore, and she'd taken all the kids, wading by Riley and Afton in the water next to them. Holden's sister was young, and at first glance, she seemed timid and shy. But the girl had confidence.

She'd sat the three older kids down and reviewed water safety. Then she'd gone over the kayak and what to expect. The spiel sounded rehearsed, and when she explained that she used to be a youth counselor at summer camps on the river, it made sense. One by one, she'd taken each kid out.

The experience so far was priceless. The kids had forgotten that their dad dropped half their weekend together.

Landon and I hadn't caught more than weeds, but between him and Afton, they'd pointed out frogs, turtles, a muskrat, and even a pelican.

"Is it time for s'mores?" Landon asked.

Holden was on the other side of me. Landon and Afton had lost interest in their rods. Afton played with Isla like she was her own personal Barbie doll. They were doing cartwheels across the lawn. Riley ran back and forth between them and the dock, trying to mimic them with Lyric. I angled my chair to keep an eye on her, not that I had to, but I couldn't not do it.

Holden had put his hoodie back on. I'd been able to stay focused on fishing after he did that. Stetson had his feet propped on the railing, his rod in a holder that was welded to the railing, and he'd tipped his ball cap over his eyes.

Landon had been starstruck when he saw that both of his coaches were camping with us.

"In the next hour," Holden answered. "But if your momma wants you to eat something healthy first, you know Stetson and I can't make the s'mores until everyone follows her orders."

Landon rolled his eyes but grinned. He draped his arms over the railing and peered into the water. "Think we'll catch a fish?"

"I dunno." Holden slowly reeled in. "This time of year, the fishing is really good by Garrison Dam."

"Mom, can we go there?"

"Maybe another time." I stuffed my hands into the pockets of my pink hoodie. I hadn't thought about Garrison Dam in years. "I used to go fishing there with Grandpa."

"What'd you catch?" Holden asked. "When you went with your dad?"

"Walleye."

He groaned and put his hand on his belly. "The filet mignon of the sea."

Stetson grunted. "If you catch a northern, throw that thing back. I don't need it sliming my dock."

"Have you seen a northern's teeth?" Holden asked Landon.

"Fish don't have teeth!"

Holden cast and put his rod in the holder. He and Landon bent over Holden's phone and pored over pictures of walleye and northern and other fish that were common in the lake.

"Mom!" Afton called. "Look!"

She did the best cartwheel I'd seen all day. Isla applauded her.

"That was awesome, honey!"

"Mama—wook!" Riley tried to do the same, putting her hands in the grass while Lyric flipped her legs into the air.

Afton gave me a *you know she's copying me, right?* look and I nodded but clapped for Riley.

Reinvigorated after the fish information, Landon took the rod and reeled it in. He cast it himself and beamed when Holden complimented him. Warmth filled me from head to toe, but it was different from the heat Holden usually caused. My son dropped the handle into the rod holder and checked its seating just like Holden and then he sat, propping his feet on the railing like Stetson.

I exchanged an amused look with Holden. Landon caught me and his expression turned curious.

"Are you guys dating?"

My insides froze like it was the middle of a January polar vortex. I met Holden's gaze. He was alarmed but looking to me to answer. Stetson kept his cap over his eyes and pretended like he was sleeping and couldn't have possibly heard the conversation.

Nora and Avery appeared around the curve, paddling closer, Nora in a yellow kayak and Avery in a red one. The other two girls were playing in the same spot.

I could blow him off. I had plenty of distractions I could use around us. But that wouldn't answer Landon's question, and he had a legitimate reason to know.

I held Holden's gaze a moment before I asked Landon, "What would you think if we were?"

He shrugged. "Dad has Jenni."

"He does," I agreed. "But Holden has his house and we have ours. If we dated, you'd be okay with that?"

"Like we'd go to his place to pet the horse and cats again? I could play with Sally?"

I glanced at Holden for help. I wanted to say yes, but I didn't want to answer for him.

"Yes," Holden said, putting his leg down and sitting forward. "But I'd like to take your mom out once in a while, just her and I. Would that be okay with you and your sisters?"

"Would what be okay with us?" Avery asked from the ramp where Nora was pushing her kayak forward so she didn't have to get out in the cold water. The kids had supersonic hearing when it was least opportune.

"If Mom and Holden dated," Landon answered.

Nora pressed her lips in as she wrestled with the kayak.

Afton ran to the dock. "You guys are dating?"

Stetson's chest shook like he was holding in a laugh. Holden was the closest to scared that I'd ever seen him. I felt the same. This conversation had a lot of witnesses.

"We'd like to," I said. "Are you okay with that?"

Avery popped a hip out, her kayak forgotten. We'd had plenty of discussions about how things were over between me and their father and that we would never be living together again. I hadn't anticipated a dating discussion. But here it was.

"Holden and I..." My throat tightened.

This was all out of my league. It was one thing to keep writing off Holden's infatuation as fleeting. No one really knew about us. This was announcing to the most important people in my life that I was moving on. Something I hadn't planned on doing. I'd be admitting to myself that this athletic, hot man wanted me, the mom who wore scrubs and pajamas most of the time.

I couldn't make myself say it.

Holden swooped in to rescue me. "I'd like to take your mom out. And I think it'd be really cool to keep hanging out with all of you. But if I, like, kiss your mom and stuff, will you be upset?"

"Ew" was Landon's reply.

Avery shrugged. "I guess. I mean, Dad kisses Jenni."

Afton wrinkled her nose. "Jenni's annoying." Did that mean she was okay with it?

Avery rolled her eyes. "Next time, don't tell Jenni you think she's annoying."

I sputtered, the dating talk mostly forgotten. "You said that to her?"

"Well, she is," Afton said as if everyone should know.

It was the same argument I'd had with Avery about

calling Afton annoying, which was probably why Afton so freely told Jenni her thoughts.

"Don't be rude." My tone lacked conviction. Some days, being an adult was hard.

"Why? She was rude first."

I chewed the inside of my cheek. "Did she say something?"

Afton stuck her lower lip out. "She called me a pill."

There were worse names, but the sentiment was there. I might have to talk to Henry and hope he cared.

Avery nodded, looking guilty. "Riley and Afton kept waking the puppy up. Jenni would get mad at us and then Dad got mad."

"He got mad at you?" I should've asked them more about how their stay had gone, but I had decided that during their visits with their dad, I would have to butt out. He was the parent in charge on those weekends.

"No, he yelled at Jenni. Said it was just a..." Her gaze darted around and she lowered her voice. "A *bleep* dog and if it was going to be a problem, then she had to get rid of it."

"I'm surprised he was okay with it in the first place." I was also surprised he'd called Jenni out on how she was with the kids, but given his history of being second best to his parents' dog, it made sense. "He doesn't like dogs."

"I don't think he likes the puppy," Landon said in his most serious voice.

"But he's soooo cute, Mommy." Afton wiggled.

"Okay." I blinked and finally remembered that everyone was watching the exchange. So. All that was out there. I didn't think they would judge. They knew what it was like when outsiders threw around opinions on their lives. "Well, I guess that's settled, then."

Holden lifted the rod and began reeling in. "Anyone else up for some hot dogs and s'mores?"

Landon sprinted off the dock to race his sisters to the firepit.

Holden saved me again. *Thank you*, I mouthed to him.

"No problem." He rose.

Stetson did the same and reeled his line in. Lyric was helping Nora drag the kayaks in. If I wasn't afraid of staring, I'd think Stetson was sneaking peeks at Lyric's ass. But then, Lyric had been doing the same to him since I'd arrived.

"Leave the chairs." Holden snagged his bottle of Coke and hooked it on the fingers of the same hand he held the fishing rod with. With his other hand, he tangled his fingers through mine. "Am I allowed to ask you on an official date now?"

I bit back a grin. "You haven't been deemed annoying, so I think you can."

He tipped his head close. "Think you can get away for an overnight?"

"I don't know about that." My body screamed yes. I slid my gaze to him. "But maybe we could go to Crocus Valley again? I hear there's a private place to park there."

He laughed and squeezed my hand. "I think I know the place."

* * *

Holden

Firelight danced in front of all of us. Stetson had tossed on a hoodie and tended the fire. Nora and Isla couldn't shake Avery and Afton if they tried, and Landon was parked in his chair next to me, trying to pretend he wasn't tired.

Emery sat farther away from the campfire to stay out of the smoke when the wind shifted a little to the left or right.

She had a sleeping Riley bundled in a blanket on her lap. Emery had put her into footed pajamas after the food was done. Riley's curls poked out around the blanket, and instead of making it hard for me to breathe, I thought she was adorable. And almost wished I could be the one to hold her like that. Someday.

The s'mores ended in less of a mess than I imagined. Roasting marshmallows quickly became a higher priority than including the chocolate and graham crackers. Nora brought her homemade graham crackers, but other than what she took, they had remained untouched until Emery took one.

She ate it and dutifully avoided my gaze the entire time.

Emery sat up, cradling Riley. "I think I can lay her down, but I might have to stay in there with her." She called to the other girls, "Guys, it's time for bed."

Avery's mouth dropped like she'd heard something tragic. "Aw, come on."

"It's late, and we'll make less noise if we all go to bed at once." Emery tucked Riley close as she stood and adjusted the blankets to keep from tripping on them.

I grabbed the flashlight and jumped up. Keeping the light beam on her path, I walked with her to the tent. Between Nora and my cousins, the other three kids were herded through the cabin for the bathroom.

"Just remember," I said as I unzipped Emery's tent and held the flap for her as she ducked in with her bundle. I lit the inside for her, keeping the beam off Riley's face. "I'm right next door if you need anything."

"Thank you."

Once Riley was cocooned in the blanket nest, Emery pivoted and crawled out.

She brushed her hair off her face. "When the others get back and settled, I'll go use the bathroom."

Nora and Isla were in the cabin. It was just me and Emery for a precious few minutes. I flicked the flashlight off.

"Ooh, it's dark," she said with mock innocence. "I'm scared."

"You'll have to stick close to me, then," I murmured as I leaned down for a kiss. I found her lips easily enough. Was it just today I'd been inside her?

Couldn't be. Because if I let my control down, I'd be hard as the rocks lining the shore. I'd tent these sweats so badly my shadow would give me away.

I didn't keep the kiss light, instead wrapping my arms around her and sweeping my tongue into her mouth.

She might've tried to stifle her moan, but I felt it as much as I heard it. I devoured her, the sweetness of chocolate and marshmallows on her lips.

When the sound of the cabin door reached us, I pulled back and swiped her bottom lip with my thumb. "You taste good. Even if you do torch your marshmallows."

She let out a scandalized gasp and tightened her grip on my sweater. "You hardly get them brown. Like, what's the point?"

"Brown, not charred."

I took my turn using the bathroom while she tucked the kids in. When I came out, country music streamed through the place. Isla was at the small island, one leg crossed over the other. She held cards in her hand. Lyric was across from her.

"Nora's gotten sneakier at pinochle," I said.

Stetson snorted. "That's why Lyric can't be partners with her. I know Isla won't let her cheat."

Nora rolled her eyes. "I don't cheat."

"But you let Ricky do it."

Lyric slapped Stetson's shoulder. "Prove it, *Stoney*. Oh, wait, you can't."

167

He gave her a shit-eating grin. He grumbled about her nickname for him, but I suspected he liked it.

I suspected he liked a lot more about Lyric than her name for him. But for whatever reason, whether it was because Lyric was the opposite of what his mother would want or because he didn't want to feel like he was getting between Isla and her closest friend, Lyric was the one woman he didn't pursue.

The cabin door nudged open, and Emery stepped inside. She was still in jeans and her pink hoodie, and she carried a little backpack.

"Hey. I was just going to clean up." She glanced out the window in the living room that faced the tent.

I knew exactly what she was nervous about. "I'll go outside in case they get scared."

She gave me a relieved look and rushed to the bathroom.

I was about to walk out the door when Isla whispered, "Holden." When I stopped, she leaned so far forward she was going to face-plant on the wood floor if she moved another millimeter. "We're going to be playing a while. So, *you know*, take your time when she's done."

I whispered back, "Okay." But I walked out of the door with a huge grin.

I wandered around by the tents, listening for the kids. There was some rustling from inside that quieted after a few moments.

Several minutes later, Emery came out, picking her way in the dark with her phone's light. I flipped my flashlight on so she could see better.

"Thank you," she said when she reached me.

I shut the light off and set it by the entrance to my tent. Then I pulled her into my arms, smiling when she came without resistance. "I have it on good authority that they'll be inside playing cards for a while."

Her hair tickled me as she nodded. "Oh?"

I whispered in her ear. "You wanna come to my tent for a few minutes of quiet making out?"

Her hot breath caressed my ear as she said, "I can do a whole lot really fast and really quietly."

The control I'd been reining in all night took a nosedive. "You'll have to prove it, Em."

Fifteen

Emery

Two weeks had gone by since the camping trip. Football was almost done, and the kids came home from school every day talking about what they were going to be for Halloween.

It was almost October, but time was flying by. The kids were supposed to be picked up by their dad tonight, and I had plans with Holden. If Henry flaked, then Holden would bring pizza over and we'd all watch a movie. Either way, I was excited about tonight.

When I wrapped up at work, I had a message from Henry to call him.

Looked like it was a pizza and movie night. I called him back when I got into my car.

He answered with a pleasant, "Hey, Emery. I'm really sorry, but a surgery went late and pushed my cases today back. Would you be able to bring the kids down? Otherwise, I'll get home late and then have to drive. My night with them would be shot."

I didn't ponder whether he was being purposely difficult. Since he was actually talking about wanting to spend time with the kids, I was willing to help. I'd have to let Holden know about the change of plans.

"I can do that. What time should I get them there?"

"Seven should work. I'll clean up at the hospital and maybe pick up some pizza. I really appreciate it."

I would've given the phone a side-eye if it wasn't up to my ear. He was nice, almost apologetic. Was he going to ask me to go to Bismarck on Sunday too? Or was he planning to drop out by Saturday? "No problem. Football Saturday still okay?"

"Yeah, no problem."

Did Henry want something he knew would upset me? I didn't know, but I wouldn't waste time being suspicious. "See you then."

I sent Holden a message. Like me, he'd be disappointed, but I didn't think he'd have an issue otherwise.

He'd called back by the time I reached the house. When I answered, he said, "Want me to come with? We can eat somewhere in Bismarck."

Ooh, an out-of-town date night. I liked Rattler's, but there were so many places in Bismarck I hadn't gotten to eat when I'd lived there. Having little kids or no time had limited us. "We'll leave in an hour."

"I'll be there."

I was grinning when I darted inside. Mom was in the kitchen, feeding the kids a snack. Her brows lifted as if she expected Henry to drop the weekend again.

"Change of plans, guys. I'm taking you to your dad's because he has to work late. Holden's riding along, if that's okay."

The news went over relatively well like I expected, thanks to Holden's presence. The kids enjoyed hanging out with him. Mom helped me get the kids ready. When Holden arrived, he loaded their bags into my car.

The drive was quick with his company. When I pulled up in front of Henry's house, Holden gave a low whistle under his breath. The place wasn't the million-dollar home Henry and I had bought after he got his current position, but it was still a large place. Two stories with a basement. Instead of being by the river, he was in a nice neighborhood surrounded by other half-million-dollar houses.

But then, he could get the financing when I absorbed half his debt and got screwed with child support.

"Little larger than my place, right?" I said loud enough for only him to hear and keeping the residual bitterness out of my voice. "Mind waiting here?"

I didn't want to add to the animosity between Henry and me by having Holden walk with everyone to the door. I knew how seeing Jenni made me feel even though I was over Henry.

"Not at all." He turned his head to speak to the kids who were in various stages of unbuckling and gathering their things. "Have a good weekend."

They piled out, telling Holden bye, and grabbed their luggage. The garage door had been opened by the time we reached the house. Henry waited by the door to the house. The older three kids gave him a quick hug and filed through the door inside to the mudroom. I approached, holding Riley.

One by one, each kid darted back and hugged me. Riley's arms were hooked around my neck.

"You're going to have fun at Daddy's." I didn't go inside. If Riley started crying, it might increase any underlying tension. I knew she loved Henry, but if she was comfortable with him, it'd be easier on all of us.

Jenni's voice instructing the kids where to put their stuff trailed after Henry as he stepped into the garage. He wore simple jeans and a UND hoodie. The dark circles under his eyes were new. They took the sting off the giant Suburban behind me and Jenni's sporty car that couldn't fit more than two of the kids. His haggard appearance helped me ignore that his garage had almost as much square footage as the first floor of my house.

"Hey, curly girl." He held his arms out, and she whined and burrowed into my arms. His smile fell.

"I think she's tired," I said, trying to be helpful. I hated what Henry had done, and I disliked how he'd acted after the divorce, but for the kids and my own stress levels, I wanted this process to go smoothly more often than not.

He nodded and tried again. "Want to go in with the others? Then I can tell you how we're going to the zoo to see the penguins tomorrow after we get back from the football game."

"Pen-gun?" Riley wiggled to get out of my hold at the same time as Avery poked her head out of the door.

"Where's the puppy?"

Annoyance flickered in Henry's expression. "He went to live with one of Jenni's friends. We work shifts too long for a dog."

I had a feeling that wasn't the reason. I was sure Jenni had gotten a puppy without asking Henry's opinion. He wouldn't like that even if it wasn't about a dog.

"Oh. Okay." Avery grabbed Riley's hand and went inside. "Did you hear? We get to go see the penguins?"

"Thanks for bringing them down." Henry's gaze flicked to my vehicle where Holden was scrolling through his phone. A line formed across his brow. "Why'd you bring him?"

It was tempting not to answer, but it would be better to

remain cordial. "We had plans tonight. We changed them to Bismarck since I was coming here anyway."

Henry's lips pressed together. "So things are getting serious?"

"Things are just things, Henry." I shrugged. What else could I say? I didn't know whether Holden and I were considered serious. Dating as an adult in my thirties was new to me. But Henry wouldn't be the one to talk to about it either.

"He's good with the kids?"

"Is Jenni?"

His scowl deepened. "She's fine." Something about the way he said it gave me pause. There was a hint of defensiveness, and I wasn't sure what that meant. Jenni was young. She could be ambivalent about the kids. She could genuinely enjoy them, though I didn't sense that was the case.

Or she could resent that four kids intruded on her time with the surgeon she'd bagged herself.

"Holden hasn't lost his temper and called them a pill. Did you know about that?"

Henry's expression darkened and his tone was hot. "I talked to her about that."

"Thank you." I'd heard his exchange with Avery, but I couldn't resist asking. "So, no more puppy?"

He gave me a *don't go there* look. "Jenni wanted him, but it's not feasible when she works twelve-hour shifts."

The way he said that wasn't a surprise. He wouldn't have helped take care of the puppy. I couldn't see him walking a dog, much less picking up its poop. He'd need to go to a lot of therapy about why he felt like he couldn't live up to the Yorkies his parents had at any given point before he'd willingly take care of a dog.

I took a couple of steps toward the garage door. "I'll have my phone on me if you need anything."

"I'll bring them back Sunday."

That would remain to be seen. He hadn't spent an entire weekend with them since he'd moved out. But I gave him a smile and a wave, grateful that this handoff went better than last time.

I got back into the car. Holden lifted a questioning brow.

"It went well. He wasn't a dick, and I didn't have to see Jenni."

"You got a twofer there. Where do you want to eat?"

I pulled away from the house. My kids hadn't fought about being at their dad's. I didn't argue with Henry. And I had the entire night to spend with a hot guy that would end in toe-curling sex. My divorced life was finally looking up.

* * *

Holden

I woke up to a round ass pressed into my side. My arm was slung over my face, and I was surrounded by a peaches-and-cream scent.

I moved my arm and blinked my eyes open. The sun was up. Shit. I had chores to do before the football game. Mom wanted to work and move cattle the next couple of weeks, and I hadn't checked all the fence or gone through my inventory to see what I needed to restock.

But I didn't rush away. Emery was passed out, breathing deeply. This was my first overnight. The first time in a long time I hadn't hurried away after sex so I could sleep in my own bed and forgo any jumping to conclusions that might happen.

I didn't want to rush anywhere. I wanted to turn onto my side and rub my growing erection into her lush ass. I'd had my face buried between those thighs for hours, and I wanted to do it again.

Emery was out, though. She hadn't twitched. I doubted she got to sleep in very often.

I eased out of bed and went to the bathroom. I didn't have an overnight kit with me, but that was the perk of being a guy. I used her mouthwash and put some of her toothpaste on my finger to scrub over my teeth. Better than nothing.

I ran through the shower until there were two of us that smelled like peaches and cream.

Her bathroom was like the rest of her house. Messy, with a lived-in feel. Toys ate up the floor in the living room, and she or the kids kicked them into the corner at the end of the day. Her kitchen had cereal boxes and bread bags lining the counters when there was minimal counter realty in the first place. Her bedroom was like the bathroom. Any flat surface was cluttered. Her house was clean but at a steady level of frenzy.

Surprising, because she was so chill.

My mom seemed like she wouldn't mind a cluttered space. Her work was outdoors and she wasn't about the frills. Yet, a mess stressed her out. Nora and I had learned early to pick up after ourselves or face her wrath. I learned a lot of swear words when Mom found a mess.

Would the clutter bother me? Or would I find it refreshing that perfection wasn't expected?

I came out of the bathroom, toweling my hair off and running a hand through the damp strands. Emery inhaled and stretched, blinking at the ceiling. Her gaze landed on me.

I didn't have any clothes on, and she squinted at my dick. If she stared for another few seconds, it'd do more than twitch to life.

"Morning," I said and flicked the towel at her ass through the blankets.

The crack it made filled the room, and she shot up to a sitting position, her eyes wide and color painting her cheeks. "Holden!"

I laughed, both at her reaction and the way she covered herself, as if I hadn't been all over that naked body last night.

She scowled and rubbed her butt, but the towel had been too thick to make a decent sting through a sheet and three blankets.

I prowled toward the bed, but she scrambled to the opposite side. "Oh, no, you don't. You showered, and I bet you have minty breath."

I breathed against my hand and sniffed. "Minty fresh."

She held her hand up like she was a crossing guard and I was a five-ton truck bearing down on her. "Then don't get close to me until I do the same."

"Morning breath doesn't scare me off."

"I'm dying inside enough as it is. I need a toothbrush, a hairbrush, and a shower."

"In that order?"

"Any order is better than I am now."

Laughing, I backed off the bed and grabbed my pants. "Want to come to my place after the game? I can show you how to fence."

"Is that a euphemism for sex?"

She hadn't been to my place other than to ride with the kids. Otherwise, she made sure we weren't alone in my house. This was the first night we'd had sex since the camping trip.

If she wanted to fuck every two weeks when the kids were at their dad's, there wasn't much I could do about it. As much as I wanted to be with her in my place, in my bed, I wanted her to be comfortable, and she wasn't the only one who thought that sneaking me in and out of her bedroom while the kids were sleeping wasn't right.

But it was the principle behind why she wouldn't come home with me when her mom was babysitting. The significance of being the first woman I would have sex with under my roof. That would mean we were serious.

If we weren't serious already, what were we?

I'd known her only two months, and I wasn't going to push. Eventually, the question would grow so large in my mind, I'd have to ask. This weekend was not that time.

"No sex—unless you want, then I'm always willing." I grinned like I didn't know she would avoid my bedroom. "But no, I have a lot of work to do, but I also want to spend time with you."

She pushed her tangled brown hair out of her face. "I'd love to, but I have the never-ending pile of laundry."

Her laundry was no joke. I thought I went through a respectable amount of detergent for a single guy. I worked outside and with animals. That sometimes required a few more outfit changes than an office job. Add in towels after cleaning myself up and all the rags I used for work, and my washer and dryer were never neglected.

Emery could lose a couple of kids in her laundry pile.

"I need to get groceries and make our meals for the week too." Her regretful expression eased the thought of going home alone. I had my work to do, and she had hers.

"Okay. Go shower, and I'll show you that I make killer pancakes."

She paused. "Pancakes?"

"If you have frozen fruit, I'll even make homemade syrup."

Delight lit her eyes. "You can do all that?"

"I can, but I won't make a chocolate chip smiley face for you like I did for Nora."

A wistful look crossed over her face. "I would've loved to have a sibling like you."

"Yeah?" Nora appreciated me, but she never said it. I didn't need to hear it either, but I couldn't deny that it was nice to be acknowledged.

"Yeah. It's one reason why I kept agreeing to more kids."

I waited for her to continue, but when her gaze strayed to the bathroom, I got it. She wanted privacy. "Pancakes coming right up."

I left her in peace while I started on breakfast. I made the pancakes from scratch. The same recipe I used to make for Nora each weekend.

I thought Emery would take longer than ten minutes. She entered the kitchen with her damp hair brushed off her face. On a wave of sweet peaches, she passed by me. "Smells good." She kept going to the basement door. The laundry.

In a few minutes, she was back. She set the table for both of us. I was flipping pancakes when she appeared at my elbow. "Ooh, did I have strawberries?"

"Not frozen, but I found some strawberries and blueberries in the fridge."

"You're resourceful."

I gave her a wink. "Thought you knew that by now."

"In the bedroom." She slid her arms around my waist. "And with the grill. But not in the kitchen."

I took the cooked pancake off the skillet and poured more batter one-handed. This was domestic bliss. I could imagine the kids roaming around while we prepared breakfast. Maybe the TV would be going or music filtering through the house. Riley talking. Avery and Afton arguing over sharing their toys. Landon rattling on about football or his Hot Wheels.

I hadn't let myself want this for so long, I almost stopped and envisioned what it would look like in my house.

Emery tipped her face up. "What are you thinking about?"

I hadn't noticed I was smiling. I didn't hit her with complete honesty. We'd come this far in a relatively short time. I couldn't scare her off. "Just thinking about how nice this is."

She chuckled and released me to stir the simmering berries. "That's only because it's just the two of us."

"No, I was factoring the chaos in. It's nice. It would be nice."

She concentrated on the syrup a little too hard. "Yeah."

I studied the bubbles forming on the top of the pancake I'd just poured. "Our house was always pretty quiet, and it was Nora and me. I didn't realize how much I missed cooking for more than me."

"I like the quiet. But by tomorrow, I'll be glad to have them home." She spun away from the stove and opened the fridge. "Score. I have whipped cream."

She busied herself, finding serving spoons and extra napkins. I couldn't escape the feeling she was avoiding the subject of her domestic bliss and me. I flipped the pancake and poured another, wondering if she'd ever think the two should go together.

* * *

Emery

. . .

I had messaged Henry to double-check that he was actually bringing Landon to the game. I let him know I'd be there so he could speak now or forever hold his peace about sitting in the stands with me.

Parking in the lot, I scanned for Henry's red Suburban, but couldn't find it. The game wasn't going to start for twenty minutes, but the coaches usually wanted the kids there early. There was time, but that didn't stop the anxiety-churning acid in my stomach.

I got out and grabbed my fleece jacket. Holden's pickup was parked next to Stetson's.

Shaking my head, I shoved my hands in my pockets and walked to the bleachers. That man had stamina. He'd gotten up earlier than me, made breakfast, and then while I did dishes, he'd gone home to do chores, whatever that entailed. Now he was back to coach, and then he'd go work all day.

I was ready for a nap.

I wasn't used to such a late, strenuous night. At all. My sex life with Henry hadn't been that enthusiastic. And it wasn't like I could look back on it and think that Henry failed in the bedroom or that I'd been the issue. The difference was Holden. He attacked sex with the same unquestioning determination he did everything else in life. When he committed to something, he stuck it out.

That thought rang around my head. *When he committed.*

While he was cooking, he'd made that comment about how he'd like to wake up to me and the kids, and I hadn't known what to do.

It'd been a year since I'd caught Henry cheating. Six months since I'd been divorced. Two months since I'd moved to Coal Haven. I'd gone from a relationship I had expected to last until the grave, to heartbroken and wondering what was wrong with me, to determination that

I would be fine, to acceptance that *single, hardworking mom* was my identity.

Not only had I lost my partner, but Henry had been clear he was done with me. It had felt like he'd gone out of his way to show me that I was on my own, from requesting only every other weekend with the kids, to getting his lawyer to carve away at the child support with an obsidian scalpel.

The idea of fitting another man into my haphazardly pieced-together life left me in a tailspin. My pulse kicked up and I wanted to run. I couldn't get my hopes up only for them to fall out of the sky like last year's fireworks.

Holden had tried to cover his hurt, but he'd been quieter through breakfast while I'd shoveled his pillowy pancakes into my mouth to keep from dipping back into the subject. And he made awesome pancakes. And homemade fucking syrup.

A girl could get used to that.

Wasn't that the issue?

"Mom?" I spun even though there were kids all over calling for their parents.

Landon rushed up to me.

"Hey." I hugged him, glad he'd made it. "Good luck today."

He ran off, and I spotted Henry. Riley clung to him, and Afton and Avery trailed behind him. I looked around but didn't see Jenni.

"Do you have gloves for the girls?" he asked when he reached me, sounding harried and stressed. "I think Afton left hers at home."

"Sure. You guys go sit, and I'll gather whatever's in my car." It wasn't like I could, or wanted, to clean my car every week. Most of the year, I could outfit half the football team in winter weather gear from what the kids left behind on the floor.

I found two pairs, along with my own. That was enough for all the girls. I grabbed the extra hat I found. The sun was rising higher in the sky, but the wind this time of year cut through the clothing. Before I shut the door, I yanked out a blanket.

Henry and the girls were sitting in the same spot I had first chosen. Thanks to the chilly morning, the stands were sparser than they had been at the rest of the games. I met them and was stripped of hats and gloves. I spread the blanket out, and when all was settled, I was next to Henry.

"Jenni didn't want to come?" I kept my tone pleasant. Part of me was curious in a petty sort of way. The other part wanted to make polite conversation. It was better for the kids if the adults could get along.

"No. I thought I'd keep the girls at home since it's kind of chilly, but...she's busy."

I bit the inside of my cheek to keep from smirking. Busy. There was more to the story, but I'd rather she wasn't alone with the girls anyway. "Thank you for bringing Landon."

"The drive is a pain."

I wished fixing Henry's cranky attitude was as easy as giving him a Snickers bar, but when he got like this, he could stay in a funk all day. The reality of the mundane parts of life was a downer compared to his day job.

"The next time you have them will be the last game."

"You mind bringing them down that Friday so I'm not making three round trips?"

Since he asked sort of nicely, I said, "That's fine."

The game started. Holden was dropped in a crouch, directing kids, while Stetson roamed up and down the sidelines. When Landon wasn't playing, I had a hard time paying attention to the game.

"The kids say you're still seeing Coach B."

"Yeah, they gave us their blessing."

His jaw flexed. "Is it serious?"

"Don't, Henry," I said quietly.

He kept his voice low. "I'm just asking."

He was just asking, but I was angry that I didn't have an answer. I'd just been thinking about how I couldn't do serious with Holden. It was a mindfuck because of Henry. I didn't want to tell my ex that and let him know how much power he still had over my life.

"What about you and Jenni?" I countered. Inwardly, I winced. What if he answered thinking I owed him an answer about me and Holden?

"Jenni's...young."

I couldn't keep my snort in. The girls looked at us, but I kept watching the field like I'd done nothing. "She's still an adult."

"Yeah, but she's not like you. You had your shit together at her age."

"We were having our second kid at her age."

"I know. It's, just, sometimes I don't think she understands why my job requires all the time it does. I can't just take a tropical vacation every couple months."

Poor thing. I kept the sarcasm to myself. For all of two seconds. "I bet she likes payday well enough."

His expression flickered, but he covered it quick enough. "To answer your question, though, yes, it's serious. I wouldn't have ended our marriage and bought a house with her if it wasn't."

His answer gnawed at my brain. He was so serious about a young nurse he'd met when he swung by the ICU where I worked that he'd started meeting her outside the hospital. And when I'd seen them leave together while I was in a patient's room, he'd been so serious about her that he'd lied. I was sure it wasn't a coincidence that he didn't move in with her until I filed for divorce and told him he couldn't sleep in the bedroom anymore.

I inhaled a calming breath. I wasn't the bitter ex. But I would answer his question honestly. I had to reclaim the power he had over me. "Honestly, I don't know how serious it is with Holden. I have myself and the kids to think about, but I do know that he makes me feel good about myself. He treats me well."

Henry's jaw tightened. "I asked around about him, you know. One of the residents at the hospital is from Hazen and knows of the Barrons."

Hazen was twenty-five miles away, but the small towns in this area were like one big small town. "Okay?"

He dropped his voice to a whisper. "Holden has a reputation."

"I'm aware."

Surprise flickered in his dark eyes.

I shrugged. "He's not just arm candy. We talk."

He ground his jaw together. "I don't know this guy. You barely know him, but the kids talk about him all the time."

"Is that what's upsetting you?"

"No, I'm worried that a guy like him is going to leave their lives as fast as he entered."

Henry could raise all the alarms he wanted, but I had a big ol' firehose ready to snuff out his bogus concerns. "You cheated on me. Is that what you're going to do for the rest of your life? Cheat on your partners?" I tilted my head. "Would you think it's fair if that was how you were labeled for the rest of your life?"

"Once," he said between clenched teeth. "I did it once. How long has Holden been a fuckboy?"

I glanced around, making sure Henry's words hadn't been heard. The girls huddled over the snacks, and the bleachers around us were clear. "What upsets you the most?

That I've moved on? That I'm unrepentant about it? That he's successful and handsome? Or that I'm not letting you push me around in a relationship you have no business in?"

"Em—"

"No, Henry. You keep trying to exert some kind of control over me, to insist on some sort of say in my private life, and you use the kids as an excuse. But you lost access to my private life for good when the divorce was final. How often are we going to have this argument?"

His nostrils flared, but he couldn't raise his voice. I doubted he even had a rebuttal. I'd hit on exactly what he was doing. It was hard to see me move on. He could buy a house with another woman and plan tropical vacations, but I couldn't do the same.

I ripped my attention off Henry at the same time Holden glanced into the stands. His gaze jumped from me to Henry, and he lifted a brow as if he was asking me if I was okay.

I gave him a tight smile. One of the kids tugged on Holden's hoodie and he had to turn away. That was fine with me. I wasn't okay.

I wanted to tell Henry that hell yeah, Holden and I were serious. I wanted to smugly inform him that Holden was giving me everything that Henry had destroyed. Trust. Reliability. Respect. But because of Henry, I was too afraid to want it.

It was hard to concentrate on the rest of the game. I stayed with it enough to clap and cheer when I was supposed to. At the end of the game, I gave the kids hugs goodbye and helped Henry load them up. We hadn't argued, and he wasn't snapping at the kids. Overall, the morning was a success.

By the time I got to my car, Holden was there. He'd

finished high-fiving the rest of the team and making sure sweaters and water bottles weren't left behind.

"Glad Landon made it," he said.

I nodded. "Yeah. I have to pay by taking them all to Bismarck again next time they stay the weekend, but that's okay, I guess." I summoned a smile. "Thanks for coaching today."

He leaned against the door, his long, lean body on perfect display. "What are you doing tonight?"

My smile turned wan. I wanted another night like last night. Another morning like this morning. I willed myself to say yes. To quit being scared of how a guy could hurt me because of one man.

However, that man had been my husband and the father of my children. Holden was neither, but he was sweeping me away faster than Henry had in college.

"Laundry and meal planning. Tomorrow I execute the meals." I had to bite my tongue to keep from inviting him over, but I needed to get used to being alone.

Disappointment filled his eyes, but he returned my smile. "I can take care of one night by bringing a meal over after practice."

"You don't have to."

He pushed off the car. "I want to. Have a good weekend, Em."

"You too," I said weakly as he walked away.

I got behind the wheel and slumped. Why hadn't I invited him over again? Laundry could last long past wild sex years. But I didn't have to worry about laundry leaving me.

Sixteen

Holden

My finger hovered over my phone. It was Saturday night. I could spend one night without her.

I didn't want to. That was the issue.

I was leaning against my pickup in its normal parking spot outside my garage.

For the last two weeks, I'd taken soup and breadsticks from Rattler's to her place after practice. I'd watched movies with them last weekend. And last Sunday, I stopped by in the afternoon to help rake and haul leaves.

I had plenty of work to do at my place.

Stetson messaged me. **Rattler's?**

I had nothing else to do and it'd be nice to catch up with him, so I sent back **Be there in an hour.**

I ran through the shower, debating on shaving since I hadn't this morning, but decided to let the scruff stay. I used a comb on my hair this time, since I could only get away with not combing it once before I looked like I hadn't used a brush in years.

After I was dressed in jeans and an orange Tractor Supply hoodie that was so bright it could double as a hunting coat, I met Stetson at the restaurant.

He was in his normal spot. Both Shawn and Remington were at the table.

I pulled a chair out. "Stetson, both owners are giving you a talking-to? What'd you do?"

Shawn stretched his arms above his head and rose. He was almost as big as Stetson. He kept a short goatee, which was the only hair on his dark head.

"He gets all of us tonight." Shawn's wife, Tenielle, appeared next to me. She wore paint-splattered overalls that weren't purchased that way. Tenielle flipped houses, and there were plenty in the county that kept her busy. She did much of the work herself, from framing to painting to home decor. A slower pace, she had claimed, after she and Shawn had lived in Chicago for years.

"Date night at your own restaurant?" I asked.

She laughed, a loud and free sound that made me miss Emery. "Yes and no. It's tough when Shawn's BFF works here too."

I leaned close and lowered my voice. "Does Shawn realize how close Remington and Stetson are? What if Remington found another BFF?"

She grinned. "He says Stetson keeps Remington out of trouble."

I glanced at Stetson. "You never did that for me."

"Half the bad ideas were yours," Stetson said, folding his arms and leaning back in his chair. "The other half were just coincidence."

"It wasn't a coincidence to move the Andersons' tractors across the field in the middle of the night."

"Dan Anderson shouldn't have left his tractors vulnerable to bored teenagers. Besides, that was Evander's idea."

"The worst ones were," I agreed, and we both nodded.

Remington shook his head. "I really want to meet this Evander."

"He talked about moving back," Stetson said. "Then shit went down with Liam and Kennedy, and he re-upped for three more years."

Evander was good at evading. Always had been.

Tenielle rose. "If you'll excuse us. Shawn's taking me to Bismarck for our real date night...that he's writing off as a research expense."

Shawn's grin was unrepentant, his brown eyes sparkling. "Guilty."

The couple left, and Remington got up. "I gotta go check on the back. Then I'm actually going home early for once."

"Oh, yeah? Who with?" Stetson asked.

Remington slapped him on the shoulder. "No one. She's already there."

I looked at Stetson, but he shook his head. Remington's love life was as uncomplicated as mine used to be.

"Just you and me?" I asked as a server slid my usual drink in front of me. Damn. Coal Haven was a small town, but that was a sign I came here too much.

"It looks like we're getting company." Stetson leveled a steady stare on me.

I was about to ask him what the hell that look was for, but a hand brushed across my shoulders.

"Hi, Holden." Holly planted a kiss on my forehead.

I automatically brushed it away and frowned at my fingers. Red lipstick was smeared across them. I wiped them off on a napkin. "Hey, Holls."

Sienna took a seat next to Stetson, but she was looking at me. "Are you alone tonight?"

"Yes, Emery's staying in tonight." I thought she was, anyway.

Holly ran her fingers through her long, blonde hair. "You're still seeing her?" When I nodded, her red-stained lips curved up. "That must be a record for you."

Stetson stared into his beer. People had given me a hard time about my free bachelor ways over the years, but none of them had noticed that Stetson sat the conversation out. None of them assumed I was three-dimensional enough to have a past, to have a valid reason to protect my heart.

It had never bothered me before. Why now?

Because I had more people who cared and who knew the real me. Holly and I hadn't reached the friend stage. She was a buddy I'd had sex with a couple of times.

"It's not a record, believe it or not." I'd admit that much. "So, what are you two up to?"

Holly rolled her eyes. "What is anyone ever up to in Coal Haven?"

"Right?" Sienna grabbed Stetson's beer and took a long pull off it.

He flagged the server for another drink, refusing to share. It was a subtle but clear message that they weren't at the sharing stage of hooking up. Sharing body fluids wasn't as intimate as sharing a beer.

Holly reached for my beer. I tried to beat her, but she snagged it and watched me while she took a deep drink from it. And just like that, I was back in high school. Tina Pearson was trying to steal my breadstick to make the girl I was taking to prom jealous. I was in my thirties and had been over that shit for a long time.

"Keep it," I said, digging out my wallet to leave cash on the table. "I'm taking off soon."

She pouted as she set the glass down. "You're no fun, but thanks for buying me a drink."

My stomach fell. I didn't need Holly telling the town I bought her a drink when I was trying to be serious with Emery.

Laughter rang through the place. I spotted Aspen, Lyric, and Isla at the bar. Three guys who looked vaguely familiar were eyeing them. They weren't from Coal Haven but probably worked at the plant, the mine, or the refinery. I'd seen Lyric and Aspen flirt and leave with some of the guys, but never Isla.

I glanced at Stetson. A heavy scowl was etched into his face. I almost joked about how he was going to cockblock his sister, but when I followed his gaze, it was Lyric he was pissy about.

That was his fault. Everyone knew she'd had a thing for him since she'd been old enough to know she liked boys. But Stetson's baggage blocked her out further than anyone else.

Between the women at our table and Lyric's group, I didn't need to get involved. I loved my cousin, but there was only one person I wanted to be with right now.

"See you for practice?" I said as I stood and pushed my chair in.

Holly's roaming eye had moved on to the guys eyeballing the other three. It was after ten, and Rattler's had become a meat market.

"See you. Excuse me, ladies. Gonna go say hi to my sister." Stetson grabbed his beer and stalked toward Isla's table. Out of the group, Isla might not appreciate his interference the most.

I was at Emery's in minutes. The light was on in the living room. Should I leave? Maybe I should've messaged. Given her some warning and let her have a chance to turn me away. Perhaps that was why I hadn't.

I was here now, so I knocked.

* * *

Emery

I peered out the door and immediately wished I wore something other than flannel pajama pants and a long-sleeved shirt with pumpkins all over it. I was trying to keep my heating bill down as much as possible. Cuteness didn't factor into my Saturday nights home alone.

Holden had seen me in similar clothing before, but with his wide shoulders blocking out the door's peephole and the shadows giving his face an extra-rugged appeal, that thought didn't make me feel better.

If I kept staring at him, he might leave, thinking I was ignoring him. And I wouldn't get a wink of sleep wondering why he stopped by. I pushed open the screen door and stepped back. "Is everything okay?"

He came in. "I was at Rattler's, and Holly showed up."

I closed the door on the brisk air that followed him in. My brain spun around Holly's name, wondering how jealous I should be—and why. "Okay?"

"She drank out of my beer, and when I said she could just have it, she joked that it was nice that I bought her a drink."

I pressed my lips together, fighting a sudden and inexplicable wave of rage. It was just a beer, and I wasn't fighting over any guy. But part of me thought *This is it. He realized he could do better.* "Okay."

He studied me, his gaze jumping between my eyes. "Does any of that bother you?"

I feathered my fingers over the hem of my top. Yes, it bothered me, and that was a state I didn't want to be in. But I wasn't sure why we were standing in my entrance talking about it. "Should it?"

His brow furrowed. "No. I'm not interested in anyone but you."

I nearly pumped my fist in the air. Ha! He didn't want her more than me, and I was *ecstatic*. And I should admit that—to him and to myself. "I'm not interested in anyone but you either."

He tensed like he was balancing on a precarious ledge. "So, we're exclusive?"

"I'm not seeing anyone else. And I don't want to."

"Okay." Satisfaction gleamed in his eyes, but he didn't grab me in a hug or swing me around. Did couples celebrate being exclusive? *Yay, you're not fucking anyone else...*

No, his shoulders were tight, and the crease was still in his forehead. Something was on his mind. "Holden, what's wrong?"

"I didn't want to go out with Stetson tonight. I didn't want to sit in Rattler's nursing a beer. I didn't want to feel like an ass because Holly was there and I didn't know what you'd think. I wanted to fold laundry and watch a movie with you."

Oh. I wasn't ready for the stark vulnerability that yawned in my belly. I'd been home wishing he was here, too, and wondering why I thought distance was best for me when I spent that time missing him. "I wanted that too. Too much."

"How could it be too much?"

I twisted my hands. "Holden, my life has pivoted so many times in the last year and a half. If this—if you and I

194

—" I let out a gusty breath. I would get the words out. He needed to hear them. "If you feel like moving on, I don't want to sit and talk myself through another man walking out the door. I don't want to have to explain to the kids why another man doesn't seem to want them in his life." Tears filled my eyes and I swiped at the corners. This was why I had suffered loneliness instead of being with Holden. "I don't want to lie in bed crying again. And I hate that I'm so scared because of Henry. He shouldn't be a part of this."

He closed the distance between us and cupped my face. "Henry is a part of this. He's always going to be a part of your life. I don't know what you're going through, and I won't pretend I do. All I know is that there's something between us I don't want to walk away from. And if you want to take it slow, we'll take it slow. I just want to know that you're not going to shove me out without talking to me first."

I hadn't talked to him first. He was considerate with me and the kids. He'd put me first and given me space. And I'd blocked him out. "Henry asked if we were serious today. I didn't know what to say."

He stroked my lower lip with one of his thumbs. "Do you want to be serious?"

The tears were back. Being exclusive was one thing, but committing to another relationship terrified me. "That's the problem. I'm scared."

He pulled me into his arms. "I know. I'm scared too. How about we start with me folding some shirts and pants?"

I could handle folding laundry with a handsome man. And wasn't that where most relationships leveled out? "Can we end with you making more of your pancakes for me to save for supper tomorrow night?"

Seventeen

IT WAS SATURDAY, and after a chilly week, the day was on the warm side for fall. I'd walked with the kids to the school playground for a break after cleaning the house.

Avery sat on a swing. She kept her toes dug into the small rocks and swayed from side to side. "I wish I could ride again."

"I know." She'd missed last weekend, and this weekend, Holden was busy moving and working cattle. Snow would be on the ground soon. Holden said they might have to pause with lessons until everything melted and there was no ice left next spring. He wanted the safest conditions possible for her.

Avery had deflated. I wasn't sure whether I was going to have to console her or Holden. He'd hated disappointing her.

Riley was in the baby swing next to Avery, and Afton was on the other side of us. I gave Riley a push, and her little hands gripped the chains. When I was mostly certain she wouldn't try to crawl out, I stepped to Afton and pushed her.

"Underdog!" Afton cried.

I dragged her swing back and ran forward, pushing her high and ducking under her. Then Riley demanded an underdog, and I gave her a modified version that wouldn't land her in the ER with a concussion.

"Mom!" Landon called from the bottom of the slide. "Can we play catch?"

"I've gotta stay by Riley."

Avery got off her swing. "I've got her, Mom."

"Thank you." My guilt from the early days after the divorce lowered since she still wanted to help when she didn't have to.

I threw the football with Landon until it was getting close to dinnertime. We were walking back to the house when my phone buzzed.

It was Holden. I answered, "Hey, I didn't think I'd hear from you again this weekend."

"Are you and the kids able to come over, like, right now?" His excitement vibrated over the phone until I was smiling and didn't know why.

"We're a block from home. We were at the park, but I can just load them up when we get back to the house."

"Awesome. See you in a few."

I wasn't sure what he had planned, but it didn't take the kids much convincing to drive out there.

Avery speculated the entire way. "Do you think he wants to show us the cows? How do you think they move them? He said they use horses. Do you think Pittance is scared of the cows? Is Pittance the one that works them? Or does he use Poppy?"

I didn't have much for answers, and I wouldn't need them. As I coasted down Holden's driveway, the kids' attention was captured by the people and the horses. Nerves twisted my belly until I made out familiar faces. Colt, Stetson, Isla, and Nora.

I parked by Holden's garage. His pickup was hooked to a horse trailer by the barn. Several horses were in his arena, still saddled, and people milled around the outside.

Stetson and Colt were talking to each other. It was the first time I'd seen them standing side by side. Both were big guys, but even in broad daylight, Colt looked like a guy I'd cross the street to keep from getting close to. I was glad I had met him while he was sitting and without his cowboy hat pulled down low to shade his eyes.

Isla was perched on the corral with Nora. They weren't dressed like I'd seen them before. Their polish was gone. They wore dusty blue jeans with sweatshirts so stained and grimy I could see the dirt from where I was parked. Isla had a cowboy hat on. I couldn't tell if the color was supposed to be a mottled brown or if it'd fallen and gotten trampled earlier.

Holden stepped out of the house with a huge smile on his face. "Nora and my cousins heard how disappointed you all were when you learned you couldn't ride this weekend."

Avery's face lit up. "I get to go riding today?"

His grin widened. "Not just you. We figured that since the horses were all saddled up and we had plenty of adults—"

"I get to go too?" Landon squealed.

Afton jumped up and down. "And me?"

"As my cousin Archer would say, 'all y'all' get to ride—if your mom says it's okay." He winced. "Sorry, I should've talked to you first."

He was comfortable surprising the kids. As if I'd turn this down. "No, it's okay. I trust you guys to know your horses."

I managed to keep the kids calm as we approached the arena. I picked up Riley.

Holden fell in step next to me. "I can take Riley with me, on Poppy."

Holden had been around the kids several times, enough for me to know that he was hesitant around Riley. He didn't pick her up. He didn't carry her. He didn't even really talk to her, and I was fine giving him time. He needed it. Oddly, that had endeared him to her. He wasn't in her face, trying to be her friend, and she was comfortable around him.

She wasn't a baby, but she was young enough that he'd have to hold her at all times. He'd have to be responsible for her. And while it was nothing like what he'd gone through, the experience was enough to bring memories back.

How much of a scene should I make? It was a big moment for him. "Only if you're comfortable."

"Riley's been patient with me. Haven't you, kiddo?"

She rewarded his effort with a cheeky grin and reached her arms to him. He swooped her up and settled her on his hip. Tears pricked the backs of my eyes, but I blinked them away. There was nothing chill about this moment, but I tried to play it cool.

Several emotions rippled over Holden's face. Trepidation. Surprise. Then delight. He cleared his throat. "I was, um—I was worried that she wouldn't want me to hold her."

"She'll definitely let you know. But you're golden." Those pesky tears.

The corner of his mouth kicked up and he looked at Riley. "This is nothing like holding a little baby. Maybe I needed to work my way backward. Get used to older kids and work my way down." He gave her a little bounce, and her answering smile pushed her chubby little cheeks up. "Thank you, Em."

"Thank you for today—for all the kids."

His grin broadened. "Come and meet the horses."

When we neared the arena, Nora jumped down. If she was concerned about how Holden was dealing with Riley after what he'd told her, she smothered it with pride.

"I used to hold you like this, Nora." He smiled like he'd missed those memories.

"I know." She laughed, and I could picture the little girl with the golden hair who adored her brother. "I'm attached to you in all the pictures from my childhood."

Stetson chuckled. "You two should recreate one of those pictures and give it to your mom for Christmas."

Nora snickered. "That'd be too sentimental for her."

Holden handed Riley back and murmured, "Thanks for not making a big deal out of it." Louder, he said, "Avery, you're going to ride on Colt's horse today. Colt looks like he'll bite, but his horse, Cutter, is the calmest of the bunch."

Adults might be scared of Colt, but not Avery. She marched up to Colt. "I'm gonna guess which one Cutter is."

Colt threw an elbow up on the top railing of the corral. "Give ya five bucks if you guess right."

Nora tsked. "Don't teach kids how to gamble, Colt."

"Why? Then she won't have to cheat like you in poker."

Nora's cheeks flushed. "I do not cheat. You're not as good as you think you are."

Colt opened his mouth, but snapped it shut and glanced at the kids. I'd been around enough guys to know he was probably going to back up how good he actually was by referencing something inappropriate. And from the triumphant look on Nora's face, she was glad he hadn't been able to.

Stetson shook his head and pushed off the gate. "You both suck at poker. Landon, buddy, you're with me."

Isla hopped down. "Afton, you're coming with me on Pittance."

Nora hooked her arm through mine. "And you get to ride with me."

"Me?" Alarm shot through me. I hadn't come prepared to ride a horse. "I'm not in, like, boots or anything." I had on black leggings and an oversized hoodie.

"Don't shove your feet all the way into the stirrups and you'll be fine. I'll walk right next to you. Right? You've never ridden before?"

"No." I'd never planned to. I liked horses, but I wasn't obsessed with them like Avery.

"Cool. You'll have fun. Wait here. I'll lead Midnight out."

Holden led Poppy to the end of the arena away from the group. He looked at Riley. "Ready?"

"Ho-sey." She wiggled and I lifted her up to him. He settled her in front of him with an arm banded around her.

"You okay with this?"

"Of course." My belly was doing weird flips seeing him with a little kid about to ride off. It wasn't a trust issue. I loved the image in front of me. I wanted to see more of it.

I heard Avery's *aw, man* and Colt's deep chuckle. Avery hadn't won the bet.

Nora came out with her horse. I had expected the horse to be black with a name like Midnight, but he was gray and spotted with black, like a reversal of the night sky with the black dots as stars.

My stomach settled down as she introduced me to Midnight and let me get to know him. Just like with the kayaks, she was competent and responsible. She coached me through putting my left foot in the stirrup and swinging up. She was like her brother, too responsible to throw me onto the back of a horse and let me go.

Nora took the lead rope and started down the driveway. I craned my neck around to look after the kids. Holden was staying close to the arena. Stetson was leading his big brown horse with Landon on top around the back of the house. Colt stalked next to Avery as she concentrated on the reins. Afton and Isla were giggling. Isla stayed in the arena and stuck close to Afton's side.

"I feel like I'm more scared than they are."

Nora's laugh was like a silver bell. "You're doing fine. You don't mind that I tossed you up?"

"No. It's not usually me doing the fun stuff. I arrange it for the kids and then make sure everyone survives."

"Our mom wasn't like that." Nora's smile slipped. "She still isn't. But I don't think I would've survived childhood without Holden. Mom's an 'only the strong survive' type of person."

"But a parent is the one who should nurture a kid to be strong."

"Holden was that person for me, but according to Mom, he failed." She adopted a sunny smile before I could say anything. "You seem like an awesome mom."

If she wanted to change the subject, I'd go along with it. From what little I'd seen and heard of Kira Barron, I didn't think Nora was exaggerating. "Thanks. I worried so much with the older two, and I still do, but now it's just so busy with all of them that I let the idea of perfect parenting go."

"I'm really glad Holden met you."

"Me too." But Nora's approval meant a lot. She was important to him.

The dried wild grasses crackled under her boots. "I worried about him. He's such a good brother and he loves being around people, but he was always alone in his empty house. It was like he built it to have a family, yet he never dared to have another girlfriend."

Being called a girlfriend was a little trippy. I relaxed into Midnight's sway.

Nora kept walking. "I thought maybe it was Coal Haven, and there's no way he's leaving, so he might be single forever. This has been his life since before he was born. Mom even hated him going to college."

"Isn't this what he wants to do?"

"Oh, it is. He loves farming and ranching. But I always thought he wanted what we didn't have growing up—a close warm family and a business that he, not our uncle Cameron, ran. Mom does whatever Uncle Cameron says."

"I haven't met your mom."

She gave me a rueful look. "If you ever do, hold your ground or she'll stomp you into it."

"Okay. I'll pretend I'm facing off with an arrogant med student who thinks he's so far above nurses."

"Good. Don't let her scare you off. I like you."

"I like you too." We exchanged smiles.

Nora turned us around, but we took our time heading back. She talked to me about college and how she didn't have plans afterward. When anyone asked, she said she was job hunting, but she secretly hoped things would fall into place.

The ride lulled me into imagining what it'd be like to be part of this family. Henry and I had decided to have four kids so they would have people. Holden had people, and they were amazing to me and to each of my kids.

When I factored that into my relationship with Holden, I should've been terrified. I'd lose all this if I lost him. But the way Nora talked, Holden knew what he wanted. He didn't change his mind. He wasn't the type of guy who'd decide he wanted something different and didn't care who he hurt to do it.

I wanted to sit with that, to think about how it changed the way I was holding myself back.

Eighteen

Holden

Only the wild kids changed oil on a Friday night. I was getting the snowblower ready for winter. Stetson had asked if I had plans, but I passed even though he said he was meeting Colt and Remington. I wouldn't mind a night out shooting the shit with them, but until we were all taken and didn't attract all the single ladies from twenty to fifty years old, I wanted to avoid the meat market.

I could picture Stetson settling down. He wanted to but was more scared than Emery about it. Remington, maybe. He didn't talk about his private life much. He joked and he flirted, and we pretended like we didn't notice that he never seemed to take anyone home. And Colt let out his soft side as often as a blood moon during a leap year. Leading Avery around on his horse was probably his limit.

So, my nights with the guys might be a little limited. The only dipstick I was waving around was the snow-blower's.

Emery had taken the kids to Bismarck. I had anticipated an invite, but she hadn't asked. I might have been sulking, but I was grown enough to admit it. I wanted to spend all my time with her, but it wasn't feasible.

The last football game was tomorrow. I'd have to wait to see her until then. I wanted an overnight with her. Desperately. Maybe tomorrow night?

An engine approached. Sally barked and ran outside. Maybe the guys had decided to bring the party here. I wiped my hands off and went to the open shop doors to check. My breath puffed out the farther away I got from the heater.

Emery pulled in.

The grin that stretched my lips had to take up my whole face. I was pathetic, but I didn't fucking care.

When she got out, she spotted me. "You don't mind that I dropped in, do you?"

She was at my house. Alone with me. "Not at all. Let me close up the shop."

"Am I interrupting?"

"Nah. I was just finishing up. Come on in." She wandered behind me with that black fleece jacket hugging her hips and black yoga pants covering her lower half. "How'd drop-off go?"

"Good. Henry seemed happy you weren't there, so I didn't get interrogated."

"He's saving up for tomorrow."

She chuckled. I put my tools away and added the discarded oil to the stash that I'd take to town for disposal. I wanted to pull her into my arms, roll down those leggings of hers, and put the workbench to good use. But I was greasy and didn't want to ruin her clothes.

She wandered around and stopped to study the tractor I used for cutting hay. That was next to ready for winter. She stopped at the posthole digger and tilted her head. She ran her hand over the backhoe. The nervous energy didn't leave her. Was it because she thought she was disrupting my night? Or because we were at my place?

I hoped she'd talk to me when she was ready.

When I was done, I turned to her and held my hands out. "I need a shower."

She nodded but didn't move.

I closed the distance between us until I towered over her. "I can't touch you without getting you dirty."

The tension drained out of her, and she got a playful, flirty look in her eyes. "Oh. That's too bad."

"But once I'm done in the shower..." There it was. The tension. I didn't back off. "I won't do anything you don't want me to."

"Oh, no. I want you to." She grimaced. "I packed an overnight bag. Is that too presumptuous?"

She'd planned this. To be with me at my place. I must have been wearing the same grin I had when she arrived. "You're worried I'll mind that you want to stay here?"

She shifted her stance. "I turned you down last time. I know staying here is still a big deal."

"Hell yeah, it is. We need to celebrate with sex." Elated, I reached for her and snapped my hand back. "Shower first."

I locked up the shop and herded Emery to the house while Sally ran to the barn to bed down for the night.

"Make yourself comfortable." I almost told her to make herself at home. It would've flowed naturally off the tongue, but she was nervous about staying one night.

We'd get there eventually. I hoped.

I stripped inside the bathroom and tossed my clothes in a pile. With the water on, I waited for it to heat up and stared at the ceramic tile. I wanted Emery to feel at home here. I wanted the kids to feel at home here.

Was I in love?

It'd been so long. I had thought I loved Teagan. What I had felt for her had been far beyond what I had felt for my high school girlfriend. But what I felt for Emery was growing beyond what I had with Teagan.

Maybe the stress of Teagan's pregnancy overrode the memories of the emotions. The excitement. The optimism. The obligation. That was what our relationship had dissolved to. Defending her to Mom. The stress of expecting when we hadn't discussed much about marriage. The heart-wrenching angst of the pregnancy. And afterward, I was left with a sense of abandonment.

Had I not loved Teagan? Was that why I hadn't fought for us? Had I known that after our daughter was gone, there would be nothing left between us but memories?

I didn't want to be that guy again, checked out and unwilling to admit it. But with Emery, there was a sense of safety. She shared her thoughts and fears with me. I wanted to do the same with her. But I also wanted the good times.

I walked into the shower and scrubbed off. Dirty water swirled around the drain. I didn't waste my time with shaving. I had a sexy woman with an overnight bag under my roof.

The warm spray was hitting my face, rinsing away the last of the shampoo, when there was a tentative knock at the door. "Can I come in?"

I froze, stunned for a moment. She couldn't be doing what I thought she was doing. I'd had fantasies about this. "Absolutely. Is something wrong?"

She slipped in and shut the door behind her as if we weren't the only two living beings in the house. "Nothing's wrong. Just thought I'd join you."

I kept the water on and leaned against the shower wall. Blood quickly rerouted to my groin as I watched her hesitantly look around. Emery might have been nervous, but she was determined.

I liked that I brought out her fearless side. Had she suppressed it because of her ex? Or had life gotten in the way and I reminded her that she could be herself, not just a mom or a nurse, with me?

Whatever the reason, she stripped down as I watched her through the shower door.

When I built this house, I'd wanted an open concept, something opposite of the closed-off old farmhouse I'd grown up in. In my house, the living room flowed into the kitchen, and both rooms flowed into the dining room. The tub and shower were separate, and the shower wasn't closed off from the rest of the bathroom. The ceramic tile space had a large panel door that was completely see-through.

Perfect for watching Emery bare every inch of her skin.

She didn't toss her clothes like she was desperate to get under the spray with me. She laid each piece neatly on the counter. Same with her pants and underwear, topping the pile with her socks.

She lifted her gaze to me, and while I didn't like the insecurity in her clear green eyes, I didn't move. I let her watch me soak in her body. Like those full breasts she was unsure of. I would never know how perky they once were, and I didn't care. They were her tits, and I got to taste and touch them.

My erection grew harder the longer I looked at her lush curves.

She had referred to a part of her stomach as a pooch before, but I couldn't see what she disliked. She had a mature, curvy body that cradled mine perfectly. She had flesh and muscle that would protect her while I leveraged myself against the tile and pounded into her against the wall behind me.

I crooked my finger and beckoned her to me. "Come here."

A smile played over her lips, but her gaze darted around like she wanted to reverse the last couple of minutes and get dressed. The foggy haze from the warm water gathered, masking my view.

"Em, get in this shower with me."

She lurched forward like she'd been pushed. I steadied myself, worried she had tripped on the gray mat under her feet. She made it to the door and let herself in. Finally.

Tension radiated from her body. I knew one way to relax her, but I began by turning her into the cascade of water. I took the bar of natural soap that Nora got me for my birthday and lathered it up in my hands. I wasn't a body-wash guy, but if I were, then Emery would smell like me and I didn't want to cover her peaches-and-cream scent.

I started at her shoulders, kneading tense muscles, and worked my way down her back.

Her head dropped against my neck, and she moaned. "I haven't had a back massage in forever."

In an instant, I changed everything I'd planned. This moment called for restraint. I wasn't dropping to my knees and licking her until her cries echoed off the walls. I wasn't pounding into her until I came so hard I had to worry about my feet slipping out from under me.

I lathered up more and continued to rub her down until she was boneless and pliant. When I shut the water off, her surprised gaze jumped to mine.

"Two things," I said, interpreting the question in her eyes. "One, I wanted to give you that long-overdue massage. And two, regrettably, as much as I want to sink into you here, I don't want the septic system to back up from all the water."

"That would not be sexy."

"A mood killer," I agreed and opened the shower door to snag a towel. The air was so fogged up, it could start raining in the bathroom. I gave her my oversized towel. Mom hadn't believed in creature comforts, so when I moved into my house, I went out of my way to get the fluffiest towels and the softest sheets. I'd never been so glad for them before now.

I wanted to spoil this woman. A woman who could've been scared off by just another guy hitting on her at the bar. A woman who could've listened to the gossip and walked away from me. A woman who had every right to build walls around her heart but who'd let me in. I wasn't taking that lightly.

I grabbed another towel from the closet and tied it around my waist. I took a second to add to the one she'd wrapped around herself.

"We'll get to shower sex." I swung the towel over her shoulders, and she scrunched it around her hair. "But I wanted to take the massage to the bed."

Mostly, I wanted her in my bed. She'd come to my home with an overnight bag. She'd come into the bathroom. Yet, nerves twisted my stomach. She could back out, and it'd hurt more than I wanted to admit.

* * *

Emery

I was wrapped in the biggest, softest towel I'd ever touched. The second one I'd twisted into my hair. The towels matched the floor mats. A steel gray. Plush, yet masculine.

And this bathroom. The house I'd lost in the divorce had been nice. A million-dollar house in Bismarck had space and luxury. But it'd been a partially furnished house Henry had bought from another doctor. It hadn't been mine. The furnishings hadn't been ones I would've selected, and my time in the house had been spent trying to make as much of it kid friendly as possible.

I pictured the kids running through Holden's house. Would we all fit? There was a partial second floor. Maybe another bathroom. How many bedrooms were upstairs? I gave myself a mental shake.

But it was easy to imagine. So damn easy.

The man. The property. The animals.

For the first time, I let myself think about more than dating Holden. What if I trusted him with my heart? What if it worked out? What if what I'd had with Henry paled against what I could build with Holden?

Fear didn't spike like I'd thought it would. And it stayed away as I entered Holden's bedroom.

Cool air chilled my wet skin, but he was a wall of heat behind me. Holden's bedroom was like the bathroom. Done in shades of gray, it emanated masculinity, but comfort. A large bed with a few pillows and a pewter comforter was flanked by nightstands built out of gray-toned wood that matched the box of the bed. Blinds were sunk into the window frame and thick, like they needed Holden's permission before they let a ray of light in.

"This is nice." I went to the bed and pushed down. Like the towels, he didn't skimp on luxury. Lying in this bed would be like sinking into heaven. "Wow."

"Mom didn't like... She didn't do..." He pushed a hand through his wet strands. "She couldn't be bothered with what went on inside the house. I did a lot with Nora, but all the belongings we had when we left home were the same ones we'd had when we were kids, unless Nora or I bought ourselves something." He lifted a shoulder. "Or one of Mom's boyfriends gave her something."

His gaze stuck on the bed. He was a few feet behind me, and I closed the distance between us. People who'd grown up with him thought he'd had everything. And he had a lot. But he hadn't had the most basic aspect of childhood— parental support. Unconditional love. He gave it, but it hadn't been returned.

I framed his face with my hands. The man in front of me wasn't a playboy who lived a carefree life. This was a guy who'd helped raise his sister, who'd defended people he cared about against a mother who should've supported him. He cared about his family. He cared about me. And he cared about my kids.

This wasn't a commitment-phobe. This was a person who committed hard to everyone in his life but had no expectations they'd return the feeling. He'd lost his daughter and the person he thought he'd weather the storm with had gotten into her own life raft and rowed away.

"You're an amazing person," I murmured.

"Because I have a nice bed?"

I shot him a playful smile and yanked his towel off. It'd been hanging by a thread with that erection anyway. "I'm totally digging you for the bed."

"I knew it." He crowded me toward the mattress. "That's the real reason I never had anyone over. I wanted to know they wanted me for me and not my high thread count."

I giggled as he tipped me back and hooked his finger around my towel. I was stripped of both towels, but he flipped me onto my belly. I yelped and worried for a millisecond about my ass jiggling until his weight settled beside me.

His big, warm hands stroked along my sides, just shy of

tickling. "I didn't get to give you much of a massage in the shower."

I hadn't come here for a massage, but it was a nice bonus. Even nicer that he seemed unable to keep his hands off me.

I closed my eyes and forgot about my wet hair as he rubbed the tight knots in my back. I should be cold, but he kept me warm enough, and I melted into the comforter.

God, this bed was comfortable.

Before he could lull me into a light sleep, his hand slipped between my legs.

His touch sent a bolt of energy ricocheting between my thighs. I looked over my shoulder and cocked a brow. "Does that come with the back massage?"

His heated gaze met mine as he slid a finger back and forth through the gathering wetness. "It comes with anything you want."

He shifted to stretch out next to me, his body half-covering mine. The friction his hand was creating made me lift my ass into the air and spread my legs a few more inches to give him better access.

I wasn't facing him, but the intimacy of this position was undeniable.

"I love how responsive you are, Em."

"It's not me, it's you." I wiggled to urge him to do more than tease me. I needed him in me.

His low chuckle rumbled right into me. "Do you want more?"

"This is a slower, more torturous version of the night we met."

"I wanted to hold you that night," he said.

I opened my eyes. Our faces were close. The soft scent of his mint-and-basil soap surrounded me and mixed with the whiskey-barrel smell of his shampoo. The throb between my legs intensified. "I wanted to cuddle too. I wasn't sure what came next, but I didn't want to leave."

"I thought about you every night until the day of the game." He circled my clit, steady strokes that I rocked my hips with.

"I tried not to think about you." I ground into his hand, and he rewarded me by smoothly pressing a finger inside. He was so damn good with his hands. "I thought it was some fantasy other girls get that I got to have for a night." I let out a long moan as he hit all the right spots at the same time.

"I'm going to fuck you from behind just like our first night together. Only, there's no clothes in the way and I get to see everything." He practically growled the last part.

"Yes," I panted. I was careening to my peak, but his voice anchored me.

He kept the same pace. "And afterward, I'm going to hold you. I'm not letting you go." He raised himself to his knees. I arched my ass higher, about to slam headfirst into my orgasm. "Unless you have to leave, but this time, I'll know where to find you."

"Oh, God, Holden!"

I catapulted into my climax, somehow ending up on my hands and knees as he coaxed out a long orgasm. How could every time with him feel like I was shattering records? It'd never been this strong before, never this long before, and I'd never left my body and sailed into the atmosphere before.

But I did, and he held me. He was all around me, consuming me but setting me free at the same time.

I didn't have a chance to come down before he placed himself between my legs. We weren't in a cramped back seat, and I wasn't hidden. All of me was on display, but he'd seen it all before.

His broad head pushed at my entrance but was suddenly

gone. "Shit. Sorry, shit." His hands gripped my hips, his fingers digging in like he was waging a war within his body. "I forgot to grab a condom."

"So... I never quit taking the pill after my divorce." I didn't bog Holden down with the details of how much nicer it was to know when my cycle would be and that it would be lighter. I was grateful for the pill for different reasons right now.

His stunned silence made me wonder whether I'd misread the situation. People talked about him so much I figured I'd have heard about any sexual issues, too, while working at the clinic. Confidentiality in small clinics went only so far.

He stroked my hip. "It's been a long time since I haven't used something. And I get checkups."

I craned my head to look over my shoulder. Strain that had nothing to do with the topic and everything to do with his pulsing erection was etched across his face. "Do it."

His fingers tightened in my skin. "Are you sure?"

"I'm sure."

He didn't look away, nor did he enthusiastically plunge inside. He entered me slowly, filling me inch by inch until he pressed against all the pleasure centers. It was a form of foreplay on its own.

When he was seated fully inside, he draped himself over me. A deep groan resonated through him and into me. "You feel so fucking good."

A strong arm came around my waist like a vise, and his other hand pressed into the mattress next to mine. Before I knew it, I was consumed again, only this time it was different. This wasn't a quickie in the back seat where we hoped we wouldn't get caught.

I gave myself to him and he took. He dominated. This was just us being us. I wasn't some lonely, divorced mom, and he wasn't some guy who routinely picked up women and moved on with someone different each time.

He plunged in and out of me. My arms shook. He laid kisses across my shoulders, and his scruff deliciously scraped my sensitive skin.

"So fucking good," he murmured.

I was filled by him, surrounded by him, and when he lightly placed his finger back on my clit, I gave in to him.

I had no idea if he was close to release; I couldn't hold back the climax.

"Holden!" I savored the freedom to shout during sex, to let the exploding ecstasy out somehow.

He continued to piston his hips behind me until his arm cinched tight and he buried his face into the nape of my neck. A few hard thrusts and he went rigid, his hot release filling me.

I was locked against him, absorbing his pleasure into my own. I felt every pulse, every tremor, until he sagged and rolled us both to the same side.

"Don't get me wrong," he rumbled behind me. "I liked what we did in the pickup, but this was pretty fucking fantastic."

I giggled and cuddled into him. "I agree."

His waning erection was pressed against my back. We'd probably have to clean up even though we'd just showered, but neither of us made a move to get out of bed.

He trailed a finger over my side. My head rested against his firm biceps. We lay together.

He flattened his hand on my hip. "Is it too early to invite you to stay tomorrow night?"

I smiled and hooked my hand through his. "I could lie and say I'll think about it, but yes, I'd love to stay tomorrow too." I twisted my head to look at him. "Besides, I heard you get more TV shows than I do."

He laughed and hugged me closer. "First my bedding and now my streaming services? Is that the only way to your heart?" His smile faltered as if he worried he'd said something he shouldn't have.

I squeezed his fingers. "It's a good start, but you've got some other advantages."

He nuzzled his nose into my neck and made me shiver. "Mm. I'll have to work on those advantages the next couple of nights."

I couldn't wait.

Nineteen

Holden

The last football game had been played. Our team won, but regardless of how we would've done, Stetson and I had planned a pizza party with the kids afterward.

Stetson was inside Rattler's. He'd arranged the party with Shawn and Remington, and one of them had met Stetson inside. I was lingering by the hostess stand to direct kids and parents to the back section that had been cordoned off for us.

Landon hadn't arrived yet, and I wasn't sure he would.

I had pretended not to notice after the game when Landon had excitedly asked his dad if they could pretty please go. The way Henry had frowned and glared at Emery. She held her hands up. I wasn't a lip reader, but it had seemed like she said something along the lines of *I told you about this*.

I didn't doubt that she had. I doubted that Henry had

taken seriously the enthusiasm of a kid wanting to be included in a group he enjoyed being a part of.

A familiar Suburban pulled in, and my phone buzzed with a message from Emery. **Henry and Jenni are bringing the kids, but Henry's pissed. It's probably best if I don't go so he doesn't think it's a you-and-me thing. I want this party to be about football.**

I swallowed my irritation. It wouldn't be about football to Henry. I instinctively knew that about the guy. He didn't like being told what to do. It was how he'd chosen his career. Emery had told me enough about her marriage. She'd been the compliant one. Henry wanted to go to med school, so it had been her job to work her career around his. Henry wanted to have more kids, so it was her job to figure out how to have more kids and still do what she wanted in life. Henry wanted to fuck around, so it had been her job to pick up the pieces for the kids.

But Emery wasn't compliant anymore, and I would be at the party as a reminder that he didn't hold sway over her.

Landon ran through the door ahead of the others. "Hey, Coach B!"

I high-fived him and pointed him to the crowd. "Go pick a booth for you and everyone else."

Henry strode in, his nostrils flaring and his glare taking in Rattler's open beam work and the tasteful modern western decor. It was like he got more pissed because he couldn't find fault in the place.

Avery skirted around her dad. "How's Poppy and Pittance?"

"He's ornery as ever and she enjoys irritating him."

Avery snickered. Pittance wasn't an ornery horse, and she liked being in on the joke.

"Ho-den." Riley held her arms out for me. I didn't know what to do. This wasn't my past freezing up when I was faced with holding a baby. She was with her dad, and I didn't want to make things worse by making him feel like I was taking his kids. Even Jenni's eyes were wide. I had to tread carefully.

"Hey, kiddo." I double high-fived her chubby hands in a move that was just shy of awkward. "I heard you cheering at the game." I booped her nose. She giggled and curled into her dad. Crisis averted.

Until I caught the dark look on Henry's face.

Shit. I searched out Afton. She was holding Jenni's hand.

"Or was that you cheering on your brother?" I asked. She grinned, showing a gap where her two front teeth used to be. I let out a fake gasp. "Someone stole your teeth."

She giggled and jumped up and down. "I lost both of them last night and the tooth fairy gave me five bucks—for each tooth!"

Was that the going rate nowadays? All I'd gotten was a *Clean all that blood up, will ya?* but I'd left a couple of quarters for Nora whenever she lost a tooth.

"So what I'm hearing is that you're buying?" I laughed at her astonished look. "Nah, it's on us. I think Landon picked your booth. Help yourself."

Henry plowed through the restaurant, the kids in tow. Grateful he didn't make a scene, I mingled with the players and their parents. I'd graduated with a couple of them. Stetson had gone to school with a few more. Other parents had moved to town, and the evening gave us a chance to chat a little. Normal small-town stuff. I gave Henry a wide berth until Landon flagged me over.

"Can you eat with us, Coach B?"

Were Jenni's eyes perma-wide? Henry had one half-eaten slice of pizza in front of him. Shawn had lived in

Chicago too long for that pizza to not be delicious. "I can't, man. I'm the host."

"Are you coming over Tuesdays and Thursdays now that practice is done?"

All eyes were on me—the kids and the parents. I squatted. Landon was on the edge of the bench seat, practically hanging out of the booth so he could visit with friends. There was no place for me to sit anyway.

"I'll have to talk to your mom."

"How often are you over there?" Henry asked, his gaze calculating.

"Not often," Avery answered absentmindedly as she played with a string of cheese.

I'd given her riding lessons for free, but I owed her.

Remington strode by, carrying another pizza to add to the stash on the big round table Stetson and I often used. "There's the main man," he said as he neared. "Leave it to you and Stetson to throw the biggest party this place has ever seen."

"You know it." When I turned back, I caught the flash of jealousy in Henry's eyes. He was used to being the big shot, but in Rattler's I was the guy people looked to. Me and Stetson, but Stetson wasn't dating Henry's ex-wife. Any other day and Henry wouldn't care. But he hadn't gotten to be a surgeon by not being competitive and maybe a little egotistical.

And of course that was the time Holly picked to show up for lunch.

"Holden!" she called, spreading her arms wide as she sashayed toward me where the restaurant was obviously full. "I keep running into you here."

I pushed up in time to intercept her hug, giving her only a quick one-armed squeeze. She was still sort of a friend, and she'd done nothing wrong other than raise Henry's suspicion of me.

"I'll be right back," I told Landon, then turned and herded Holly toward an open booth. "What's up?"

She glanced around. "I'm meeting Sienna for lunch. What's going on here?"

"Our football team's last game. Stetson and I are treating them to pizza."

"That's so nice of you." She dropped into her booth and peered out the window. "I knew I should've picked her up, otherwise she'll be late." She smirked at me and scanned through the restaurant. "Still seeing that girl?"

"Emery? Yes. Those were her kids and her ex I was talking to."

"Oh, shit." She dropped her voice to a whisper. "That's her ex? Are you two cool?"

"No. Believe it or not, he's not into me."

She laughed, and I didn't have to look to know that Henry clocked everything. "Hard to believe, Holden. Go, then. He's going to get all kinds of wrong ideas, and I'm not out to fuck up relationships."

"He shouldn't be the one jumping to conclusions, but thanks."

She leaned out of the booth and snagged the sleeve of my hoodie. "Can you let Stetson know that Krystal is harassing Sienna? She won't tell him, but Krystal is getting weird. Sienna thought she saw her drive by her place twice."

I didn't want to get dragged into Stetson's shit, but he was too much like me. He'd weather it all without telling anyone. "Can you let me know what else Sienna thinks Krystal's doing, and I'll pass it on? Also let her know that if she needs to involve the police, we'll support her."

She bobbed her head. "I told her the same. We're too old

for this shit, and the sooner she cuts it off the better. But if Stetson doesn't hear it from me, she'll be okay with that."

"I'll talk to him."

I approached Landon's booth, but Henry's glare wasn't exactly welcoming. Landon was gone, probably at the table with ten boys surrounding it watching another kid play a video game. But Afton was scooting out with her plate. "Is there more pizza?"

Jenni was sliding out to go with her, but she stopped and glanced from me to Henry.

"Let's go see." I didn't bother to look at Henry. He'd interpret anything he saw in my expression as challenging him, and the last thing I wanted to do was to make Emery regret meeting me.

* * *

Emery

"And then what happened?" I curled my fingers through Holden's. We were both on our backs, but my head was on his shoulder, and I stared at the shadows on the ceiling. It was technically Sunday, but we were still awake.

We'd tried to get through a show, but I'd ended up naked and on his lap. Then we moved to the bedroom, and now we were postcoital and just talking. This was something I had taken for granted when I was married. The moments we could talk late into the night. Our schedules had gotten in the way. Kids waking up at all times of the night. We'd let it slip. But instead of finding our way back to this, Henry had just found someone else.

I couldn't believe how neutral the thought had become.

223

If I went looking for the anger, for the hurt, it'd still be there, but it was weak and fading. It served no purpose.

He folded his long fingers around mine. "I helped Afton get more cheese pizza and didn't have to talk to Henry the rest of the time. That guy doesn't like me."

"I don't know what his problem is." As long as Henry dealt with his pissy emotions and didn't let them spill over onto the kids, I'd ignore it. But I couldn't shake the sense of foreboding. Henry had been hired in Fargo and it would've been a job with more pay, but we'd moved to Bismarck because he'd been passed over for a residency slot at the same hospital in Fargo. Henry held grudges. "What about Stetson? Is that going to get bad?"

"I have no idea. Krystal's gotten more unpredictable over the years, and it accelerated when they were dating."

"Glad Holly isn't like her. If someone wanted to spy on me, I'd rather just put them to work. They could clean out my flower beds or unpack the boxes in the garage."

His body shook as he chuckled. "If they're going to stalk you, they could help carry groceries in?"

"They could get the groceries and find out all my dirty shopping habits." I laughed, grateful he didn't mind humor for serious subjects. It was how several of us survived working in health care. "No, I know it's not funny. I'll take the issues with Henry over what Holly's friend is dealing with."

He let out a breath. Holden saw more than I wanted him to, and the heavy silence after what I just said told me that he thought Henry might be vindictive.

But he'd cheated, made me and the kids move out of our house to sell it, and finagled a lower child support payment than should be feasible for a man who earned what he did. There wasn't much more he could do.

I rolled into Holden. "So, Halloween. You got plans?"

"I usually go to the bar and get an eyeful of all the skin the costumes don't cover, but I'm hoping to have my very own naughty nurse."

I laughed, trying to picture myself dressed in a revealing nurse costume. "I'll keep that in mind when I put my scrubs on Monday morning. The best I can do is to wear flats instead of orthopedic shoes."

"Keep talking, baby, and you won't be able to walk in the morning."

I swatted his chest, but still I beamed. He had a way of making me feel sexy, no matter what. "Want to go trick-or-treating? Mom's going to stay over, and she said she'd hand out candy while I walked through the neighborhood with the kids."

"That sounds fun."

I lifted my head. I couldn't see much of him in the dark, but I had to know he was serious. Instead of going to the skin fest of a bar's Halloween party, he'd carry Riley and maybe even Afton because they were tired but refused to give up. "Really?"

"Serious. I've been avoiding it for almost ten years, but I used to love taking Nora around town. Seeing all the costumes. Kids are clever as hell. Nora trick-or-treated with her friends until they graduated."

"It's a date, then?"

"It's a date."

He didn't say anything, and I closed my eyes, thinking it was time to drift off, but his chest went tight under my cheek like he was going to say something. I waited, but he didn't speak. My eyelids drifted shut and the same thing happened.

"So... We're getting into the holiday season, and you don't seem sick of me."

I didn't think it was possible. "And you're not sick of me."

"Okay, so, um, about Thanksgiving. We have this big family get-together. Stetson and I have taken over deep-frying turkeys, and Nora and Isla cook. Aunt Willow brings over her asparagus hot dish, and I shit you not, it's got crack or something in it. It's like the one day of the year that my family isn't uncomfortable around each other. We eat and watch football."

"Sounds nice."

"Does it sound nice enough for you all to come over? Your mom is invited too."

We'd been together for long enough that it shouldn't be weird to meet his family. But my first thoughts were to come up with excuses why not. It wouldn't be just me meeting everyone but also the kids. He sounded so hopeful, I hated to ask for time. "Can I think about it?"

"Yeah, no problem. I'm sure you and your mom already have plans."

I let out a scornful laugh. "Either Henry or I, or both of us, have worked Thanksgiving for the last ten years. We don't plan much other than time and a half. Your plans sound intimidating, to be honest."

"If it was any other holiday, I'd say yes, we're intimidating. Last summer, when Archer met everyone for the first time, my uncle Cameron ran him out of the barbecue. Mom wasn't much better. But Thanksgiving is the most relaxed the Barrons get as a group."

He didn't have a small house, but it'd be cold toward the end of November and we'd all be crushed inside. Would I spend my time refereeing the kids? Wouldn't his mom have an issue? I hadn't given her much thought. In my list of people I had to deal with, she was barely on it.

"Nora and Isla will be there," he said quietly.

If he wanted to reassure me, he succeeded. His mom intimidated me, and if her brothers were only slightly better or worse, they would still be a lot. I hadn't had meet-the-parents anxiety for more than a decade. I was too old for that shit. But all of that was an excuse.

He'd been so generous, and my only reason for hesitating was that I was scared. I'd been wearing big-girl underwear for years. I'd dealt with blood and death and fear of the medical unknown. I could deal with a Barron Thanksgiving. "Okay."

His grin grew. "Okay?"

"We'll be there."

"It'll be fun. I promise."

I trusted Holden, and I fell asleep with a dreamy smile.

Twenty

Holden

It was Halloween, and, like Afton, I had been excited about it all last week.

I even dressed in a costume of sorts.

Emery opened the door and stopped, her eyes wide. She broke into laughter, and her mom appeared behind her.

"Oh my," Lynnie said. "You look quite the part, Holden."

I held my arms out. "Huh? I didn't have to buy anything extra."

When I worked, I usually wore a ball cap and a hoodie. When it got cold, I'd throw on a stocking hat and a coat. Yeah, I wore cowboy boots, but not flashy ones. I wore a pair that protected my feet and were easy to clean off mud and cow shit. I didn't look like a stereotypical cowboy.

But tonight I did.

I'd dug out my black Resistol cowboy hat from high school. I had found a red plaid button-up shirt and an old western-style sports coat that one of Mom's boyfriends had left at her house. My jeans were Wranglers, and I put on the boots with the wide calves so the bottoms of my pants pooled inside them. The cherry on top was a red handkerchief tied around my neck.

I had dug out my tan leather gloves since tonight would get chilly. But for the end of October in Coal Haven, we couldn't ask for better trick-or-treating weather.

Emery pushed the screen door open. "Come on in, hoss." She was still in her purple scrubs, her hair tied back in a bun. "I'm going to change. Mom's got hot dogs cooking for a quick supper before they really load up on junk food."

Landon bounced out of his bedroom, still in his school clothes. "Yeah. Trey said there's a house on the next block that gives out full-size cans of pop every year." He disappeared inside his room.

I heard buzzing, but my phone was quiet in the big pocket on my shirt. Emery patted herself down before pulling her phone from a cargo pocket of her scrub pants.

"It's Henry. Sorry." She answered and turned to walk to her room.

By the time she reached the doorway, she was shaking her head. She disappeared inside, her voice low. The kids were supposed to go to his place for the weekend tomorrow night. Was he backing out?

I wandered into the kitchen. Lynnie was at the stove. Riley was already at the table, helping herself to peas.

"Can I help with anything?" I asked.

Lynnie turned the burner off and lifted the pan. "Having another adult to monitor the chaos is enough. Did you eat yet?"

"I grabbed a bite." I hadn't, but I didn't want Lynnie to worry about me. She had more important mouths to feed.

Setting the table was one of the kids' rotating chores,

but since it was an off night, I put out plates and cups. I cut up the hot dog for Riley as Lynnie called the other kids to eat.

By the time the kids circled the table, Emery still wasn't out yet. Talking to Henry and changing clothes didn't usually take her that long. I waited until Lynnie sat to eat before I said, "I'm going to check on Em."

Emery's bedroom door was only partially closed. She sat on the edge of the bed still in her scrubs, staring at the floor.

Worried, I knocked lightly, and she jumped.

Relief crossed her face when she saw it was me. "Can you come in and shut the door?"

I did as she asked and stayed standing as she rose and rushed to her dresser.

She tossed jeans onto the bed and started digging through a drawer. "Henry wanted to pick up the kids for some private school Halloween party." She yanked out a long-sleeved red shirt and threw it on top of her pants. Then she ripped her scrub top over her head. My gaze stuck on her creamy tits jiggling in her plain white bra as she spoke. "And I said that we had plans, and he was a dick about it. Like, what am I supposed to do? It's the last minute, and we have plans."

"Did he think they'd miss school tomorrow?" I watched her shrug into her shirt until every last inch of skin disappeared.

"Oh, the school." Her tone grew more incensed. "Then he started quizzing me about the programs that Coal Haven's school has. Do they have advanced math? Do they have AP English? What about their science programs?" She stepped out of her pants and chucked them toward the laundry with a sneer. "And he goes on about how we shouldn't have left the precious private school all his doctor friends send their kids to. As if he gave much thought to the kids and their schooling before I pissed him off by telling him no." She rammed her feet into her jeans.

"And this is the school that's having the party."

She straightened and puffed loose strands out of her face. "Of course." She folded her arms and kicked a hip out. "Then he started on Thanksgiving."

"And he wasn't happy when you told him you had plans."

Her jaw tensed. "He brought up how close you and Holly seemed at the football party. And I maybe..." She rolled her eyes to the ceiling. "Instead of basically telling him to butt out like I have been, I said you were involved with trick-or-treating and that we were going to your place for Thanksgiving and that Mom was even going and... He's so angry, Holden."

She almost sounded scared. I crossed to her and pulled her into my arms. "He can be pissed. He made his choice and is facing the consequences."

"I could give him Thanksgiving," she mumbled. "He asked ahead of time, and I don't want to discourage him from being involved in their lives."

"Do what you feel is right. You and your mom can still come over."

She curled her arms around my sides. "I don't want to give him the satisfaction, but this is for the kids. That would be his weekend anyway, and I could take them up in the morning." She exhaled like she was deflating.

"It's all right."

"It's not how I saw tonight going." She said it like she was really saying that this wasn't how she saw her life going. Fighting with an ex on days that should be fun for the whole family.

"I know." I couldn't make her problems go away, but I

could be the one keeping them from weighing her down. "Once you message him, forget about it and have fun."

She nodded but let me hold her for another minute before we broke apart. Worry lingered in her eyes, but she gave me a small smile. "I'd better get out there or they'll come looking for us."

"And I don't need your mom thinking I'm up to no good." I led her out, hoping the remnants of her conversation with Henry stayed behind.

* * *

Emery

I tried to root myself in the moment and thrive off the excitement of the kids, but the message wars with Henry weren't helping.

If I had expected appreciation for cooperating with him about Thanksgiving, I was wrong. **I want them Monday night through Thanksgiving weekend. We're going to Arizona.**

It was cool he was actually visiting his parents and that he wanted to take the kids. But he couldn't just announce it and expect everyone else to do the work for the trip. **Let me know what time you want to pick them up. Also, remember to contact their teachers so they can bring the schoolwork they'll miss.**

You'll need to bring them down. Just send any schoolwork with them.

I took a steadying breath as I read his last message. I slipped the phone into my pocket. Holden gave me a side-long look as Afton showed him the full-size can of grape pop she got from the house we were standing in front of.

My breath puffed in front of my face, and I pivoted with the rest of my family as we tracked to the next house with its outside lights on.

"Everything okay?" Holden asked as the kids ran to the door. Riley was still going strong, running after her siblings on her own. I'd brought the stroller, which functioned as storage for winter clothing the kids might need to put on or take off. And extra candy bags. Avery had insisted.

"Just Henry flexing." I gave my head a shake. "I'm done with him for tonight."

A couple with two young boys walked toward us. The dark-haired woman was dressed as a fairy with gauzy wings on her back and sparkly face paint. She wore a loose Tinkerbell dress over thick leggings and a black sweatshirt. I wouldn't have recognized Kennedy if Liam wasn't next to her. He wasn't dressed up, but Kennedy was a teacher. She'd probably been in that outfit all day.

Liam aimed his grin at Holden. "I thought for a minute Bruce was out here trick-or-treating."

"That's a low blow, Liam." But Holden laughed and looked down at himself. "I do look a little like Uncle Bruce, don't I?"

"Subtract thirty years and you could pass as twins." His attention was snatched away as his boys—Woody and Buzz Lightyear—ran to the same house my kids were finishing at. "Remember to say thank you," he called.

"I love your costume," I told Kennedy.

She smiled and did a little curtsy. "All the cool fairies wear thermals."

"Winter fairies, for sure."

Kennedy peered at my kids as they rushed from the front door to us. "There's Avery. I didn't see her costume since she's at the middle school, but I saw Afton's Black

Widow costume. And Landon told me how Holden helped score some football gear to borrow."

Landon wore a Vikings jersey over the football gear he'd used this season. Holden and Stetson had procured it from the club. Avery was a witch for the third time.

"You guys just start?" Liam asked.

Holden pointed down the street and the path we'd taken. "We started at her place and have only made it this far."

"Want to combine forces?"

"Sounds great." I didn't have to ask Holden whether he wanted to. I liked Liam and Kennedy, Afton talked nonstop about Eli and Owen, and socializing would help take my mind off Henry.

Holden and Liam steered the kids to the other side of the street so the group could trick-or-treat together without hitting up houses we'd already been to.

Kennedy fell in step beside me. "I have an appointment with Dr. Abdallah soon to start my OB visits."

I'd seen her on the schedule, but of course I couldn't mention anything. It was new to me, knowing the patients that came to the clinic. "You'll like her."

"I was so glad to hear that she does prenatal care and I don't have to run to Bismarck for every appointment. It makes it easier for Liam to come, too, with his shift work. And I'm really glad you're her nurse."

I smiled. Stetson might not talk to Liam, but it seemed the dislike of Krystal ran heavy through the Barrons. "If I have to put up with another doctor on the regular, I'm glad it's her."

Kennedy chuckled. "It's going well, then? The move and the new job?"

My gaze landed on Holden's broad back. Riley was hanging on to two of his fingers as she walked next to him, and my heart nearly burst. "Yes, I'd say it turned out better than I imagined when I planned the move."

"I haven't met your mom. She works at the seed co-op?"

I nodded. "She moved here after I was in college. My grandparents were from Stanton, so she's known the area. Cheaper housing and a job with benefits."

"Laney would know her, then. We should meet up with her sometime."

"That'd be fun." I succeeded at sounding casual when I really wanted to take out my phone and get her info and Laney's info and set a date. I might have been a little friend deprived. "I don't get out much."

"I don't either." She stopped a few feet behind the guys as the kids ran to ring another doorbell under Avery's supervision. "To be honest, I didn't really have a close friend until a year ago. I was a sick kid, and my mom moved a lot. But then I met their cousin Derek in high school, and we were tied at the hip. Where he went, I went, and vice versa. Then he died, and I was so alone."

Holden had told me the tragic story. "Except for Liam?"

She nodded. "He was the only person my age I really socialized with. Then I started going out with coworkers— Aspen being one. And I met Lyric. Then Laney barged into my life again."

Our stories weren't the same, but they were so similar. "I met my ex, Henry, in college, and we weren't tied at the hip, but the kids kind of isolated us. Between our jobs and their activities, I was close to a few coworkers, but they're in Bismarck with their own busy lives." I shrugged. "Life just gets in the way."

"Let's do it, then. Next weekend?" She grinned. "The guys can babysit."

"If you've already found a sitter, then absolutely."

We laughed, and Holden glanced at me. The secret smile

he gave me, the one that everyone could see but was just for me, warmed me better than any hat and gloves could.

My phone buzzed again, and I was wrenched into the real world. Maybe it was Mom telling me she ran out of the party pack of candy I'd bought for her to hand out.

I checked the message. Nope. Not Mom.

You'll need to pick the kids up Sunday night at 7.

I shot back, **Why can't you drop them off?**

I'll be on call and Jenni has the night shift.

I rolled my eyes and resisted bartering with him. Fine.

I tucked my phone away and glowered at the sidewalk.

"Everything okay?" Kennedy asked quietly.

"Yes. Just a little bit of a power struggle going on."

We wandered to another house. The kids were going hard, and Riley was half a block away from being carried by Holden. I didn't know why I kept talking, but I did. The kids couldn't hear. The guys were busy with them, and I had someone who seemed like she'd listen. When I was going through Henry's affair and then the divorce, I hadn't been able to be open about it. Sure, some of my coworkers were friends. But they were also in the same hospital as Henry. They were still his coworkers of sorts. Just like I didn't rant about Henry around the kids, I hadn't been able to do it around them.

"He started off by being almost negligent of the kids after we split. But once I started having a decent life without him, he's gotten more difficult."

She gave a sympathetic hum. "And a guy like Holden would only make it worse for an insecure ex."

"Exactly. It's like it accelerated what was probably coming in the first place."

"So...confession. I kind of hate the saying 'let us know if you need anything.' If I'm not already the type to reach out if I need help, I'm not going to do it. But I'm serious. Liam and I are here if you need anything. If you need help with babysitting, if you need an ear to rant to, if you need someone to drive with you to Bismarck. I know Holden will be first in line, but Liam and I will be second and third."

"Thank you."

She smiled, and the streetlight caught the glitter around her eyes. Her brown stocking hat and thermals blended in with the shadows. She looked like my own Fairy Godfriend.

Afton ran to me to throw her gloves in the stroller and sprint away. As we walked up and down the streets of the neighborhood, Liam and Holden stopped and chatted with other adults. People they'd gone to school with or they knew from the businesses in town. Kids would excitedly wave and greet Kennedy. Some kids who were Avery's age would swing by and give her hugs.

Another mom passed me, herding three kids ahead of her. She looked vaguely familiar, and then she reached out to tap my sweater. "Hi, Emery."

I blinked. She was the X-ray tech at the clinic, but she only worked part-time. "Nisha, hi."

"You working tomorrow?" She did the *half-turn, sort of walking backward to keep up with kids who weren't stopping for their mom* to chat.

"Yes. See you there?"

"You bet." She turned back to her kids and trotted to keep up.

I hadn't thought I'd know anyone. But I had plans for next weekend. I had a Thanksgiving invitation. And I could walk along the street and greet people.

Months ago, when I'd reconciled my time and expenses and realized I had to make a change, I never imagined the shift would lead me here. When I'd interviewed, I hadn't felt like a part of Coal Haven. It would be my new home, but it was where I would help just my kids have a life.

In such a short time, however, Coal Haven had woven itself into the fabric of my being. The town had taken a lost mom and four wandering kids and given us a place. If I could go back in time and tell Mom that her move here would help me and the kids more than anything in our lives, I'd do it. I'd tell her that this move would help me in ways neither of us would see coming. I could still tell her, but I thought she knew.

I'd gone from wondering what the rest of my life was going to be like to being excited to live out my life in this place.

Twenty-One

Holden

Stetson was outside getting the fryers ready for the turkeys. I also had a turkey roasting in the oven. After the year both Stetson and I fucked up the turkeys, we always had a backup. One turkey didn't go far with a group this size, but it was something to throw at them when they were pissed about a half-burned, half-raw fried bird.

Nora pushed her way through my front door. She held a pan of something gluten-, milk-, and sugar-free that no one but me would touch. Emery would take a pity bite and earn my eternal appreciation.

"I have to make another trip, but this can sit out." She set the glass pan down and pushed her golden hair behind an ear. "It's like a pumpkin pie."

I paused at the oven before I opened it to baste the bird. "How can it be *like* a pumpkin pie?"

"I used honey and—you know what? It's better if I

don't say. Stetson might overhear and then he'll blather to everyone about my 'weird' ingredients."

She wasn't wrong. Stetson had a close relationship with his gluten, milk, and sugar. "Is Colt coming?"

She wrinkled her nose like she always did when we talked about Colt. He'd arrived when she was fourteen, and she'd gone from terrified of his burly nature to "I can't even" with his gruffness. The death knell had been when he'd gagged and spit out the special cake she'd baked for her nineteenth birthday. She'd forbidden me from buying her anything, insisting on doing the organic, grass-fed, free-range thing with every ingredient possible.

The cake had been memorable. That was all I could say. I'd never eaten chalk as a kid, but I hadn't missed a thing if that cake was anything to go by.

Her "clean" cooking skills were getting better, but try as I might, I couldn't stop the dread of the first bite with any of her food. None of us could after those early years, but no one else tried anymore.

"Colt disappeared like he always does," she said.

He never spent holidays with us. I had invited him ever since my house had been finished and I'd been in charge of the guest list. "All right. Mom on the way?"

"I hope not," she muttered as she went to the door to grab another concoction of hers. "She's in rare form."

"Shit."

She paused with her hand on the doorknob. "I hate to even say anything, but I think you should know, just in case I'm right. I think she's salty that Emery's coming."

"Why? Emery's not seducing me to live a city life like she blamed Teagan for. Can't she give her a chance before she acts like a ranch diva?"

Nora lifted a shoulder. "Who knows? It's Mom, so it's all about her."

"Thanks for the warning." How could our grandparents raise more than one self-centered, egotistical kid?

Mom and Emery had nothing in common, but they didn't have to. Mom could be civil. That was all I asked.

People started arriving.

Aunt Willow breezed in and set the Crock-Pot with her asparagus hot dish on the island. Then she wrapped me in a warm hug. "I always look forward to your Thanksgivings. And did I hear correctly? I get to meet your girlfriend?"

"Yes, she's coming."

She pulled away, and her delighted smile eased the tension Nora's warning had caused. "Kennedy has said wonderful things about her."

"Likewise." I hadn't known Emery long, but she wasn't one to gush over anything. She was steady with her emotions. But after her girls' night with Kennedy and Laney, she'd talked about the night with a huge smile on her face and her hands flying, and she'd laughed when she relayed stories. Downright giddy.

I wished at least Laney and Archer would feel comfortable joining us for the holiday. I'd invited them but said I completely understood since Uncle Cameron and Mom hadn't exactly been welcoming and they'd never apologized for the way they behaved. I didn't invite Liam and Kennedy. I couldn't care less about the ripples it'd cause in my family, but it would be worse for Liam. He'd been through enough.

Aunt Willow rushed outside to direct Uncle Bruce with the pies he was carrying, but she hadn't needed to worry. Stetson was on it. He wouldn't let anything happen to the sweets with Nora's food as the only backup.

"Your woman's here," Stetson said as he carefully placed two pumpkin pies on the island. "So's your mom."

Shit. I rushed outside. We'd gotten a dusting of snow last night that might melt by the weekend, but I didn't bother with a jacket. I tucked my face down to avoid as much of the bitter wind as I could.

Emery got out of her car, her hair tied in a knot at her neck and tucked into her winter coat. She rushed to her mom's side. I gave Emery a quick kiss and held my elbow out to Lynnie. The path was icy.

"Oh, thank you, Holden." Lynnie gripped my arm. "I'm walking like I'm twenty years older than I am, but when I first moved here, I fell in the parking lot of the grocery store and broke my leg. A broken leg in winter. Ugh." She shuddered. "I'm so paranoid now."

Quick bootsteps crunched past us and Mom grunted. She walked like it was the middle of June and she had special shoes with extra-grippy tread.

I pretended like I hadn't heard, and I hoped Lynnie hadn't either. "No worries at all. Best to be careful."

Inside, Nora greeted Emery with a hug. "So glad you came. Ooh, is this the Lynnie I've heard so many good things about?"

Pride could've punctured my chest. How could my sister be so sweet when she was raised by a mom like ours? Stetson told me once that I should take credit for it, but I didn't see it that way. I'd left for college when Nora was ten and came home on the weekends and holidays. When I moved back, she was in high school and Mom had given up on her. Nora had been constantly under the weather as a kid, but she'd learned to take care of herself.

Now Nora never wanted anyone to feel unwelcome like Mom had often made her feel.

She engaged Emery and Lynnie in conversation while Stetson and I got the turkeys ready. Willow always hustled into the kitchen and never left on a holiday. I suspected it was her safe spot. She'd been married to Bruce for decades, and she'd learned to navigate his siblings, but that didn't mean she wanted to.

Before the food was served, Cameron, Naomi, and Isla arrived. Isla carried in a plate of cookies and jumped into the chat with Emery and her mom. Naomi had a couple bottles of wine. She coolly took in the crowd as she wove through the main area to the island.

"Do you have a wine opener, Holden?"

She asked every year. Every time she was in my house. It didn't matter how many times I told her to help herself, she wouldn't.

"Sure thing." By the time I got the cork out, Naomi had been absorbed into introductions with Emery.

Cameron appeared by my side and took over opening the wine. "Still have some corn in the fields?"

It was the same conversation every Thanksgiving. I didn't recall ever discussing anything personal with Uncle Cameron. It was the ranch side of business or the farming side. It was a new pickup or whether I should upgrade one of the tractors. When I was in high school, Cameron had sometimes asked about football, but that was the extent of him getting personal.

"Yeah, there's no reason to let it sit at the elevator. How about you?" It wasn't like we went to different grain elevators or farmed in separate states. Mom's property and Cameron's used to be one large chunk.

The corner of his mouth ticked up. "You'll have to ask Stetson about that. This is the first year I haven't done much."

"Busy at the refinery?"

He nodded, but something flickered in his gaze. I couldn't identify it. Usually, Uncle Cameron was as unflappable as his wife. Today he looked tired. There were faint rings under his eyes that weren't there before, and the lines that fanned from the corners were just a little bit deeper.

I almost asked him if he was feeling alright, but I knew the answer. He could be crawling into his deathbed and he'd confidently reply that he was fine.

When it was time to eat, I made sure Emery and her mom were next to me. I had an open floor plan, but seating eleven people wasn't easy. Nora and Isla sat at the island, murmuring to each other. Cameron and Bruce took seats on the couch and used the end tables for their plates as they discussed weather and what Bruce was going to do through the winter.

If Stetson wasn't at the table, it'd be awkward as hell, but he had turned his personality on. This was the Stetson from the bar, the guy who made everyone feel comfortable and welcome, the guy who cracked jokes. He did what he was best at and kept the peace.

Until Emery's phone buzzed. She shifted in her chair but ignored it and shot me an apologetic smile.

"It's okay to answer," I said quietly.

My mom was across the table from us. She chewed and watched us, her expression flat as if she was ready for an eye roll or an *I told you so* look. She was territorial. She'd been that way as a rancher and as a mom, like she wanted me and Nora to be as lonely as her.

"The kids are with their dad. You and Mom are here. I'm sure it's nothing."

Her phone buzzed again. She bit the bottom of her lip and discreetly pulled the device out of her pocket. "Oh. It's Henry."

"Think everything's okay?"

"I hope so." She sighed and pushed her chair back. "Since he's calling again, I'd better make sure."

I lifted my chin in the direction of my bedroom. "You can go in my room."

"Thank you." She hurried away.

Mom speared a piece of turkey. "She talk to her ex a lot?"

Dammit. Lynnie looked up like she was going to answer, but Mom's challenging stare was on me.

"Some dads are involved in their kids' lives," I answered. Despite the troubles Emery was having with him, Henry had done more with his kids in the short time I knew him than mine ever had.

Stetson grunted. "Some don't butt out."

I recognized the signs. Our typical family interactions. Little comments meant to ruffle feathers. We didn't do this on Thanksgiving, and I wasn't going to let it start. One holiday a year where we acted civil shouldn't be too much to ask.

"Pass the cookie salad, please." It was a weak attempt to divert attention, but maybe it would be enough. Lynnie handed the bowl of pudding and fruit mix with fudge-striped cookies over. It was a dessert, but right now called for a sweet moment.

Emery's voice rose from the bedroom. I set my fork down. Lynnie's head jerked up. Stetson tried to pretend he didn't hear anything. Mom's shrewd gaze was directed at the alcove that housed my bedroom door.

"And you chose Thanksgiving to talk to me about it?" Anger amped Emery's volume up. "Well, then when? Christmas? You got everything you wanted and suddenly you change your mind?"

"Oh, dear," Lynnie said under her breath.

I should check on her. I pushed my chair back to move in that direction.

Lynnie patted my arm. "Give her a moment."

Mom cocked a brow as if asking me whether I was going to listen to Lynnie. What else could I do? Talk as if nothing's going on? I should be used to tense family times by now, but the tension was usually caused by one of our parents.

"You do that, Henry. Talk to your fucking lawyer, and I'll talk to mine."

I glanced around. Everyone had gone silent. A hint of respect entered Mom's gaze. Emery wasn't taking shit from Henry, and that scored a point for her in Mom's eyes.

I didn't hear any more talking, but Emery hadn't come out. My stomach cramped. Something was wrong. "Excuse me."

I found Emery with her back to me, much like she'd been sitting on Halloween when Henry had been a jackass. Only this time, she was pale and a small tremble shook her body.

"Em?"

She looked up at me, her green eyes watery. Tears spilled over and she buried her face in her hands. I rushed to her side and gathered her in my arms. It was in this moment I realized there was nothing I wouldn't do for her.

If seeing her this upset bothered me as much as it did, it was the final sign I needed to know that I loved this woman.

* * *

Emery

This couldn't be happening. Henry was destroying the life I'd built—again.

I sobbed into Holden's chest, and that made me cry harder. The reality of what he'd said growing more apparent.

"What'd he do?" Holden asked after several minutes when I'd finally calmed down.

I couldn't tell him while I was ensconced in the safety of his arms. This might affect him too. Affect us.

It would end us.

I sat up and blinked my vision clear. "He plans to change the parameters of our custody agreement so the kids live with him."

Holden reared back. "The fuck he is."

Tears trailed down my cheeks. "I knew he hated being shown up. I saw that the day I fought with him on the sidewalk, but this is over the top." I sucked in a hard breath and tried to calm my raging emotions. "Avery was the one who called. She was distraught and sobbing. She took her dad's phone after she heard him and Jenni talking about how they're going to juggle their schedules when the kids are with them full time."

"He can't do that, can he?"

"He's not going to be happy until I pull up stakes and move back to Bismarck. He even said that."

"What? Why?"

"Oh, he has his reasons. The kids' school. Said the traveling is hard on them." My eyes burned, but I held the tears at bay. What if Henry was right?

"It's an hour," Holden scoffed. "It's not like you moved across the country."

I let out a gusty breath. "I said we could go back to mediation if he wanted more time with the kids. I'd be happy to. Yeah, it'd be more complicated, but it's the best thing for the kids."

"And?"

"He wants the kids back in private school." I'd seen the signs when I met Henry. He'd wanted to achieve a certain status and he'd wanted the status symbols to go with them.

The wife and kids. The house. The kids in the same private school and expensive activity clubs as his coworkers. Only I had thought there'd be more sincerity than concern over his image.

"What's wrong with Coal Haven?"

I rolled my eyes because the answer was so Henry. "It's not the same school all his friends' and mentors' kids go to." I rubbed my fingers beside my eyes. "And if he doesn't agree to mediation, then we'll have to litigate and I...can't afford that. And he knows it. You know we didn't get married until we were done with undergrad? His parents paid for his bachelor's degree, but not medical school. I took out loans for nursing, and I'm responsible for those. But since his med school came after we got married, I get to pay for half of those too. Even though I had to use my degree to support us while he continued school." And I probably wasn't going to find any better representation than I had before. I'd get screwed again. Tears welled up and spilled over. What if Henry tried to push me out of their lives?

"I don't get it. How can he do that to them and to you? I get that his ego's bruised because you're standing up for yourself and I'm around and the kids like me." He shook his head. "Doesn't he understand that I'm not replacing him and I'm not trying to?"

"He needs to be number one. His parents gush over their dog. They've been that way his entire life. Always their pet over him. But you're a real person, and that's worse. When they gush about you, I'm sure it's the same feeling for him." I let out a bitter huff. "It's why he was drawn to a young, single woman who could dedicate her time to him."

"Jesus, Em, I'm sorry. What can I do to help?"

I couldn't fight my tears. "Do you know that I was just thinking about how awesome this move has been? How it was exactly what the kids and I needed? They're making friends. I'm making friends. I like my job, and it doesn't run me into the ground. I met you. Things couldn't have been better."

He rubbed my back. "It'll be all right. You're their mom."

I wanted to believe Holden. To hang on his words and lean into his comfort. But the phone conversation pinballed in my head. Henry's anger that Avery had contacted me. His defensive tone, one I recognized well from when I'd confronted him about the affair. The tone he used to explain how I was at fault and that was why he did what he did.

I wasn't the young, compliant girl he'd met in college who was excited to start her career in nursing and support her husband through medical school and through his residency and into the early years of his career. I had been a mom to young kids. I hadn't had time to gush over him and fawn over his lab coat, impressed that he was a surgeon. I'd been proud of him, but I'd been drowning in the obligations of my life.

And now, I wasn't the overtired, overstressed, haggard mom I'd been when we divorced, and that upset him. He claimed I had moved without consulting him and I changed the lifestyle of the kids while he had to keep paying the same amount of child support. He wasn't wrong. It was enough to revisit our agreement in the court's eyes.

I lifted my head from Holden's shoulder. I was in his room and his family was right outside the door. How much had they heard? Mom was probably worried and trying to cover it.

I wiped off my wet cheeks, wishing I could scrub the embarrassment away. "I don't think I can go out there and pretend nothing's wrong. I just want to go home."

There was a little tap at the door. Mom peered inside. She must've heard the pause in our conversation.

What a way to introduce myself to the rest of the family.

Mom's smile was gentle. "Henry's causing problems?"

I nodded and fought back another onslaught of tears.

Holden gave my shoulder one last squeeze before he rose and held his hand out for me. "If you need to leave, don't worry about it. I'll bring over some desserts later."

"Thank you." I rose with the help of his strong grip, leaning into his strength, soaking up as much as I could.

Holden was grounded in a way that Henry hadn't been when I met him. I was older and knew better now. If I had met someone like Holden instead, I wouldn't be in the position I was in now.

I straightened my clothing. I was dreading walking out and getting the stare. It would be a hundred times more uncomfortable than the small-town stare I still got when I went to new-to-me businesses in town. Everyone outside this room knew I'd taken a call from my ex and had heard me crying.

But I straightened my shoulders and strode out. Kira watched me like a hawk ready to swoop in for an easy meal. I didn't have time for her bullshit too. In another life, maybe. Willow's kind expression drew me to her, but I kept my gaze from lingering on anyone.

I put on a small, apologetic smile. "It was nice to meet you all, but I have to get going."

Nora slid off the barstool at the island and crossed to me with her arms out. "So glad you could make it. And sorry about whatever's going on."

I squeezed her back. Isla was next in line. She gave me a hug. "Did you bring anything? I can grab it for you."

"No, it's fine."

I beelined for the door and stepped into my snow boots.

Mom said her goodbyes, blocking me from the openness of Holden's house, as if she was giving me as much privacy as she could.

I shrugged on my coat. Holden had kept his boots on and he followed me out, giving my mom his elbow again.

God, that guy was considerate. No wonder Henry was intimidated.

I got in my car as Holden helped Mom into the passenger side. When she was in her seat, he leaned down. "Want me to call before I come over?"

"No. Just come over whenever. Don't rush your time here, though." It wouldn't matter what time he came over. I wasn't going anywhere. I was going to throw myself an enviable pity party, get a little lost in the past to fuel the woe-is-me feeling, and prep myself for the fight that was coming.

I didn't want to cast any more negativity on a day that was usually a good one for Holden.

With a nod, he shut the door and went back to the house. I didn't take my gaze off him as I started the car. He disappeared inside.

Our breath puffed around us. Mom rubbed her gloves together. "I thought the sun was going to come out today."

The overcast weather fit my mood. I put my hands on the steering wheel, and the hard plastic leeched the heat from my hands. I reached into my pockets for my gloves, but they weren't there.

Should I go without? Cold fingers would take my mind off Henry. But I didn't need Holden worrying about crap I'd forgotten when he came over later.

"I have to run inside. I forgot something."

I rushed across the yard with my hands tucked into my jacket. I didn't want to knock and have everyone's attention on me. My gloves were probably on the bench right by the door. I quietly opened it, planning to shoot anyone who saw me a quick smile as I ducked in and got out in seconds.

The warmth of Holden's house surrounded me. Everyone was focused on the dining room. I couldn't find Holden right away, but I found my black gloves were right where I had set them under my jacket.

I glanced up to see if I could catch Holden's eye and wave my gloves so he knew what I was doing, but Kira's voice stopped me in my tracks. "It's for the best, Holden. It's not like she's gonna give you kids or anything, and I'm not letting the ranch go to some other man's kids."

"What the hell, Mom?"

Nora's gasp made heads swivel to follow her gaze right to me.

Holden's eyes grew wide, and his mouth tightened so hard color bled from his lips.

"I forgot my gloves," I said weakly and slunk out the door.

"Emery, wait."

I didn't. I scurried to the car, stuffing my hands into my gloves. A few snowflakes landed on my cheeks. The weather was going to release its load, and the day would continue to shit on me.

It's not like she's gonna give you kids or anything.

It wasn't like I hadn't thought of the subject if Holden and I stayed together. But he had his past experiences and I had mine, and it wasn't worth converging until we had to. We had enough to consider in the present.

"Em!" Holden's rapid footsteps behind me made me turn around only out of fear he was going to slip and fall. But he jogged to me with the same confidence his mom had used earlier.

"I didn't mean to listen in on a private conversation." I sounded calm and collected. I should have won an award.

Kira had deftly jabbed at what could be a major issue between me and Holden. As if anxiety wasn't squeezing my heart already, her words had cracked it. Because it wasn't something Holden and I could ignore forever.

Bewilderment entered his expression. "Mom's not worried about privacy. You don't need to be. I'm sorry for what she said."

"She's not wrong."

His expression went blank. "What do you mean?"

"I mean that I'm solidly in my thirties with four kids. Trying for a fifth..." My heart rate sped up thinking about it. I put my hand on my chest as if willing the organ to stay in my rib cage, but I couldn't stop shaking my head. Sleepless nights. Colic. Being at the beck and call twenty-four seven while having other children and a spouse to take care of.

Yeah. Having another kid was a thing for me. It wasn't a decision I could make lightly.

His brows drew together, and I drifted closer to him even though we were the only two outside. "And that's me. What about you? Have you thought about what going through the pregnancy would be like for you? Are you ready to think of another baby? There's an entire family business tied to one little baby."

I didn't have to say the rest. His mom had gotten the ranch from her parents. He would get it from his mom. Then what? I had learned enough about Kira and Nora's relationship to know there wasn't much more of a chance that it would get passed on to her than to *some other man's kids*.

"I don't even know if I'm going to be in Coal Haven much longer. I just..." I let out a hard breath and the cloud drifted away like I wished my worries would. He was tied to this town. His roots ran deep. My roots went wherever my kids would be. "I just have to deal with me right now."

"Can I still come over later?"

I couldn't bring myself to say no. I didn't want to let him go, but that sounded like what I was doing. He was a good thing. Such a good thing. But there was a mountain growing between us, and as important as he'd become to me, I had four others I had to take care of first. I shouldn't be in a place where I had to choose, but I didn't have the money to give me options.

Twenty-Two

Holden

I charged into the house. "What the hell, Mom?"

Cameron had stayed on the couch with Bruce, his empty plate on the end table. Stetson had migrated to the island, along with Willow, to hang by Nora and Isla. Mom sat at the table, not one ounce of guilt showing on her face.

I should have waited for everyone to leave before I confronted her, but I couldn't. We'd all seen what happened. I figured they might as well be here to watch the rest play out.

She folded her arms across her chest. The cream turtleneck she wore didn't soften her harsh visage. "Someone's gotta be thinking about this. You get serious with these girls that don't want to live in Coal Haven. Then you're going after the ones who don't want kids. And now one that has a full brood."

"I get that you want me to stay in the family business,

but you can't predict the future." My volume ramped up as I spoke. "You didn't know that I wouldn't come home again."

"Not if Teagan had any say."

"Well, you don't have to worry about her," I said bitterly. I'd been left to support myself once I left college and didn't move home right away when I was done. And I'd been left to get myself through the worst thing that had ever happened to me.

Mom snorted. "Oh, I still worry because of Teagan. She left you high and dry after that baby died, and here you are, single with no kids, in your thirties."

The place went quiet. The only movement was Willow putting her fingers to her mouth as if she could stuff words she didn't say back into nothing. Nora looked just as horrified, but Isla was the only one left in shock. Bruce and Cameron took Stetson's method of staying out of it by staring at the floor.

"You knew?"

Mom's expression turned incredulous. "You think something like that can happen without us finding out? You were listed as the father in the obituary."

Teagan hadn't wanted a big funeral, but her parents had taken over a lot. Perhaps they'd done an obituary. I'd been lost in a haze of grief and coasted through that time until Teagan walked out.

I gave my head a shake. Mom had known and offered me nothing. No *I'm sorry*. No hug. No sympathetic pat on the shoulder.

Hadn't I wanted it that way? She'd given me the room I had asked for with my lack of explanation and distance. And I'd returned home like she wanted.

I stuffed a hand through my hair and curled my fingers

into a fist. Frustration and confusion raged with so many other emotions I couldn't identify them all. "So you've been waiting it out? For me to get over it and give you a grandson like this isn't the twenty-first century?"

"It's not like that and you know it," Mom shot back. "This isn't exactly the refinery that Cameron works at where we can just hire a new CEO when he decides to retire."

I didn't bother with the *well, actually* rebuttal. Both of us could retire and we could hire a ranch manager. Colt functioned as one for Mom anyway; we'd just hire more. I knew the point Mom was trying to make. She wanted to make sure the ranch stayed a family business.

I couldn't fault her for wanting to have something to hand down to me and to her grandkids. But I could fault her for getting between me and someone I cared about in order to get her way.

"Emery's important to me," I said quietly.

Mom's expression softened, but the underlying hardness didn't go away. "I know. She seems nice. But we all heard it, Holden. Her priority is her kids. If you stay with her, your priority will be her. She might have to move, and then what? You wait until you fall in love before you realize that you're living her ex's life in order to stay with her?"

I didn't have a good reply. Hopelessness threatened to fog my brain, but it wasn't like this was a decision I could make overnight. I didn't know whether there was a decision to be made.

"You're my priority," Mom said, and from the corner of my eye, I saw Nora's head drop down. Dammit, Mom. "I'm not apologizing for it."

"If I'm your priority, maybe quit trying to run off people I fall in love with because they don't tick all the boxes you think are important. Just because you can't let anyone in doesn't mean I should keep them locked out unless they can shoot out children and irrevocably tie themselves to this place."

I yanked my coat off the hook by the door. "You all are welcome to stay and enjoy yourselves, but I'm heading to town."

"Wait." Nora jumped up. "Go get your pickup warmed up. I'll bring out some dessert for you to take to her."

Grateful I had some support in my immediate family, I left a flurry of activity behind in the kitchen.

I was in my pickup waiting for the windshield to defrost when Nora rushed out. She had a bag filled with containers in her hands.

She opened the passenger door and climbed in, carefully setting the bag on the floor. "Whatever you decide, just know that I'm here."

She was what I'd needed when my daughter died, but she'd only been a kid herself.

"About what Mom said—"

Nora waved a hand. Resignation filled her blue eyes. "Mom is Mom. I won't change her, and I don't want to be like her. Once I accepted that, life got easier." She opened the door and slid out, hanging on to the oh-shit handle. "I packed some leftovers in case you stay there a while, and I packed some of every dessert in case you don't like mine." She had a knowing look on her face when she closed the door.

A smile ghosted over my lips. I'd eat every last crumb of her pumpkin pie.

There was almost no one on the highway, and town was quiet as I drove through.

Lynnie's car was still in front of Emery's house. I parked behind her, grabbed the food, and rushed to the door.

Emery let me in with a frown. Her eyes were red, and her face was pale. "Don't you still have company? I didn't run everyone off, did I?"

I gave her a kiss on the forehead. "No." She didn't need to know what went on after she left. "They were happy to clean everything up."

Her mom rose from the couch. "I'll head home."

I didn't want to chase her mom away. Emery needed to be surrounded by people who cared about her while her kids were with Henry. I lifted the food. "I've got pie. Might as well enjoy some."

Emery didn't give her mom a chance to argue. "I'll get some plates. Do we want to eat at the table or in the living room?"

"I feel like it's an eat-in-the-living-room kind of night," Lynnie said.

Emery didn't crack a smile but disappeared into the kitchen. Lynnie squeezed my arm as she passed. She stopped. "Henry never would've checked on her like this. He used school and work as an excuse to hide from his obligations."

I wasn't surprised. Henry and my mom were a lot alike.

Emery turned on the game as we ate. I didn't pay attention. Stetson shot me a message. **Don't worry about anything here. I'll make sure it's all cleaned up. Nora and I will do your chores tonight and tomorrow morning.**

Thanks.

When we were done eating, Lynnie left. Emery stared at the TV like an ambitionless zombie. I racked my brain for something to say to make her feel better, but there was nothing. Just a looming uncertainty that could change her life.

She didn't look at me when she spoke. "You know when

I confronted him about the affair, he called all over town for a lawyer."

"He knew the divorce was coming?"

"Yes, I told him I couldn't trust him anymore, that I realized that was where our marriage had been heading. And he'd called around so when I went looking for a lawyer, no one could work with me because they had prior knowledge of the case."

That son of a bitch. I vaguely recalled hearing about people doing that. Holly had laughed about doing the same to her ex. Only he had deserved it. Emery hadn't. "That's fucked up."

"Yeah." Dejection hung heavy around her. "I doubt any offices will be open on Black Friday, but I wouldn't be surprised if he's already done the same thing." She sighed and stretched across the couch. "I'll make some calls tomorrow, then I'll find out for sure."

"You can't use the same lawyer?"

"She didn't do much for me. It's like she went through the motions to get to the payday. She didn't care about what kind of job she did." Emery glanced around the house as if she was already cataloging all the tasks she'd have to do to break her rental agreement and move.

The thought of her moving was as heavy as an anvil on my chest, caving my ribs in until I couldn't breathe. "Can I stay with you tonight? Until the kids come back?"

She blinked at me. The kids wouldn't be back until Sunday, but I didn't want to leave her alone for a minute. "Yeah, but you don't have to."

"I want to. I want to be with you as long as I can."

Her expression wavered and she teared up. I hadn't meant for that to come out sounding like this might be the last weekend we'd have together. I knew little about mediations or litigation or how long they took.

I gathered her into my arms and let her cry.

* * *

Emery

I slammed my phone on the table. "That asshole." I seethed. I'd been on a roller coaster of emotions for a solid twenty-four hours and there was no sign the ride was going to stop.

Holden had run to his place to get some work done. I had waited for him to leave before I started calling law offices. There was one left in Coal Haven, but I didn't doubt that Henry had fucking called them too.

He'd planned this. When would I have found out if Avery hadn't called?

He would've dumped the news on me Sunday night. So I'd have to drive back to Coal Haven a complete mess.

Regret beat through me. I shouldn't have stood up to him like I had. But Mom's advice rang through my mind. What would that have shown my kids? To let the person who was supposed to be a life partner treat them like they weren't worthy of respect?

But was the cost too high?

Henry couldn't take the kids away completely. He worked sixty-hour weeks and had to be on call. He didn't take them to practices and appointments or sit through rehearsals. He hadn't been part of traditions like pictures on the first day of school or ice cream on the last day of school.

If he wanted to do all that, I wouldn't interfere as long as I also got to be involved. But he wouldn't. He had the same job. He had the same personality. He'd hire sitters and nannies, and he'd have Jenni take over when he wasn't around.

As long as Jenni was a responsible adult in their lives, I'd get over our past. But I knew Henry. He'd use the kids to control me. I wanted to talk to them. To hear their voices and pretend like I had more power and money than I did and could keep the nice little life we were building in Coal Haven.

I steeled myself to pick up the phone again. I called Henry.

He answered with a rushed, "Hello?"

"Can I tell the kids good night?"

"Why?"

I ground my teeth together. "Because they're gone for four days, and I'd like to say good night before Riley goes down." They were used to their dad being gone. Not me.

"Well, we're eating supper."

Avery's "Is that Mom?" sounded from the background.

Henry gave a disgruntled snort and handed the phone over without saying anything to me.

I talked to Avery first and heard all about Arizona and how they went to the zoo and how nice the weather was. I got passed down the line until Riley. Avery helped her hold the phone without cutting me off. It was a blissfully normal conversation free of tears and worries. I'd needed it.

When she put her dad back on, I felt slightly better about the fight that was coming.

"Are you going to call every night?"

If I could stuff his attitude back into his smug mouth, I'd have a lot of fun doing it. "I don't have to call tomorrow if it's going to disrupt your plans."

"We might be busy."

I held in my sigh. "Okay. Thanks for letting me—"

He hung up.

And the anger was topped off once again.

The front door opened. Holden came in. He'd changed clothes after doing chores and held an overnight bag.

"No luck?"

I shook my head. "I'll try the lawyer in town. If they don't do family law, maybe he'll have recommendations of someone good."

His expression flickered. "I don't know if you'll have much luck with him. He's not exactly progressive. The colleagues he recommends might be more likely to empathize with Henry."

I shoved my pen and notepad away. It was better than throwing it. "This is so frustrating."

He came up behind me and put his strong hands on my shoulders. I rotated my neck as he massaged. "You're so good with your hands."

His voice dropped low. "Tell me what else you want me to do with them."

I tipped my head back and let my gaze caress the hard angles of his face. "Can you make me forget what's going on for a little while?"

He spread his hands flat over my shoulders and stroked down my arms, bending over me. "I can't make you forget, but I can give you an outlet to vent your emotions."

"I'll take it."

I rose, but he caged me by the table and moved my phone closer to my notepad and pen.

"Aren't we going to the bedroom?"

His smoldering gaze landed on me. "You expecting company?"

"No?" I glanced out the window facing the street. The neighborhood was usually quiet, but there was no school. What if some kids went outside to play?

He reached over and tugged the cord. The blinds fell shut. Instant privacy.

We didn't waste time after that. I wound my fingers through his hair as our mouths clashed. My ass bumped into the table, and he lifted me the rest of the way, managing to get my leggings rolled down.

I was about to undo the clasp to his jeans, but he released my mouth, leaving me bereft for a second before he kneeled. Peeling my pants off, he dropped them, his hot gaze not leaving my center.

He pushed my legs apart, and I swallowed hard. Broad daylight, kitchen-table sex. It wasn't like I was in a sex club with twenty strangers watching, but my mind didn't believe it. My heart raced and my self-consciousness peaked, but typical Holden—he wiped all that out of my mind.

He descended on me, burying his face between my legs. I twined my fingers through his hair once again and gave in to the storm of sensations. He did what he'd said he would and gave my emotions an outlet.

We were alone. I was free to cry his name, holler my pleasure, and pant and moan—all things I needed because he brought me to climax hard and fast.

When I exploded, he didn't give me a chance to float down from my peak. He was up and ripping open his pants. Shoving them down only far enough to free his hard erection, he plunged into me. Pleasure surged in response. He had his thumb on my clit, doing nothing but resting it there while he thrust in and out.

This wasn't a sweet and intimate interlude. This wasn't a sexy quickie. This was a release. Just what I needed.

I came again, bucking hard against him. I would've slid across the table, but he captured my legs and held me in place as he growled and braced himself on the table as he came.

He stayed inside me and continued to hold my legs. "Feel better?" he asked, breathing hard.

"Yeah. The pressure is definitely off." I felt less like I was going to crawl out of my skin or hide in a corner and cry about the path my life had taken and more like I could don my armor and go into battle.

He eased out of me. "We can do that every hour if you need it. All fucking weekend."

I believed him. Neither of us would be able to walk by the time I left for Bismarck on Sunday to pick up the kids, but I'd be too boneless to worry. I'd be too spent to care about how the upcoming legal battle would affect my life.

I thought I might even be able to ignore what the likely outcome would be. Because I hadn't forgotten what Kira had said and the unfair pressure it put on me and Holden during a time I couldn't handle much more. Her words had highlighted where I had to put my priorities and what it might mean.

I had the weekend to figure something out—or come to terms with what I might have to do if I couldn't.

* * *

Holden

It was Sunday, and Emery had been pensive and quiet all day. I showered and dressed and was about to leave to run home and do chores. I had on my coat and boots when I found her sitting at the kitchen table.

She was stirring a cup of cocoa and staring out the window.

"Want me to grab some lunch to bring back before you leave?" I asked.

Her haunted gaze met mine, and acid churned in my

stomach. Her expression, while distraught, was resolute. "Holden, I don't think you should come back."

I didn't have much relationship experience under my belt, but I understood the finality of her tone. Still, I asked, "What do you mean?"

"I don't want... I have so much to think about." Tears gathered in her eyes and spilled out. "I should've talked to you about this earlier, but I couldn't bring myself to tell you to leave. But suddenly I have a lot going on, and I can't let what's between us affect me."

I understood what she was saying, but I didn't. "What's between us, Em?"

She hastily brushed her cheeks. "You mean a lot to me, but between what your mother said and the fact I might have to move... I can't let my feelings affect what I'm willing to do for my kids."

"You think that if you move, it's over between us?"

She leveled a stare on me that understood way too much. "You can't just leave Coal Haven."

"It's not that long distance of a relationship." As I said it, I knew it was a losing argument. But I had to try. I couldn't let the best thing to happen to me walk out and do nothing.

"For how long, Holden?"

I wished I had a definitive answer. She'd move, Henry would back off, and then she'd have to uproot her job and her home once again and come back to Coal Haven in order to come back to me. "We don't even know how much Henry is going to push for."

"I do. I know him. It's why I didn't stay in the marriage and repair our relationship. It's why I didn't string out the divorce proceedings in the first place. It's because I know what he'll do, and I need to be able to concentrate on that, on my kids. I can't worry that you'll leave me in the middle of everything. I can't worry that if you don't leave me, maybe you and I won't work anyway because deep down you want kids of your own. I can't worry about whether I'm willing to have kid number five and what that'll propel Henry to do."

"Henry shouldn't have a say in anything that happens between you and me," I said hotly and immediately regretted it. In her expression was the acceptance I'd been hoping to fracture. I had wanted to show her that she was wrong, but I'd only confirmed that she was right.

She would be consumed with fighting Henry for custody and child support. I would be a distraction. The distraction she'd wanted to get through the weekend, but too much for the rest of her life.

"All right," I said and shoved my hands into my jeans pockets. "All right."

She tipped her head down, and her shoulders shook with silent sobs.

My heart broke with hers. Should I go to her? Wrap her up in a hug and let our hearts break together?

Or should I leave before I felt worse than before?

There was one matter I couldn't just drop. "Can you, uh, tell the kids...something. I don't want them thinking..." I didn't want them thinking I was the one who gave up.

I backtracked out of the kitchen and grabbed my duffel bag by the door. I went straight to my pickup and drove off.

That was it. My relationship with Emery hadn't topped four months, but it felt like my heart had been incinerated and stomped into mush, then burned again. When Teagan left, I'd felt empty. This was like being shredded into so many pieces I wasn't sure I could link them back together.

If I had known that last night could be the last time I held her, would I have done anything differently?

I drove through the town I'd known my whole life. I

hadn't wanted to leave when I went to college, but I'd been willing to wait until Teagan changed her mind. I didn't know what I would've done if she hadn't. Perhaps our breakup after the loss of our daughter was the inevitable end. I hadn't admitted it, but I'd been glad to come home. It had become my refuge.

I hadn't entertained the thought of leaving again. This was where I lived. Where I built a house when I got my oil money from the trust my grandparents had set up. And where I worked. But I also hadn't wanted to leave and open myself to heartbreak. To a life I had chalked up to not being for me. I'd had my chance.

Stetson's pickup was at the café downtown. I pulled in. It was either this or face my empty house and admit to the secret fantasies I'd had that it'd be full of kids and laughter after sitting so quietly since it'd been built.

I'd have to admit that maybe I had entertained a thought or two of having kids with Emery. But I would also be fine if she allowed me into her life to raise her kids with her.

Stetson was hunched over a plate, digging into an omelet. I slid into the booth across from him. He did a double take at my expression.

Jocelyn came by. "Usual for ya, hon?"

My stomach lurched. I didn't know when I'd have an appetite again. "Just water, please."

She paused for a moment, unsure of what to do. Then she patted my shoulder and hurried away.

"Who kicked your puppy?" Stetson asked.

"She broke up with me."

He put his fork down and leaned forward on his elbows. "Cuz of the ex?"

I nodded and jerked my gaze out the window. Church would get out soon. The café and Rattler's would be overrun with the lunch crowd. I had to make sure I was gone before then. If I wasn't smiling and congenial, people would wonder. They'd talk. They'd ask questions. And I wasn't in the mood for that shit.

"Was it also about the baby thing?" he asked quietly.

"More that she didn't need more to worry about."

"Harsh."

"But fair."

He arched a brow. "Is it? Yeah, she's going through some shit, but she's not giving you a chance to go through it with her. She's acting like you're just going to be baggage."

He had a point, and if I thought too hard on it, I'd get angry. "What do you want me to do, Stetson? Turn into Mom and make it all about me?"

"No, it just sucks, man. It sucks. I'm sorry." He stabbed his omelet. "Maybe your mom was right, anyway."

I jolted. How could Stetson side with my mom? "What do you mean?"

"Do you want more kids?"

"That's too deep of a topic for a simple answer, Stetson."

He stopped with his forkful halfway to his mouth. "What about moving away if she has to move?"

I scowled out the window. "There's a lot to consider." But she hadn't given me a chance.

"Guess it's for the best, then."

I aimed a glare at him. "Thanks a lot, jackass."

He shoved his food into his mouth and chewed. When he swallowed, he said, "When Teagan broke up with you, you let yourself get swallowed up in the grief and then wouldn't let anyone get close to you until Emery. I remember once when you got shit-faced you said you wished Teagan did more to get through to you. So, what are you going to do? Mope about Emery for nine more years or work harder to get through to her? Because she sure as hell doesn't have time for your ego when she's fighting for her kids."

My throat grew thick. He was a jovial good guy to most people, but he wasn't afraid to be blunt when it counted. "Harsh."

He cut another hunk off his omelet, and melted cheese gushed out. "But fair?"

I switched to staring out the window again. Traffic was picking up. I should leave soon if I didn't want to see people. "I don't want to make it harder for her."

"Then make it easier."

He made it sound so simple, I could deck him.

"Just don't ask me how," he grumbled and hunched over his meal. "I got back together with Krystal."

"What the fuck?"

"I know. I know." His head hung. "I already know it's a mistake. She left an overnight bag at my place, and her toothpaste and shampoo and shit is all over my bathroom."

Sienna would've distracted him, but he probably placated Krystal so she'd leave Sienna alone. The playground games adults played. "What were you thinking?"

He gave me a warning glare, but I read the answer in his eyes. He'd been left to his own devices because I'd been wrapped up in Emery. He might be a grown man, but that didn't stop him from being lonely. He'd made a mistake. It wouldn't change that Krystal would go nuclear when he said he'd changed his mind and wanted to break up with her.

"No matter what I'm going through, I'm still here for you," I told him.

"Thanks. I'll clean up my own mess, but I might need a few beers when it's over."

"You got it." I pushed away. I hated to leave him behind, but his words resonated.

Then make it easier.

Whether or not she wanted to have a future with me, I could still help her carve out one for herself. A future where she didn't have to play games to be with her kids.

Twenty-Three

Emery

I'd picked the kids up last Sunday, and Henry hadn't said more than a few words to me. The kids gushed about their trip to Phoenix, the plane ride, and their grandparents' pool. The dog got high praise too.

Henry must've hated that.

They asked about my Thanksgiving and Holden, but I told them I had a nice holiday and left it at that. I'd tell them that Holden and I weren't seeing each other anymore, but I'd have to do it when I trusted myself not to cry. Sunday, and Monday, had not been that day.

I parked in the driveway. A message from Henry flashed on my phone screen. **I'd like to have the kids this weekend.**

I ground my teeth together and replied. **We have plans.**

I was going to take them Christmas shopping for each other and so they could pick out gifts for their dad and my mom. They were with him the weekend after this weekend, and that didn't leave much more time before Christmas.

My phone rang. Henry.

I closed my eyes. Better to take the call out here than inside where the kids could see.

As soon as I answered, he said, "Come on, Emery. You get them all week."

"I get them ready for school and day care and then I feed them supper and get them to bed. I like to have weekends with them too."

"It's just one extra weekend."

I knew I'd regret saying this. "Those are the terms of our custody agreement, Henry."

"So you're not willing to work with me on this?"

Typical of him to turn it around on me. "We have plans, Henry."

"So you're not willing to work with me on this?"

"Henry—"

"What you're saying is"—he spoke slower this time— "that you're not willing to work with me on seeing the kids more often?"

Dread clawed up my spine until the hair on the back of my neck stood on end. "Are you recording me or something?"

"Why? Are you afraid of saying something that would make it sound like you're not willing to give me more time with my kids? That you moved them away from their school and where I lived with little notice?"

Those were the details he was using to revisit mediation. I wasn't rising to the bait. "Goodbye, Henry."

I hung up on his sputtering. He tried calling back, but I ignored it.

Inside, Mom was sitting with Riley and Afton on the couch, reading books. Landon was driving his race cars around the carpet and listening. Avery was bent over her jewelry-making kit.

Landon popped his head up. "Is Holden coming tonight?"

Shit. It was Tuesday, and I'd been trying all day not to think about how Holden usually brought us dinner on Tuesdays. "Um...Holden won't be visiting too much anymore." The kids and my mom blinked at me. I rushed on. "He's going to miss seeing you guys regularly."

Landon's mouth dropped open. "You two broke up?"

How did I handle this? They were going to blame me. *I* blamed me. I steeled myself for the truth. "I told him we should quit seeing each other, yes."

A chorus of *why*s rang out, and Riley's eyes got round, filling with tears. She might not understand what was going on, but she was absorbing the feelings.

I fought my own tears. At some point, I would quit feeling like the villain in this story, but I didn't think it'd be soon. "He's still in town. He'll always be your friend. He just won't be over as much."

Avery's jewelry was forgotten. "But—"

I threw my hands up and walked into the kitchen before I started bawling in front of the kids. "I'm gonna make some supper."

I had the door to the fridge open and was blankly staring at the contents when Mom gently closed it. She wrapped her arms around me.

I buried my head in her knit sweater, grateful she'd been there from the beginning, but wishing I could give her more happy times than tears. "Did I mess up?" I told her about Henry's call. "He's not going to make it easy. Better to end things with Holden before all of us get closer, right?"

She patted my back. "You're trying to do the right thing for them."

"It doesn't feel like the right thing."

"No, it doesn't. You and Holden worked really well together. If Henry wants to ruin that, it shouldn't be so easy for him."

But it was. Henry had the money, he had the connections, and that gave him all the power.

"I've really liked being closer to you too."

Mom pushed me out to arm's length. I'd never seen the expression she wore. Mom was mild. Mom was nonconfrontational. Mom was supportive. The hardness and edge this Mom radiated wasn't the Mom I'd grown up with.

"You've always had a weak spot when it came to Henry. I wonder, if your father was still alive, whether you'd have married that boy." She peered into my eyes as if daring me to look away. "Henry used you to make himself feel better. You've done what he wanted. When he wanted to marry, you did. When he wanted to have kids, you had them. When he wanted to sleep with other people, he expected you to deal with it. He wanted his way in the divorce to be with Jenni as much as he wanted, and when you moved on, he elbowed his way back into your life. He wants to keep controlling you, and he's succeeding. I know your reasons, Emery. But think about this—what's to stop him from getting a different job in another town and taking the kids with him?"

My rage was so swift I had to back up a step. That was what he claimed I did when I moved to Coal Haven. I could see him doing it, only moving farther away, as far as our custody agreement would allow. I wouldn't be able to move with them. My money would be gone after the new round of mediation. I'd be in debt if I had to pay for litigation. Henry could take the custody he was likely to win and move to Arizona so the kids could know their dog uncle.

It was like a premonition. My hands curled into fists.

"I have some money," Mom said, but I shook my head.

"I can't let you do that."

"It's my retirement account, and if I want to spend it keeping those kids where I've never seen them happier, then that's my choice."

"Mom, it could get ugly." Once Henry learned that Mom was backing me financially, he'd be ruthless. He had more connections, and Mom would be left penniless. I couldn't threaten her financial security.

She let me go. "Think about it. All of it. Don't give in to Henry. He only makes you regret it more the next time you stand up to him."

She left me in the kitchen. I still had no idea what was for supper. I had no idea how I was going to fight Henry with half the income I used to earn and my mom's retirement savings. I had no idea what my future held, but I didn't like that Holden wouldn't be in it.

I was trying to do what was best for my family. Mom's words from the first day Henry came over to pick up the kids ran through my head. *It's not a bad thing that your kids see you holding your own against him. You don't trash him in front of them no matter how much he deserves it, but you're also not letting him continue to be an ass to you.* Maybe showing them that someone they were supposed to love and trust shouldn't be able to ruin their lives over hurt pride was more important than I realized.

* * *

Holden

It'd been a shitty week. I came up with a million ways to make life easier for Emery, but only one was valid. I didn't know if it had a chance at working, but there was one person who would have a better idea than me. I was willing to make a fool out of myself, but I also wanted to approach my plan with the most information possible.

I was on my way to my mom's house. It was Saturday, nearly a full week since I'd heard from Emery. Regardless, I might be able to help her. No concessions. If she decided she was still done with me after that, then it was over. I wasn't like her ex. She didn't have to react the way I expected her to for me to treat her decently.

Small flakes dusted my windshield. The flurry of light snow was enough to create snow snakes that wiggled across the road in the wind, but it was cold enough out to keep the snow from sticking and making a slick surface.

I turned before I reached my place and drove toward the house I'd grown up in. The old white farmhouse stood proud, like its owner. And like its owner, it was in rougher shape on the inside than it looked.

Nora's car was parked by the house. She was home for the weekend, claiming she had to study for finals.

I pulled up next to the shop, where I was likely to find Mom. Inside, I was surrounded by the lingering smell of exhaust, oil, and fuel. Colt was wiping his hands on a rag. His pickup was on the lift Mom had installed because she refused to go to town for something as simple as an oil change. It was more because she didn't like dealing with people.

"Mom around?" I asked.

Colt tossed the rag onto the bench. "Maybe the barn?"

"Thanks." I turned to rush out.

"Holden." When I faced him, he didn't speak right away. Colt wasn't a talker. He could bullshit, but he preferred solitude. Maybe he didn't prefer it, but he sought it out. Whatever he planned to say, he wasn't telling me anything superficial.

"She's been extra hard on your sister lately." His brows drew in like he was afraid to say more. "I'm just saying it's been worse than usual and"—he glanced around the shop like he was worried the walls had ears—"I wouldn't be surprised if Nora found somewhere else to go for her next school vacation."

It was my fault, and my purpose for being here wasn't going to help. I'd have to let Nora know she was welcome to stay at my place when she wasn't in her dorm. "Forewarning —what I have to talk to Mom about might put her on a rampage."

Colt grunted but didn't look otherwise concerned.

I crossed to the giant red barn. Mom was inside, her back to me, one hand on her hip, the other braced against a horse stall. I gathered all my determination. This conversation wasn't going to be easy, and I didn't know how Mom would react, but I needed real talk, not fucking backhanded comments.

"Mom, I've gotta talk to you."

She jerked her head up but dropped it again. "If it's not about this ranch, I don't want to hear it."

"It's about Dad."

She didn't twitch, just lifted her gaze from the spot she was studying on the packed-dirt floor. "I don't have anything new to say on the subject, Holden."

"I do."

She dropped her arm and propped both hands on her hips. She made a half circle to face me, her expression guarded. "And that is?"

We faced off like in a bad western. No weapons. No other people. Just the wind outside and the dim light of the inside bulb highlighting us.

"I want to help Emery," I said, knowing Mom wasn't going to like how I wanted to help. I was Mom's support. I saw that now. She didn't let anyone get close to her, not even her own kids, but I was the only exception. My purpose was to be here to support what she cared about—our land and our business.

"So she'll stay?"

"So she can decide for herself where she lives and who she sees and when she gets her kids without her ex flexing our legal system to get her to do what he wants."

"You could ask for something worse than a parent wanting to be with their kid." She said it as if she'd given my dad or Nora's a chance to be in our lives. I blamed my dad for giving up, but I blamed Mom just as much.

I'd heard enough whispers of what had happened between my parents. I knew Mom well enough to decide what was truth, and my last interaction with my dad had shown me his side. "You know what it's like when a dad suddenly feigns interest in their kids to get what they want from a woman who isn't willing to give it."

Mom's expression hardened, and she averted her gaze. "Yeah."

"You knew about my daughter."

"I did," she said tightly.

Grief was hidden deep in her expression. She hated that I hadn't told her, that it was another thing we didn't talk about. Maybe someday we would. Maybe she'd never be that type of person. Maybe pushing back with Emery was her way of trying to keep me from getting hurt.

How this talk went would go a long way to under-standing my mother. "Did you know that before she was born, I went to see Dad?"

Her brows shot up, but other than surprise, I couldn't interpret her expression. "Did he contact you?"

I let out a scornful laugh. "No. But when I told him I

wanted a prenup like you suggested, he refused to work with me. Refused to help me."

"You should've gone to another lawyer."

I would've had to ask her for the money, but she wouldn't have helped me marry Teagan. "He's good at what he does."

"Yeah." She shook her head. "He was good. It was what made me so suspicious of him and his ideas."

"So I want you to tell me everything about him."

She narrowed her eyes. "Why?"

Dad had always been a touchy subject. I suspected he was the closest thing to the one that got away. Only Mom wasn't a woman built to settle down, and an ambitious lawyer would put her guard up permanently. She couldn't bring herself to trust him, and she had enough with juggling her oldest brother's demands and control over the business.

"I need to talk to him."

"He's not going to help you. And he definitely won't help a divorced woman with four kids. He's the guy people like Emery's ex fork boatloads of cash out for."

That was sort of what I wanted to hear. "It's either that, or if Emery ends up moving, I go with her." If she'd have me.

Mom's mouth dropped open. She hadn't thought I would risk my heart again. "Why? You haven't known her for long."

"I've known her long enough. She's special, and I'm not letting some jealous ex ruin it. But I don't think either one of us should have to play his game."

Mom's mouth flattened, and she chewed the inside of her cheek. "This ex—he really a bastard?"

"He's a controlling fuck, and he'll keep upsetting Emery's life when she stands up to him. His pride is a weapon."

"Fucking pride." She adjusted her stance, her boots grinding in the dirt. "Your dad started talking marriage when I told him I was pregnant. He was like everyone else, bitching at me when I'd move cattle on a horse at six months along."

People probably would've had issues with Mom tossing me into the bed of the pickup and bumping through the pastures. Child safety wasn't at the top of her mind.

"Then he was going on about how I'd change my last name and maybe we could rebrand the ranch and—" She sucked her lips against her teeth. "Then I asked him why he wasn't changing his name. We could rebrand his business. 'Barron Law' has a nice ring, don't you think?"

"It does," I agreed. Not quite like Rotham, McGuinty, and Partners. Jack Rotham wasn't a man who'd entertain changing his name.

"Then he started in on you. Doing what Emery's ex is doing." She gave an indignant sniff. I had heard parts of the story, but thanks to Henry, I understood it a hell of a lot better now. "I think he would've liked to have known you. But his requests always came with concessions, and I refused. If he couldn't see you without playing fucking games, what kind of mindfuck was he going to pull on you?"

Surprise ran through my veins. A pleasant surprise. Mom had looked out for me. I'd gotten used to her cold demeanor, and I had understood some of her motivations, but I hadn't recognized how staunchly she protected what was hers. It didn't explain how she was with Nora, but I could tackle only one issue at a time.

"I think he resented you, though," she said. "You didn't defy me and seek him out yourself."

"He moved to Billings." What the hell was I going to do

as a teen? Drive six hours and say "surprise" to a dad who had seemed to ignore me?

But I wasn't a teen anymore, and my eyes were wide open.

"Men don't always make sense, but one thing they all have in common, in my experience, is that damn pride." She tapped her fingers on her hips, her gloves making a dull thud against her jeans. "So if you want him to help you, cater to that."

She walked past me but stopped. "I don't want you to leave Coal Haven again."

Was that her way of telling me she loved me? "I know."

"Do you want to have kids?"

"I'd love to have a life full of them. Whether they're biologically mine or not. I'd love a big family. But did you think it was right that you were put under so much pressure to have kids to pass everything down to?"

"Right is different from reality. You want some big industry coming in and wiping everything out? Want the pastures filled with windmills and their blinking red lights?"

I gave her a *you know better* look. "I'm not your only chance at grandkids."

Mom's expression turned to stone. "If it gets out that whoever knocks up that girl gets a direct line to her oil money and all this land, you think she's gonna suss out who legitimately likes her and who's using her? She's too trusting."

Nora was trusting, and she was naive, but I didn't think she was the attention-starved girl Mom assumed she was. Nora had chosen pajamas and sleepovers instead of dating, and I doubted she was tight lipped like I had been to hide the fact that she was seeing someone. I didn't think she was dating at all, and I thought she preferred it that way.

"But I get what you mean," she conceded. "You gotta

understand, it's a lot of pressure. It was a lot of pressure when I was in my twenties and being asked when the next generation was coming. 'We have to secure the legacy.'" She rolled her eyes. "It's an indoctrination, and I've been a follower all my life. You tell me that I can trust you'll do right by this ranch, and I'll work on making my peace with it."

"Even if it includes windmills?"

Her lip curled up. "Don't mess with me, Holden. Hate those damn things."

She walked away, leaving me alone. I'd always shrugged Mom off. Endured her personality. I'd tried talking to her, but this was the first time it was actually effective.

I tried not to take it as a sign, but as my footsteps crunched through the dusting of snow on the way to my pickup, I dwelled on how to appeal to my dad's pride.

Twenty-Four

Emery

I thought about what Mom had said all weekend. I'd made good on my claim that the kids and I had plans. We went Christmas shopping. We wrapped gifts. The three oldest helped me with Christmas baking and freezing.

During my break this morning, for a Monday pick-me-up, more to build my confidence than anything, I dropped off treats in the break room. Krystal was there, bragging about her weekend at Stetson's place with his giant TV and his built-in bar in the basement and his snowmobile. Lyric was buried in her phone, ignoring the woman, and the pharmacy rep was smiling and nodding as if he knew who Stetson was.

The compliments on the candy cane cookies and peanut butter blossoms helped me fight back the swell of nerves that made me want to vomit sugary goodness all over the desk.

But work was done for the day. Mom said she'd throw

one of my freezer meals in the oven and the family wouldn't wait to eat. I had an errand to run once I left the clinic.

I peeked at my phone. I had a missed call, a number I didn't recognize, but it was probably Henry's law office. I'd been getting emails already, and I was going to have an ulcer before the year was over. Shoving all that out of my mind, I got into my car and drove out of town, taking a familiar route.

It'd been less than two weeks since I'd been here, but it felt like ages. My stomach flipped again and again. Was I doing the right thing? Was I too late?

I pulled into Holden's place. I didn't see his pickup. Everything looked locked up and like he wasn't around.

I hadn't planned for that.

Was he in town already? Was he at Rattler's? Was Holly helping him forget that I dropped him the minute things got hard?

My gut said no. People assumed guys like Holden were indiscriminate, but he'd been incredibly discriminating. He wouldn't use sex to soothe himself, and I had to believe there was more between us than a few days of hurt feelings before he moved on.

I went to his door and knocked. Sally barked from behind the barn and ran to me, her tail wagging. "Hey, girl. Your daddy home?"

Sally's tail thumped on the wooden floorboards of the porch, and her tongue lolled out. Tabby came around the corner of the house and brushed against the siding. Her fur was puffy with her winter coat, and she trotted to me like she could talk me into letting her inside.

I wasn't much different from the cat. Hanging around, hoping to be let in.

"Well, damn. What now?" Should I drive by Rattler's or

the café? Or should I just go home? I wanted to talk to him, and a message wouldn't do.

I was making my mind up when I spotted his pickup coming down the drive. My stomach clenched, and I drew in a shaky breath. I'd wanted him to be home, but now that he was heading this way, I was tempted to run.

My thinking hadn't been this chaotic about a guy since...ever.

There were so many signs that what I had with Holden was different from what had been between me and Henry. So much better. So much more real.

Holden pulled in and parked by my car. I didn't go to him. My feet were rooted in place. The house blocked the worst of the winds, and the cat and the dog fortified my courage. They hadn't run me off, which must have been a good sign.

Holden got out, not taking his concerned gaze off me. "Is everything okay?"

I almost said yes out of reflex, but that wasn't what I came here for. "No." As he walked toward me, his boots crunching in the snow, I let everything spill out. "I made a mistake. I cut things off with us too soon. I mean, not that a breakup was inevitable, but that I didn't give us a chance. Then Mom pointed out that this was what Henry did. More like, what *I* did when it comes to Henry, and you know what? She's right, and that's awful, and I just want to go back in time and smack myself."

My breath puffed out. I could keep rambling, but that was the sum of what I had to say. I tacked on, "I'm sorry."

He absentmindedly petted Sally as he approached me. "After you go back in time to smack yourself, then what?"

His brown eyes were mesmerizing. The flecks of green were even brighter in the winter sun. He was so close, his heat enveloped me and warded off the worst of the chill.

"I'd...keep myself from saying everything I said."

"You wouldn't break up with me?" he asked, a hopeful note in his question.

I shook my head. My hands were stuffed into my coat pockets. A good place for them. It kept me from flinging myself at him.

"What if you have to move?" he asked.

I swallowed hard. "I don't know. But I think that we can work it out if it comes to that."

"So you trust me, then?"

I nodded. "I think I more than trust you."

He tilted his head and softly asked, "What does that mean, Em?"

The way he said my name, I could sink into his voice and stay lost forever. The next words tumbled out. "I love you, Holden. And that terrifies me."

"It scares me too." He dipped his head to murmur, "Because I love you."

I used a gloved hand to grip the front of his coat and drag him close enough for me to reach his lips. He didn't resist. I was closed into his strong embrace, and he dominated the kiss. I let him. Just minutes before, I'd thought I had lost this—and him. But I was back in his arms. He'd accepted my apology, and I hadn't realized how tense I'd been until I melted against him.

He pulled away way too soon. I was left blinking and wondering whether I'd imagined our talk.

"Did you get a call today from a lawyer?"

I blinked at the unexpected topic change. "Um...no. Wait. Maybe. I had a missed call, but I assumed it's from Henry's people."

"What's the area code?"

"I don't know."

"Can you check?"

He was so intent on the call, I pulled out my phone. His eagerness hinted that it was important. "Not North Dakota." There was a voice mail. I pulled it up, dreading what I'd hear. Just because it wasn't a local area code didn't mean it wasn't Henry's legal team. If Holden wanted to rekindle what I'd almost destroyed, he was with me in this.

A deep male voice spoke. "This is Jack Rotham. My son recently visited my office to discuss your concerns. I'm still licensed to work in North Dakota and am willing to work with you."

The message ended and I stared at Holden. Details clicked into place with my disbelief. He'd never said his dad's name, but he'd mentioned his dad was a lawyer. "You went to see your dad?"

He dipped his head. "I went down last night and talked to him as soon as his office opened this morning."

"Holden." He'd said once he'd never talk to his dad again. He'd gone there for me? "Why?"

"Because he's a lot like Henry, so who better to work with you? And he's taking the case pro bono."

Astonishment filled me. I'd gone from worrying about paying a lawyer and draining Mom's retirement account to having a lawyer offer his services for free. "Why is he doing that?"

"Because I asked him to do it for you, not for me. I was willing to foot the bill, but I don't think he wanted money he thought was tied to Mom in any way." His grin was lopsided. "So I didn't tell him it was leftover oil trust money that I have in savings."

Not only did he talk to his dad, but he'd offered to help me financially? Fear had nearly made me give up on an amazing man. I put my hands on either side of his face. "I almost ruined something really special."

"But you're here." He wrapped his arms around me.

"I'm here. The kids are really upset with me. They miss you."

The corner of his mouth ticked up. "I can't believe how much I miss them."

"Want to come over? Mom put a lasagna in. We can talk to them about us over dinner." Paralyzing insecurity roared back. "I-if you want."

His gaze flicked to the door behind him. "Do we have a few minutes? I want a few moments with you when you don't have to be quiet."

Heat chased away the chill and pooled in my belly. I fisted my hands in his coat. "She said she wouldn't wait for me."

I let him sweep me inside, knowing this was the right move. It felt right in a way that letting him go hadn't.

* * *

Holden

Six months later

I pulled down the tailgate. Sally ran around the bottom and Landon clambered in.

Avery appeared at my elbow. "Horses are fed."

"Awesome, thanks. Once we get this off-loaded, that's the last of it."

Landon grabbed a box from the stack inside the bed of my pickup and jumped down. He ran into the house with Sally hot on his heels.

Avery hauled herself onto the tailgate. She didn't go for

a box. She leveled a solemn stare on me. "I think we should bring Tabby inside."

"She got to you."

"She didn't have to," Avery said like she won the argument. "You didn't want a pet inside because you're outside working all the time. But now you have us. I'm helping with the horses, and Landon feeds Sally. Afton can do litter boxes."

I laughed. "You're volunteering your sister for litter box duty?"

Avery chewed the inside of her lip and tried to act innocent. "No, but she needs a job like me and Landon."

"It's a tight fit with all of us."

"But you're adding on." She grinned like she'd played the ultimate trump card. Construction on the house was starting the next week. Emery and I had contemplated waiting to move her and the kids in, but the kids swore they didn't mind camping out under my roof until the addition was done.

"All right." I stroked my chin like I was pretending to think. Emery and I had had the cat conversation when we discussed moving in together. "You agree to help oversee the work that needs to be done for an indoor cat?"

Avery nodded, her dark ponytail swinging. Emery's car approached. She had finished cleaning the rental house and had picked Riley up from her mom's. I'd never get tired of seeing them all at my place—our place. Home.

I grinned, more at Emery than at Avery. "Okay, then. It's a deal."

Avery squealed and crushed me in a surprisingly strong embrace for a twelve-year-old. She grabbed a box and ran into the house, yelling for her siblings.

As Emery got out, I said, "Tabby's going to figure out she should beware what she wishes for."

"Good thing I didn't take Stetson up on his bet." She unhooked Riley and helped her to the ground. The girl crossed to me, and I lifted her up to sit on the tailgate. I leaned against it with her. Emery closed the distance between us and gave me a kiss.

I held her close. "He's trying to bet me about whether it'll rain during our wedding."

We'd wanted to wait until school was out. Then the kids would spend a few weeks in Arizona with their dad. I'd miss the shit out of them, but they needed time with their dad. Time to adjust to him living across the country.

My father had mediated the shit out of Henry. Emery hadn't been the only reason Henry had been heavy handed. He'd had problems with Jenni, and she'd ended up leaving him. When it came out that he planned to leave the state, the trajectory of the case had changed, and Henry's energy had dissolved.

The last time he talked to Emery, he'd said he was in counseling and that it was important to him to have a better relationship with his kids.

So, Emery and I waited for our intimate outdoor wedding. We'd moved everyone in together before the kids left for Arizona. We wanted them to be a part of the move, a part of the decision, essentially, but without the rush. We wanted the wedding to happen as naturally as everything else.

Emery rested her head on my shoulder until Riley wiggled to get down. Avery was walking out of the house, and Riley ran for her.

"Mind keeping an eye on Riley?" Emery called.

Avery squinted at us. "Do I have to help move boxes while I'm watching her?"

"She's good," I muttered.

Emery chuckled. "Not while you're watching her," she

said to Avery. She sighed and put her head back on my shoulder. "I'm late."

"For what?"

"*Late* late."

I spun toward her. "You're pregnant?"

I could barely breathe. Happiness turned to stark fear and back to happiness. Elation nearly made me float away, but a very real tether kept me on earth. I knew to expect the mixed emotions. I wasn't prepared for how strong they each were.

She glanced at the house but kept her voice low. "I grabbed a test from the store. Looks like the decision was taken out of our hands."

"How?"

She blew out a breath, looking as stunned as I felt. "I think going back and forth between houses and the overnights—I must've gotten off schedule." She peered at me. "Are you okay with this? It's early yet, but—"

I picked her up and spun her around. She yelped, and her arms twined around my neck.

"I'm fucking terrified." I circled us around until her ass hit the edge of the tailgate. I stood between her legs and put her hand on my chest. "You're sure?"

"The tests are pretty accurate. And it explains..." She adjusted her shoulders. "Sore boobs. Tired. I thought it was just a doozy of a *that time of the month*. But that was supposed to happen a couple of weeks ago." She shook her head. "Five kids. Whoa."

We had talked to Avery, Landon, and Afton. We'd asked their opinions about Emery and me having a kid, but also told them that it might not happen. We weren't taking anything for granted. Like the veteran siblings they were, they'd been thrilled, but also surprisingly chill about the possibility.

"Are you okay?" It would be like her to worry about me, to care more about my feelings than her own.

Her nod was slow. "I realized I was so hesitant because I'd done so much on my own. Henry was in school, or he was at work, or he was on call and needed the rest to be fresh for surgery. Being in the medical field, who was I to argue? And I hadn't argued. I hadn't demanded an equal partner. I had taken it all on myself. But when I saw that plus sign, I realized it wouldn't be like that with you. You're not like that. You're going to be as involved in the baby's life as you are with the kids. I mean, you're already getting up with Riley when she's sick in the middle of the night and we aren't even married. You're going to keep being a rock star of a dad, but no matter what, no matter what happens, we'll get through it together."

"I fucking love you."

"It's a good thing I love you too."

I caught her mouth. The quickie make-out session turned heated, and I reluctantly drew back. "If we keep doing this, I'm going to have to park the pickup in the shop and reenact our first night together."

She smoothed her hands across my shoulders. "We could do that anyway."

I did a quick calculation. Avery was in charge of Riley. Landon had been taking at least an hour to unpack each box he brought inside. And Afton had disappeared around the back of the house to hunt down Tabby.

I closed the tailgate. "Hop in."

She laughed, and I led my soon-to-be wife to the back seat.

Twenty-Five

Stetson

"Shut up and fuck me, Stetson."

That was pretty much how I ended up with my lips on Lyric and with her legs wrapped around my waist, but I thanked fuck we'd found a little corner of Holden's tack room no one could see into.

Lyric pushed her fingers into my hair, knocking my cowboy hat off. I let it go, otherwise I would have had to take my hands off her sweet ass, and these round globes had teased me since she'd come home from college to visit my sister.

I'd done my best to stay away. I called her "kid"—hell, I even treated her like my sister's annoying best friend when my thoughts had been X-rated for years.

This girl was trouble. With a capital *T*, and she didn't know it.

She made me want things that weren't mine to have. I wasn't going to make her life miserable going after them.

But I'd give myself this.

I yanked her underwear down, heard a rip, and kept going. My alcohol-fogged brain hadn't thought through the logistics of getting her lacy underwear off with her legs hooked around my hips.

She licked her tongue against mine. I tasted the Moscow mule she'd been nursing, the flavor mingling with the beers I'd been downing to dull the effect of seeing Lyric in a little pleated skirt and a tight top at Holden's wedding reception.

The alcohol had failed. Months of being abstinent after my unstable ex screamed out of my life hadn't helped my restraint either.

Her underwear came free, and I stuffed them into my pocket. Holden or one of his new stepkids didn't need to find the lacy scrap and go looking for answers.

With the fabric in my pocket, it meant she was bare.

As much as I wanted to shove inside and feel her tight little body grip mine, I had enough experience to know that sex with me could be uncomfortable. I was big all over, but I wasn't a clumsy boy learning to fuck anymore.

I knew what I was doing, and I'd need all that experience today to keep from coming in my pants. I'd been lusting after Lyric for too damn long.

I didn't waste time. I dropped to my knees and buried my face in heaven. Her hands twisted in my hair, and her thighs clamped around my head.

"Oh my God, Stetson."

I could barely hear her. I went after her like all my dreams had come to fruition at once. The muscles in her legs rippled, and she bucked between me and the wall. Her clit was mine until she was shattering around me. It'd been seconds, but I wasn't the only one hot for this.

I growled, barely louder than the sounds she was trying to suppress. The tack room was at the back of the barn, and I'd come in to check on a distraught Lyric. Her loser boyfriend—all her boyfriends had been fucking losers—had dumped her, and I'd meant to be supportive. I'd meant to give her a hug and walk away, but once she was in my arms, I put my mouth on her, she'd said what she had, and I'd been a goner.

Her legs were trembling when I set her feet down. She was panting, and my breathing sounded like a freight train as I undid my jeans. Each movement was painful, I was so damn hard.

She twined her arms around my shoulders and pulled me down. My mouth was back on hers. She was fearless, kissing me when I was covered in her release.

Blood roared through my head. How could I have any spare blood with all my reserves in my dick straining for her?

Once I was free, I lifted her. Those strong legs wrapped back around me, and my cock argued that it was too close to paradise to take my time.

I pushed in, forcing myself to go slowly. But Lyric was having none of that. She rocked her hips, groaning with each inch until she melted over me.

We hadn't quit kissing, as if we had a silent agreement that plastering our mouths together would muffle us.

I withdrew and shoved back in. She moaned into me and hugged me harder.

There wasn't a word for how phenomenal her wet heat felt stroking over my dick. My mind hadn't conjured anything this good. She was as greedy as me, taking what she wanted, riding me until her little whimpers told me she was close.

I hadn't thought I'd last this long. Prolonging the pleasure for myself was a motivator, but now that she was so close, I concentrated on her. When she tightened around me again and her walls started convulsing, I exploded.

I usually threw my head back and roared out a good orgasm, but for this I had to bend into her. My fingers tightened in the flesh of her ass, and dammit, I didn't want to bruise her, but the orgasm screaming through my body, turning my balls inside out as she milked my release, was powerful. I couldn't let go without shouting to the world and revealing what we were doing in here.

Her hands were all over my shoulders, stroking my face, in my hair. I broke apart from our kiss and lazily opened my eyes.

This sight, a freshly fucked Lyric, would stay with me forever. Hooded pale-blue eyes, a messy bun that I'd mussed up more, and a nice flush to her cheeks, all faded against the way she looked at me. As if she saw me and not what she thought I should be. It was something I could get used to every day of my life.

I swallowed the hard lump that suddenly formed in my throat.

No. I wasn't going down that road. I had too much shit going on in my life to take up with Lyric. I wanted to stay drama-free, and Lyric was a walking argument. She challenged me and everyone else in her path. I liked to witness it, but she'd also challenge everyone in *my* path. And that was the issue.

I withdrew, losing the heat of her body, and hating the distance between us. But other emotions were starting to leak in around the blinding lust that had hounded me since I'd touched her.

I helped her set her feet on the floor, and she brushed her skirt down, her movements almost shy—a word I'd never associated with her before.

I was tucking myself in when I froze. My gaze dropped to my crotch and to my extremely satisfied dick that wasn't softening as fast as it should, like it would be ready for round two if she said the word.

But blood rapidly drained from it as I realized what had happened. "Shit, Lyric, we didn't use protection."

I never skipped protection. I never lost my head during sex. I'd lived with a constant reminder of what happened when someone fucked around. Between my mother throwing my father's infidelity in his face my entire life and my half brother being born and raised in the same damn town as me, I couldn't forget.

And I never forgot. Until now.

I waited for her casual dismissal, for her to tell me that she was on some sort of birth control, but as I met her gaze, I knew I wasn't going to hear that. Her eyes were wide, and her gaze jumped from my crotch to my face.

"I-I'm sure it'll be fine..." She blanched and bit her bottom lip. Despite the growing concern that we'd majorly fucked up, I still wanted to be the one to bite her bottom lip, to run it through my teeth and feel her squirm under me. "I'm clean."

Her statement took a moment to register. I finished buttoning up. "I always wear a condom. *Always.*"

"So do I. I mean, so does whoever I'm with."

Blood roared between my ears again as I plastered my hands on the wall next to her. The last thing I wanted to hear about was her with other guys, which was fucking rich. I was almost thirty-five and had about twenty years of sexual history behind me.

I was about to ask her about birth control when my aunt Kira called, "Stetson?"

I jerked back. "Shit."

"Stetson." Kira's voice drew closer. I couldn't be caught hooking up with my sister's friend at a family function on top of the other shit going on in my life. And with the way

Mom's mouth puckered like she drank lemon juice at the mention of Lyric's name, getting caught would mess up Holden's big day.

"I'll go out first." I straightened my shirt and looked around for my hat. Giving my hair a good finger-combing, I stuffed the hat on.

Lyric was looking at me like she couldn't believe how I was acting.

"What?"

"Do we really have to hide?" Something that looked too close to hurt shone in her pale eyes. I brushed a lock of hair off her cheek, wishing I could touch her more.

"Stetson!" Kira called, her tone flat, sounding unhappy. "Krystal's here."

My body stiffened and I spun away. "Goddammit. What the hell!" I turned to Lyric, my gaze pleading. If I didn't handle the Krystal situation well, she'd make a giant scene that my family wouldn't let me forget. But I couldn't ruin Holden and Emery's night, not after what they'd been through. "All right. I'll go out. Can you give me like a five- or ten-minute head start?"

If Krystal saw us together, all hell would break loose. She'd been a jealous girlfriend, and she'd been especially sensitive about Lyric. As my sister's best friend, Lyric was on my property a lot. Isla lived with our parents, and Lyric was at their house when I was. Sometimes I had made sure to overlap her visit. Hell, maybe Krystal sensed that I wondered way too often what Lyric looked like naked.

Whatever. All I knew was that the breakup with Krystal was the longest and messiest of my life, and for some reason, she didn't think we were through. She'd probably waited until Holden's wedding, thinking I'd relent so she didn't make a scene.

Lyric's nervous gaze darted toward the entrance of the

tack room. Shit, she worked with Krystal. A confrontation could be extra bad. "I'll deal with her."

"Stetson—"

"I'm sorry. I've got to deal with this." I stuffed my hat down farther on my head and trotted out of the barn. I'd deal with Krystal, talk to Lyric about the lack of protection and how we couldn't do this again, and then get shit-faced and try to forget everything. I just wanted one night of peace, but after being with Lyric, I wasn't sure I'd get that.

———

Stetson and Lyric try to find their way through the repercussions of their one night stand in Make Me Dream.

Thank you for reading. I'd love to know what you thought. Please consider leaving a review for Make Me Blush at the retailer the book was purchased from.

For all the latest news, sneak peeks, quarterly short stories, and free material sign up for my newsletter.

About the Author

Marie Johnston writes paranormal and contemporary romance and has collected several awards in both genres. Before she was a writer, she was a microbiologist. Depending on the situation, she can be oddly unconcerned about germs or weirdly phobic. She's also a licensed medical technician and has worked as a public health microbiologist and as a lab tech in hospital and clinic labs. Marie's been a volunteer EMT, a college instructor, a security guard, a phlebotomist, a hotel clerk, and a coffee pourer in a bingo hall. All fodder for a writer!! She has four kids, cats, and a half blind Corgie.

mariejohnstonwriter.com

Follow me:

Also by Marie Johnston

Oil Barrons

Make Me Whole

Make Me Shiver

Make Me Blush

Make Me Dream

Oil Kings

King's Crown

King's Ransom

King's Treasure

King's Country

King's Queen

CPSIA information can be obtained
at www.ICGtesting.com
Printed in the USA
LVHW101216270722
724473LV00003B/139

9 781951 067427